Betrayal

Corrupt Empire

Book One

Sarah Bailey

Betrayal Copyright © 2019 by Sarah Bailey

All rights reserved. No part of this book may be reproduced in any form or by any electronic or mechanical means including information storage and retrieval systems, without permission in writing from the publisher. The only exception is by a reviewer, who may quote short excerpts in a review.

This book is a work of fiction. Names, characters, places, and incidents either are products of the author's imagination or are used fictitiously. Any resemblance to actual persons, living or dead, events, or locales is entirely coincidental.

Please note the spelling throughout is British English.

Cover Art by V Designs

Published by Twisted Tree Publications
www.twistedtreepublications.com
info@twistedtreepublications.com

Paperback ISBN: 978-1-913217-00-6

This book is dedicated to Elizabeth Bailey
She inspired me to become a writer and none of this
would be possible without her help, support and
guidance.
Thank you for everything.

Prologue

Avery

Lying here, handcuffed to the bed, my eyes blindfolded, ankles bound, I wait for him.

This isn't a story of love, sunshine and roses. This is a story of betrayal, murder, lust and deceit.

My name is Avery Daniels. I am the heir to my parents' fortune and their multi-billion pound property empire.

The clock in the hall ticks. The only other sound in the air is my breathing. This game is one I play willingly. How I came to be lying in his bed. In the bed of the man who broke me. Who ruined my life. Who stole my future.

It all started one dark night. The last night I saw my family. The night I met him. The only man to haunt my every moment.

I am the heiress who disappeared without a trace.

This is my story.

Mine.

And his.

Chapter One

Avery

The sound of laughter rang through the kitchen as my mum prepared dinner and my father set the table. We last had a chance to do this months ago. Multi-billionaire parents with a huge global company to run meant I didn't get to see them often.

"Sweetie, can you pass the pepper?" my mum, Kathleen, said.

I liked to help her cook. Ever since I'd been a kid. I grabbed the pepper grinder and tossed it to her. She grinned, her blue eyes glinting. I'd taken after my father in the looks department. Hazel eyes and dark hair, although my father's was greying at the sides now. I told him it made him look distinguished.

Mitchell Daniels was head of Daniels Holdings. A company my great-grandfather built from the ground up, mostly dealing in property development. And little old me, the heir. I'm sure my father wished for a son, but he'd never made me feel inadequate for being a woman. Things between us were a little weird sometimes. Especially when it came to the company. I tried to avoid discussions about it with him these days.

"Dad, did Mum tell you I'm going to Antigua with Gert in a couple of weeks what with it being half term?"

"No. I'm sure sun, sea and sand is what both of you need," he replied with a smile.

My best friend, Gertrude, was doing Management Science at UCL. I was studying Architecture. The only part of the property industry I had any interest in. I'd always been good at drawing. It was my real passion.

"James not going with you?" Mum asked.

"No, he's got stuff with his dad."

James Benson, the son of Zachary Benson, the famous, but reclusive designer and fashion mogul, was my other closest friend. We'd been inseparable growing up, always in and out of each other's houses. His siblings were almost like the ones I'd never had.

"Avery, can you get the glasses out of the cupboard?" Dad asked.

I turned, going up on my tiptoes to reach the top shelf and pulled out three wine glasses. One slipped out of my hand and crashed to the floor.

"Shit," I muttered.

"Don't worry about it," Mum said. "Just get the dustpan."

I moved away, careful not to step in the glass with my bare feet and snagged it from under the sink. I bent down and started to sweep up.

"Don't move an inch," a deep voice I didn't recognise said.

Betrayal

I looked up at Mum. Her face hardened. She mouthed to me 'stay down'. My hands stilled.

"Walk around the counter slowly," the voice said.

It sent a chill down my spine. Void of all emotion. Cold as steel.

Mum complied, sending me another warning look before she disappeared.

What is going on?

"You know why I'm here."

"We can discuss this calmly like adults. Just put the gun down," Dad said.

Gun. He has a gun. My heartbeat kicked up a notch. My palms began to sweat. Why did this stranger have a gun? And what did he want with my parents?

"Funny, Mitchell, you lost the right to negotiate the moment you took something that never belonged to you."

Took what?

Nothing made sense. I needed to see for myself. I carefully placed the pan on the floor and crawled towards the counter, edging along to the end. Peering around, I found both my parents with their hands up. The man holding the gun wore no mask. My breath caught in my throat.

I'd never described a man as beautiful before. There was no other word for him. His light brown hair, short at the sides and longer on top, was neatly styled. Grey eyes glinted under the soft kitchen lights. His dark suit clung to him in all the right places, tailored to absolute perfection. It left no doubt he was all hard muscle underneath. An avenging angel. Except this angel had a gun pointed at my dad's head.

Self-preservation made me freeze. If I alerted him to my presence, it wouldn't help anyone. I ignored the voice in my head telling me the real reason I couldn't move had more to do with how awestruck I was by the gun-wielding stranger.

Thanks, brain. Not!

"Look, can't we put all of that behind us? It's been over twenty years," Dad said.

The angel's expression didn't change. Cold, almost calculating. It sent chills running down my spine. Terrifying and beautiful at the same time. A deadly combination.

"No."

There was no other warning. Two shots fired in quick succession. The sound rang in my ears. My parents collapsed one after the other. I put a hand over my mouth, stifling a scream. He'd shot them right between the eyes. There was no question in my mind. They were dead.

Dead.

The word stuck in my head.

Dead.

Dead.

Blood poured out of the back of their heads, pooling on the wooden floor beneath them. Their chests were still, unmoving. Tears pricked at my eyes.

My parents were dead.

Dead.

I looked at the angel again. He stared right at me. The surprise in his eyes faded after a second. I fell back onto my hands as I tried to scramble away.

"No, please," I whispered.

Betrayal

He didn't raise the gun to me. His lip twitched. I backed up right into the counter behind me, putting my hands up.

"Please don't kill me."

In five long strides, he stood before me. His very presence made my heart hammer erratically in my chest. I could hear it loud and clear in my ears. Up close, I got a real sense of just how tall and well-built he was, muscles rippled under his suit jacket as he moved.

"I'm not going to kill you," he said, his voice quiet. "But you and I are going to have a little talk."

I nodded slowly. I'd just seen him murder my parents. The likelihood of him letting me go was slim to none. I doubted he'd counted on having a witness.

He squatted down until we were eye level. Those grey eyes cold and yet so beautiful.

"You shouldn't have seen this."

"Why... why did you kill my parents?" I whispered, almost unable to get the words out.

"They weren't good people, Avery."

"How do you know my name?"

He cocked his head to the side.

"Everyone knows who you are."

He wasn't wrong. I'd been photographed countless times by the press and had my name plastered all over social media. Still, he didn't seem like the type of person to browse tabloids.

Why did he know who I was?

Why did he do this?

His expression told me he felt no remorse for killing my parents. They'd known who he was.

Why?

I had too many questions. And I didn't think I was going to get many answers out of this man.

"What are you going to do with me?"

He stared at me for the longest moment without answering. My skin prickled. I was struck again by just how beautiful he was.

Get a grip!

You don't crush on the guy who just murdered your parents. Normal people don't go around with guns. He wasn't a good guy. Nothing about him was soft or welcoming. Nothing at all. My brain was playing tricks on me. I was just in shock. That had to be it.

He reached out, grabbing me by my neck and pulling me up to my feet with him.

"Who are you?" I whispered when he didn't let go.

"Your worst nightmare."

A sharp pain erupted from the back of my head and radiated outwards. The last thing I remember before passing out was those steel grey eyes and his expression.

Regret.

My head hurt. It was the first thing I registered when I came to. I shivered, a chill seeping into my veins. I opened my eyes. Darkness encompassed me.

Where was I?

What happened to me?

Betrayal

The knowledge my parents were dead came flooding back, causing my heart to shatter into a million tiny pieces. I put a hand to my chest, just to reassure myself it was still intact. Thinking about my parents wasn't going to get me anywhere. I didn't have time to grieve. I needed to know where I was.

I sat up, wincing, and felt the back of my head. A bump had formed.

Well, that's just fan-fucking-tastic.

There was no light at all around me. My eyes had nothing to adjust to. Only darkness. I shifted, freezing when I heard the distinct sound of clinking across the floor. I felt down my legs until I found a metal cuff around my ankle connected to a chain.

It hit me all at once. The avenging angel had hit me over the head and taken me. Now, I was chained up in a room with no windows, no lights and nothing but the cold floor to sit on. The man I'd thought beautiful was exactly what he said.

My worst nightmare.

Did he know I wasn't a fan of the dark?

The chain dragged across the floor as I struggled to my feet. Putting my hands out, I tried to get a sense of the layout of wherever he'd put me. My hands met a wall.

Left or right?

I went right, feeling my way across. I hit a corner. I moved with it until my fingers met metal. It was a doorway. The only way in and out. I banged on it as hard as I could.

"Let me out!"

Even knowing it was useless, I tried anyway. I hit the door over and over again until my fist hurt and my hand began to feel sticky. I slid down the door, feeling my knuckles. I'd split them.

Tears pricked at my eyes. I didn't have it in me to dash them away when they started to fall. I put my unhurt hand to my mouth as a sob escaped my lips.

It was useless. The entire thing. I'd known the moment I saw him, he was bad news. He killed my parents without a second thought. Who does that? He must've had some reason. What had he said? My dad had taken something that didn't belong to him, but what?

The unanswerable questions again, brain? Not helpful.

Tears fell harder. I couldn't hold back any longer. Ripping my hand away, I screamed.

"Let me the fuck out of here!"

Silence.

I expected nothing less.

I crawled away from the door and huddled in the middle of the room on the floor. I stopped caring my fist was bleeding. The pain reminded me I was still alive. Still breathing. I let the waves of sorrow overcome me.

My parents.

Gone.

The two people who'd loved me, cared for me, made sure I could have anything I ever dreamed of.

Gone.

How long I lay there, sobbing until I couldn't cry any longer, was beyond me. I heard the sound of locks turning and bolts sliding back. The door opened. The light streaming in through the doorway hurt my eyes. I didn't look up, curling my arms tighter around my legs.

Betrayal

"Get up."

The same cold voice rang in my ears. I hated him already. Hated how helpless and terrified his presence made me feel. I wasn't going to let him get to me. I had to be strong.

"Do I have to repeat myself?"

I didn't respond. What the hell could I even say? I didn't know what he wanted. All I knew is he took my parents from me and chained me up like a dog. I heard his footsteps until they stopped right next to my head.

"Get up."

Seconds ticked by. I didn't want to see him. I didn't want any of this. I knew he'd squatted down next to me because the next moment, he grabbed my injured hand and tried to tug it away from my legs. I cried out, pain radiating from my knuckles. He turned my hand over in his.

"What did you do to yourself?" he muttered.

"Don't touch me," I hissed, pulling my hand from his grasp.

I cradled it to my chest, still refusing to look his way. The sound of his footsteps echoed in my ears. I peeked out. He'd left but hadn't shut the door behind him. A blank white wall lay beyond. I had no energy to pick myself up and investigate further. It wouldn't have done me any good anyway. The chain on my leg prevented me from leaving. At some point, I'd find its limits, but I was in no mood to test it at that moment.

I turned my face back into my knees. My hand throbbed. I'd been an idiot to hit the door more times than I could count. Hurting myself wouldn't change my situation.

Footsteps in the hallway outside alerted me to his presence again. The single lightbulb above us flicked on. The harsh light hurt my eyes further. I'd gotten used to the dark.

I looked up at him. He was carrying a small box which he placed on the floor next to me. He reached out for my hand. I reared back, pushing my feet against the floor to get away from him until I hit the wall. His expression darkened.

"Come here."

"No. Stay away from me," I said, sitting up and curling inwards.

I glared at him from behind my knees. He was wearing an uncollared blue shirt, buttoned up to his neck. I glimpsed the beginnings of a tattoo peeking out from the top of it.

"I'm only going to say this once. You are going to let me see to your hand without complaint. Then we are going to have a discussion about what's expected of you. If you argue with me, Daniels, there will be consequences. Ones you won't enjoy. Are we clear?"

His tone left no room for questions. No room for disobedience. Nothing. I was expected to obey. He'd called me Avery before. I wasn't sure why he referred to me by my last name now.

He picked up the box. I didn't move as he approached me. He sat next to me and took my hand. Looking over the cuts in the light, his brow furrowed.

"What did you do?"

"Hit the door. Repeatedly."

His eyes met mine, the disapproval in them making me flinch. He rested my hand on his knee before opening the box. It was full of medical supplies. Carefully, he cleaned my split knuckles. His touch was gentle, completely at odds with his appearance. I wasn't about to try work him out. Wanted absolutely nothing to do with him. He'd murdered my parents.

He bandaged my hand when he was done and gave it back to me. I held it to my chest, staring at him with narrowed eyes. He closed the box.

"Next time you want to hit something, try not to make it a reinforced steel door."

"No shit," I muttered.

I wasn't planning on hitting anything else except maybe him.

He stood up, walking around and standing in front of me. I craned my head up to look at him.

"You saw something you were never meant to see or be a part of. So, Daniels, I have rules. You will obey me in all things. You will not talk back to me. You will stay here until I decide otherwise. Simply put. You. Are. Mine. As I said before, there will be consequences if you break these rules and any others I decide are appropriate. Have I made myself clear or do you have questions? This is your one and only opportunity to ask."

My heart thudded in my chest at the finality of his words. His? Was he certifiable or just a psycho? Either way, I wasn't a piece of property or someone he could own.

"What the actual fuck is all that supposed to mean?"

His expression didn't change. I wasn't sure what I expected.

"Are you deaf?"

"No. I just don't understand anything. You killed my parents in front of me and now you've chained me up in a room with nothing but the clothes on my back. I didn't even do anything. Why? Why are you doing this to me? Give me one fucking good reason."

I'd had enough. The hold I kept on my temper snapped entirely. I dragged myself off the floor. I only came up to his chest, but I didn't care. He wasn't going to get away with any of this.

He took a step towards me, backing me right up against the wall as I tried to get away from him. He slammed his hands against the wall by my head, effectively caging me in.

"Do not take that tone with me."

"You're insane."

"And you are a spoilt brat."

I spluttered. How dare he make assumptions about me? Spoilt? The last fucking thing I was. Did he think I was some rich kid who thought she was better than everyone else? Hell no.

"Fuck you."

His eyes hardened to steel.

"Listen very carefully, Daniels. I am going to let that slide because you're clearly not in the right frame of mind to understand your situation. Make no mistake, you talk to me like that again, it will not end well for you." He paused, appraising me for a moment. "In answer to your question. Why am I doing this to you? I don't need you running off and telling tales. What happened last night will stay between us."

It most definitely wasn't going to stay between us. The moment I got out of here, I was going to the police. Not only had this man killed my parents, but he'd essentially kidnapped me. No way I would allow him to get away with either of those things.

"I'm just supposed to accept that?"

"Yes."

"Well, let me make something clear to you. I am not your slave. I will not bow down to you. Go. To. Hell."

He straightened, his hands falling back to his sides. He shook his head.

"Perhaps a little time to reflect on your circumstances will put you in a better frame of mind."

He turned away and walked towards the door. He gave me one last look before he flipped a switch from outside, plunging me back into darkness.

"No. Don't put me in the dark again. No."

I couldn't face it. I started towards the door but it slammed shut, stealing away the last bit of light I had. I let rip and screamed. I raged until my voice was hoarse and my throat hurt. I collapsed on the floor in the middle of the room and cried again.

When my tears dried up, I turned on my back, staring into the blackness.

My parents were dead.

I was a prisoner.

And I didn't even know the name of my tormentor.

All of those things made my head hurt and my heart feel tight.

My life as I knew it was over.

Nothing would be the same again.

Chapter Two

Aiden

I slammed my hand against the wall beside the door as I heard her muffled screams. That fucking girl would be the death of me. The wild look in her eyes when she told me to go to hell made my blood boil and my cock stand to attention.

What the fuck was I doing? Never in my life had I felt more out of control. If I had any other choice, I'd get rid of her in an instant.

The problem was… her. When I'd seen those doe eyes staring back at me after I'd executed her parents, my entire world shifted on its axis.

She wasn't meant to be there. No one else but Mitchell and Kathleen Daniels were supposed to be in their penthouse. My entire fucking plan had gone tits up the moment I realised she was there.

Now I was stuck with Avery Daniels. The daughter of the fuckers who stole my life. I couldn't kill her. I wanted to, but she just happened to be innocent of all the crimes the rest of her family had committed. My moral code wouldn't allow it. I might be a fucked up bastard but killing an innocent girl would be a whole new low.

Thing is, I was going to do something so much worse to her. So much fucking worse.

Avery would become utterly dependant on me for everything. Then I was going to use her to destroy the Daniels legacy for good. Sick. I was sick, but nothing would stand in my way. The twisted pieces of shit needed to be stopped. Mitchell and Kathleen were only the beginning.

I walked away from the room I'd put her in, unable to listen to her screaming any longer. She'd wear herself out eventually.

I had every intention when I went in there to feed her and let her see to her needs. The stupid girl had hurt herself. First mistake. And then she'd openly challenged me after I'd laid down the rules. I wanted to pin her down on the floor and shake some sense into her. Hell, I wanted to do things I really shouldn't to Avery.

I needed to break her. Break that girl so she'd be mine. Mine to use. Mine to manipulate. I had a new plan and Avery was key to its success.

She would learn the hard way if she decided to keep up this little act. That's if she didn't fucking break me instead. She'd already tested my patience and it had barely been eight hours since I'd taken her.

Doe eyes. Fucking doe eyes. Behind them lay a girl who'd watched me kill her parents. Of course, she was going to hate me for it, but she didn't understand. Literally no clue about what her family really did. Innocent. Too fucking innocent for this.

I couldn't stray too far. Avery would need me sooner or later. She'd grown up pampered. There was no way she'd cope in that room alone for long. It was the very reason I put her in there. The fact I even had it installed was fucked up. I'd done unspeakable things to people in there. All at the request of fucking Chuck Daniels, Mitchell's younger brother. I wasn't sure who was worse. Him or Mitchell. Both of them were sick fucks.

I didn't want to put her in there but needs must. Enough time alone and she'd be begging me to let her out. Exactly how I wanted her. Obedient. Only then would I tell her the truth. The real reason her family needed to die and their entire company razed to the ground.

I had the heir to Daniels Holdings in my hands. And nothing would stand in my way as I took them all down with me.

My phone rang. I pulled it out of my pocket, looking down at the display.

Chuck.

"What?"

I knew why he was calling.

"Shit has gone down."

There was a long pause.

"Someone killed Mitchell and Kathleen and my niece has gone missing."

I smiled. With the exception of Avery, everything was still going to plan.

"Shit, man. I'm sorry. Missing you say?"

I wasn't sorry. Not at all. Not one bit. Fuckers deserved it. Chuck didn't need to know that.

"The police went to see her, but she's not in her flat. No one has heard from her. She's the fucking heir to the company, Aiden. Mitchell refused to change the fucking papers even though she's not ready. This is all fucked up."

When I took Avery, I knew plans needed to change. Chuck hadn't told me anything I didn't already know.

"No trace of her at all?"

"As of right now, no. Anyway, it's all fucked. I don't know how long it will take for the media to get wind of it."

"Do they have any idea who did it?"

They wouldn't. I'd covered my tracks well. No CCTV footage existed. Nothing. I knew how to take that shit out. The only issue I'd had was getting a passed out Avery back to mine without anyone seeing her. It was fucking lucky I'd brought the car instead of my bike.

"As if the police would tell me anything. I don't even know how they died yet. The housekeeper found them. Fucking bitch went to the police. She should've called me first."

I stifled a laugh. I knew the housekeeper would freak out. I pitied the woman finding her employers dead by a single gunshot to the head. That gun was long fucking gone now. I wasn't stupid.

My careful planning was working, except for the girl in my cell. The girl with doe eyes who made my cock so fucking hard when she'd challenged me, it hurt.

"Can't get the staff."

"No, too fucking right. I'll need you when I find out more."

"No problem."

Chuck hung up. I'd help him, but not in the way he thought. Help him to his fucking grave along with the rest of those involved in their sick operation. Chuck was a motherfucking scumbag. Living in the shadow of his brother his whole life. Now, I'd see just how fucking much he could take before he snapped.

And I was going to enjoy every moment of it.

I opened the door to her cage. Avery lay on the floor, staring up at the ceiling. I flipped on the light. She blinked as the room lit up. Her long, dark hair fanned out around her head like a halo. The sight of it made me feel things. Things I shouldn't fucking feel for the girl I chained up.

I'd left her for an hour, hoping it'd be long enough for her to calm down. She didn't move when I approached her. Up close, I could see her face was tear-streaked and red. She'd been crying again.

"Sit up."

Surprisingly, she complied. Her eyes were bloodshot. She stared at me with almost unnerving intensity.

"Do you need anything?" I asked.

A blush crept up her neck. She looked away.

"Water… and the bathroom, please," she whispered, her voice a little hoarse.

It hardly surprised me given how long she'd raged for after I left her alone.

"I will take you on one condition."

"What's that?"

"I'm not leaving you alone. Either you have me there or I give you a bucket. The choice is yours."

Her eyes widened, her face growing redder. A dimple appeared in her cheek.

Fuck.

"I don't like either of those options."

"You don't have to like them."

After a long moment of silence, she looked at me.

"A bucket is too degrading."

I slipped the key to her ankle manacle out of my pocket.

"You're going to behave if I take this off you, Daniels."

"Yes."

She shifted, giving me access to her ankle. I knelt down and unlocked it. The manacle dropped. I grabbed her arm and pulled her to her feet.

"Let go of me."

I ignored her. She could get pissy with me all she wanted. The moment I gave her an inch, she'd bolt. I dragged her out of the room and down the hall. She struggled to keep up with me.

"Slow down, I've got short legs compared to you."

It made me smile, but she couldn't see my face thankfully. I opened the door to the bathroom and shoved her inside. Standing in the doorway, I watched her teeter on her tiptoes for a moment.

"Get on with it."

"How can I go when you're watching me?"

Betrayal

"I'm not watching you. I don't trust you not to do something stupid. So go."

She walked towards the loo, looking at me from over her shoulder. I knew it made her uncomfortable, but until she'd learnt her place, this would be her reality.

"Can't you at least avert your eyes?" she asked.

"Avery, stop making this harder on yourself."

I hadn't meant to use her name again, but her expression made me feel weird. I didn't want to watch her pee any more than she wanted me there.

She unbuttoned her jeans and shoved them down just as I turned my head away from her. I couldn't look. Seeing any part of her would fuck with my head. She'd already started fucking with it the moment our eyes met.

When she was done, she washed her hands and walked over to me.

"We can go back now."

I took her arm and this time she didn't object. I didn't have to drag her. She followed along and walked back into the concrete room. She sat down and put her leg out for me. I replaced the manacle, chaining her to the wall again.

"Was that so hard?" I asked.

"No. Can I have some water now, please?"

"Wait here."

I'd give her more than just water. She needed to eat. I'd interrupted her dinner with her parents. Who knew how long it had been since she'd had her last meal?

Stalking back down the hall, I went into my kitchen. Unsure of what she might eat, I played it safe and made pancakes. Who didn't like them?

I poured her a glass of water before snagging the plate and a fork. She'd have to make do. A knife could be used as a weapon. I didn't want her getting any ideas.

When I returned, she was still sitting where I left her. I squatted down in front of her. She looked at the plate in my hand.

"Is that for me?"

"Who else would it be for?"

I handed it to her and placed the glass of water by her feet. The first thing she did was grab the glass and drain half of it.

"Why are you feeding me?" she asked when she placed it down and looked at the plate.

"I need you compliant, not starving."

I rocked back on my feet, watching her cut the pancakes with the fork. She ate slowly, taking her time over each mouthful. Did she think I wouldn't feed her again?

Fuck.

I needed her to obey me, not be scared I wouldn't look after her. I wasn't an animal.

She handed me the plate when she was done. When she'd drained the glass, I took that too. Standing, I eyed her for a moment.

"Since you've decided to be good, light on or off?" I asked.

She looked down at her hands.

"Off."

Walking away to the door, I tried to work out why she'd want to sit in darkness. She told me not to leave her in the dark before. Avery was a bit of an enigma. She wasn't what I expected from a girl who'd grown up with every privilege imaginable.

"Wait."

I paused in the doorway, turning slightly to look back at her.

"What do I call you?"

I smiled.

"Aiden. You call me Aiden."

Chapter Three

Avery

His name whirled around and around in my head as I sat in the pitch black cell. The cell he'd put me in. *Aiden.*

I finally had a name to hate. Except the name made my heart fucking ache.

I'd seen him as an avenging angel. I couldn't reconcile the man who'd fed me with the man who'd shot my parents. I hated how conflicted I felt.

His. He'd said I was his. The completely fucked up part about it. I was beginning to think he was right.

I didn't know how much time had passed since he took me, but he'd mentioned it had only been last night when I saw him kill my parents. I was already losing my mind and it'd barely been twenty-four hours. How the hell was I going to survive this?

The glaringly obvious answer to that question was simple. I wasn't meant to. Not if Aiden had his way. The fucking prick was in for a wakeup call. I didn't have the energy to fight him earlier. Next time he wanted to start with his bullshit, I'd be ready for him. I had to make it out of here so I could turn him in. That meant surviving. Surviving a man like Aiden was impossible, but no one could blame me for trying. I had time to work out how. Too much time.

I shifted back until I hit the wall. I brought my knees up and rested my head on them. Exhaustion settled into my bones. Everything I'd been through suddenly felt like too much. Perhaps I'd just rest my eyes for a little while. Who knew when Aiden would grace me with his presence again. I needed to regain my strength.

I let myself drift. Fading in and out of consciousness.

⁜

I snuck into my daddy's office when he left for a moment. I loved the smell of his cigars and whisky. Crawling under his desk, I smiled. My nanny, Esme, would be looking for me.

"No, now isn't the time to move the date forward," I heard my dad's voice and his footsteps on the carpet. "I told you, we have to be careful. Things are delicate right now."

There was no one else with him so I assumed he was on the phone.

"Listen, the girls are our most lucrative trade. If I fuck this up, Nick will give the business to Chuck. No one wants him in charge of operations."

I put a hand on my mouth stifling a giggle. Daddy said a bad word. I crawled out a little way from his desk. He had his back to me, staring out the window with the phone to his ear.

Betrayal

"Yeah, well, we both know my brother has a loud mouth and will get us into more shit."

Was Daddy talking about Uncle Charlie? I didn't feel right around him. He always looked at me strangely. Daddy turned. His eyes fell on me, widening slightly. He gave me a smile.

"Look, I have to go. Something has come up. No. We can deal with it later. All right. Bye."

Daddy slipped his phone in his pocket and crossed his arms over his chest.

"Now, Avery, you know you're not supposed to be in here."

I crawled the rest of the way out from the desk and stood up. I brushed my dress down.

"Sorry, Daddy."

He squatted down and put his arms out. I ran towards him, squealing with delight when he wrapped me up in a bear hug. He set me down, putting his hands on my small shoulders.

"Where is Esme?"

"I was hiding from her. She said it's lunchtime, but I wasn't done playing."

He chuckled, squeezing my shoulders.

"Are you angry with me, Daddy?" I asked, folding down my bottom lip.

"No, you're my little angel."

He kissed the top of my head before standing and putting his hand out to me. I placed mine in it.

"Let's go find Esme."

I smiled, following him from the room.

The sound of the bolts on the door jerked me awake. My cheeks felt wet. I put my hand to them. Great. Now I was crying in my sleep.

I looked over at the door. Aiden filled the frame, blocking out most of the light. I wasn't in the mood to deal with him again. Not after that dream.

The full force of my emotions hit me like a punch to the gut. My dad was gone. I'd never see the little crinkles at the corner of his eyes when he smiled at me. Never get to have one of those bear hugs.

Aiden walked slowly towards me before coming to a stop by my feet. The shaft of light streaming in from the door lit him up. The avenging angel was back. I looked up at him.

"What the fuck do you want now?" I muttered.

I wished I'd controlled my mouth because the next moment, he squatted down and was right up in my face. His expression made me flinch. Cold and heartless.

"Do you want to rephrase that, Daniels?"

I'd started down this path. If I turned back, it'd be admitting he had control over me and I was never giving that to him.

"What. The. Fuck. Do. You. Want?"

His expression darkened. Even in the low light, I could tell he was pissed with my outburst. Served him right. His rules were bullshit. I wasn't obeying anyone let alone the man who'd chained me up in a concrete cell.

He grabbed me by my hair and hauled me up to my feet. I yelped. My scalp burned from where he was holding my hair in his fist.

Betrayal

"Is this what you get off on, huh? Chaining up women and forcing them to do your bidding?" I spat.

He spun me around so fast, I felt dizzy. Slamming me against the wall, his hand wrapped around my throat. I froze, my heart thudding against my chest.

"Oh, Avery, you really have no idea," he said, his breath dusting across my cheek. "No fucking idea at all."

His chest was flush with my back. I could feel the solid wall of muscle, pinning me in place.

"This little tough girl act isn't going to fly with me."

"I'm not afraid of you," I hissed.

"You should be."

His other hand was at the bottom of my t-shirt. He released my throat only to tug it off me. He tucked it in his pocket.

"Clothes are a privilege. Each time you break a rule, you'll lose something else. You think I'm playing games? I'm not."

The concrete wall was cold. I shivered, goosebumps appearing all over my exposed skin.

"Fuck you."

He grabbed both my hands, forcing them behind my back. I felt cold metal against my wrists. When he released me, I realised he'd handcuffed me. I struggled against them. He shoved me to my knees.

"I'm not going to give you any more warnings. If you want to do this the hard way, be my guest."

I tried to turn to look at him, but he pushed me over on the floor. I might not have use of my hands, but I sure as hell still had use of my legs. I kicked out at him. He narrowly avoided my knee to his face. In response, he sat on both of my legs, stopping me in my tracks. I continued to try to struggle against him, but it was no use.

"Let go of me."

His eyes raked over me. My bra was still intact, but it didn't make me feel any less exposed. I could've sworn I saw a hint of longing in his expression for a millisecond before his eyes met mine.

"I will if you behave yourself. The rules are very simple, but you seem to have trouble following them."

"Your rules are bullshit."

He shook his head slowly as if disappointed in me.

Did I care what he thought?

Absolutely not.

"I told you not to make this harder on yourself."

"And I told you, go to hell. If you think I'm going to do anything you say, you're fucking delusional. You murdered my parents."

His eyes flashed momentarily with anger. He leant down, his hands pressed to the floor at the sides of my head. I could feel his breath across my face.

"It's no worse than what they've done."

His words hit me square in the chest. That couldn't possibly be true. They weren't monsters like the man on top of me.

"The girls are our most lucrative trade."

My father's words rang in my ears. It hadn't registered when I was a child what that meant, but now, now my mind raced with possibilities. What did that mean? Girls? We dealt in property, not... people.

"I don't believe you."

"I don't need you to. The only thing you need to do is shut up, listen and do as you're told."

"Or what?"

"There are worse things than this cell, Avery."

My name on his lips sent a shiver down my spine. My cheeks felt hot all of a sudden. His closeness affected my senses. His body radiated heat. The chill of the bare floor no longer seemed to matter with him practically lying on top of me.

His finger ran across my jaw and down my throat.

"Much worse."

The air felt stifling. All the fight left me in an instant. A very small part of me wanted him to trail his fingers lower. My lips parted on a silent plea. What I was begging for? I had no idea. Something to end the tension building inside me.

His eyes mesmerised me. I was sure I wasn't misinterpreting his expression. Burning, molten silver seared holes into my own hazel eyes.

"Are you going to behave now?" he asked, his voice strained and barely above a whisper.

I was done. I needed him off and away from me. The only way that was happening is if I did as he said. It went against all my instincts. I fucking hated him and myself for it.

"No? Do I have to give you more of an incentive?"

The words were on the tip of my tongue. All I had to do was tell him I would stop fighting him.

His fingers brushed lower, across my collarbone. My breath caught in my throat. His touch left a trail of fire in its wake. Fire which burned its way down my stomach and lower to places I tried not to think about.

"Please."

No sooner had the word left my lips than I wanted to shove it right back in my mouth.

What the fuck?

Aiden's eyes darkened further. He had me at his mercy and I'd just begged him for something. I didn't even know what.

"Please, what?"

A question I couldn't answer. I shook my head. The beautiful monster above me smirked.

"Please stop or perhaps… please don't stop?"

The answer to that question was so complicated, it made my head hurt. Yes, I did want him to stop, but no, my body didn't want him to stop. My body was a fucking traitor. It was time to get a grip and pull this right back.

"Please get off me. I won't fight you."

He cocked his head to the side.

"No? I don't trust you, Daniels."

"Seriously, you've made your point. Do I look like I'm in a position to argue with you further?"

His eyes roamed down my chest.

"Well, no. In fact, you're rather compromised right now, aren't you?"

I wanted to glare at him but I didn't think it would help my case.

"Just a little."

He shifted back, sitting up on my legs. I could finally breathe again. The tension between us slowly dissipated.

His hands found the top button of my jeans.

"What are you doing?"

Betrayal

"You might have given in for now, but you've still disobeyed me more than once."

For now.

So he knew I was only giving in now because I had no other choice. I didn't stop him tugging off my jeans. He had to unlock the cuff so he could remove them completely.

His eyes fell on me lying there with my hands behind my back in my underwear. It was uncomfortable and cold now he'd got off me. I didn't want to give him the satisfaction of knowing just how embarrassed I was being so exposed in front of him.

He didn't say a word for a long time. The two of us stared at each other. The muscles under his shirt rippled as he shifted on his feet. Did he always wear a shirt? It seemed so at odds with his nature. Almost as if he was hiding behind a façade of civility.

I knew he had tattoos on his chest because I'd seen one under his collar. Curiosity pricked at me. How far did they extend and where else were they lurking?

"I didn't come in here to fight with you," he said.

"Why did you?"

"Mostly to make sure you hadn't done anything stupid like hurt yourself again."

I wanted to say, 'thanks for the vote of confidence', but instead I settled for rolling my eyes. Hurting myself wouldn't help me get through this ordeal with him.

"Mostly?"

"You are alone in here with nothing but your own thoughts. It can do things to a person."

"I'm fine."

Liar.

I wasn't fine at all. My entire world had changed in the space of a day. I had no idea what was up or down any more. Nothing made sense. Nothing seemed real. I knew it was because my imagination wouldn't dream up something as twisted as this.

"If you say so."

"Are you going to leave these on me?" I indicated my hands behind my back with my head.

"Do you think you deserve to be let off?"

I didn't think yes would be the right answer.

"No…?"

His lip quirked up at the side, eyes sparking with amusement.

"So you are learning."

I wanted to wipe that smile off his face. Partly because it annoyed me how sarcastic his tone had been, but mostly because his smile made him seem human. I couldn't afford to think of him that way. Aiden was making it his mission to break me. He'd said it himself. He needed me compliant. I had no idea why. He should just kill me and be done with it. Then he wouldn't have to deal with me being the only witness to murder.

"Why are you keeping me alive?"

The smile left his face. His expression hardened.

"I gave you an opportunity to ask me questions. You wasted it."

I didn't point out he'd answered the questions before that one.

Betrayal

"Fine, be all mysterious about why you're keeping me here. I mean aside from the obvious part where you took me because of what I saw."

The absurdity of my situation wasn't lost on me. Lying almost naked on a cold concrete floor with a man who looked at me like he wasn't sure whether he wanted to strangle me or… fuck me.

I wasn't about to let him do either. Not that I would have much choice. He'd already shown me how easy it was for him to overpower me. Even so, I was sure Aiden wasn't planning on raping me. He'd had ample opportunity to do so.

"You're not what I expected."

I thought I'd misheard him for a moment. What did he expect? A girl who'd just lay down and take it? I'd certainly given him a wakeup call if that was the case.

In all honesty, he wasn't what I expected either. Especially not the part about my body's traitorous reaction to him. Normal people didn't want their captor. Normal people fought tooth and nail to get away. Perhaps I wasn't normal. I was going to try my damn hardest to keep from falling under whatever spell was between us because I was almost one hundred per cent sure he had a similar reaction to me.

"That makes two of us."

He picked up my clothes from the floor and walked away to the door. I didn't want him to leave me like this. Arguing would only land me in further trouble. I wasn't about to lose any more clothes to him. He said nothing as he shut the door behind him.

I was alone in the dark again.

I was freezing cold.

And a huge part of me didn't want to admit he'd left me high and dry.

Stupid traitorous body.

Chapter Four

Aiden

Holy fuck did I feel like beating the shit out of something or someone. My skin itched. Pacing the living room to stop myself from going straight back in that fucking cell, I tried to tamp down my frustration. Tried and failed.

Avery fucking Daniels had successfully fucked with my head. I'd left her alone all day, not that she seemed to have noticed. I figured I'd go talk to her before I went to bed, perhaps even feed her again. Avery had other ideas. Ones that got completely out of hand.

Taking her clothes had been a stupid idea. I didn't think. All I'd wanted to do was show her I owned her now. Instead, I'd proven to myself just how fucked up I really was. Having her beneath me, handcuffed and half naked had done a fucking number on me.

She was so soft and delicate. Too innocent. Too pure. And I wanted her. I wanted her naked. Completely at my mercy. Legs spread wide so I could fuck her.

Sick fuck.

I wanted to fuck the daughter of the man who'd ruined my entire existence. I'd always known I wasn't normal, but this went far beyond the rest of the shit I'd been involved in. Anyone else would think it was poetic justice after what they'd done, but to me, it wasn't justice at all. No. It was pure fucking torture.

I might want to use Avery to bring down her family, but that was supposed to be it. I wanted nothing more to do with the Daniels when this was over.

I had to do something. Anything to stop this feeling. This need to take everything from her. Make her mine in every sense of the word. Possess her.

I stripped out of my shirt, throwing it on the sofa before shucking my trousers. I walked over to where my boxing bag hung in the corner of the room. Hitting it was better than finding some randomer to take my anger out on. It was too bad Chuck had no work for me. I growled. No way I wanted to think about that sick pervert right now.

Putting my hands up, I started slow, jabbing left and right. It wasn't enough. I hit the bag harder, using the full force of my fists until they ached and I'd built up a sweat. My entire body radiated tension and my stupid fucking hardon wouldn't go down. It wasn't working.

How had this happened? A fucking day she'd been here and I was all kinds of messed up over her.

It was no use. I stormed into the bathroom and turned the shower on. Kicking off my boxers, I stood under the water, hoping it would help. It didn't. The longer I stood there under the spray, the stronger the urge became until I couldn't take it any longer.

Slamming my hand against the wall, I fisted myself and thought about Avery half naked on the floor, her hands cuffed behind her back.

Fuck.

I imagined her naked in my bed. Wet. Wanting. Begging me to give it to her.

Fuck.

I wanted her hands cuffed to the headboard so she couldn't stop me. I wanted her to want me so fucking bad, it hurt. Only then would I let her have it. I'd bury my cock so deep in her hot, tight pussy, she'd still feel me there for days. I'd make Avery scream.

I shuddered all over as I pumped harder.

Fuck.

Images of me pounding her tight pussy with no mercy sent me over the edge. I grunted when hot, sticky streams erupted from me, mixing with the water rushing down from the shower head. Washing away the evidence of my sickening desire for someone I should never want. It didn't stop me wishing it was all over her tits rather than down the shower drain.

I needed to get her off my brain or the release would only be temporary. There was no way I could allow these thoughts to consume me in the way they had been.

The big fucking problem with that plan?

I'd seen the goddamn look in her eyes when I sat on her. When I touched her skin. The way her breath quickened and her tongue darted out, wetting her bottom lip. The one I wanted to bite. I'd seen her just as she'd seen me.

On some level, she wanted me to fuck her.

Screw her.

Ruin her.

And she'd deny it with every breath she took.

I shut the shower off and snagged a towel, wrapping it around my waist. When I was dry enough, I stalked into my bedroom and tugged on a pair of shorts. I got into bed and lay there, staring at the ceiling. It was late and I should be tired. Instead, I was wired up to the max.

Perhaps I was still running off the adrenaline from finally exacting revenge on those sick fucks. I hadn't slept in forty-eight hours. Sleep had never really come easy to me. Not when memories plagued my dreams. If I ever saw a psychologist, they'd have a field day with me.

I needed sleep if I was going to survive another day with her. I closed my eyes. It took a while. I forced myself to take long, slow breaths and the tension in my limbs melted away. I drifted off with thoughts of her running through my mind.

The screaming woke me up. I huddled under the covers with my hands over my ears.

"Please, my son is sleeping, please," she said.

"That boy is none of my concern," the voice I'd heard so many times before replied.

Betrayal

It was a man who always visited us late at night. I'd never seen his face.

"But he is. You know his father wouldn't be happy."

"Don't you bring him into this."

"Please, I will do as you wish."

"Fine. Sweetheart, arrange a nanny for her son."

"Of course, darling," came the voice of the woman who always arrived with him.

"Thank you, sir. Thank you."

"Don't fucking thank me. I'm not doing this for you. Get on your knees."

There was no more talking. Only the sounds of grunting and moaning rang in my ears. I didn't understand what was happening, only that the man did bad things to her.

Later, when the front door slammed, she came into my bedroom. She climbed into bed beside me and hugged me to her chest.

"I'm sorry," she whispered. "I'm so sorry."

"It's okay, Mummy. I love you."

"I love you too, sweetie. Go back to sleep now."

My eyes flew open. I felt hot. A dream. Just another fucking dream. I wasn't stupid enough to think they'd ever stop.

I shifted, grabbing my phone from the bedside table. It was four in the morning. At least I'd managed five hours. No way in hell was I getting back to sleep after that shit.

I hauled myself out of bed and pulled on a t-shirt before picking up a set of keys. My footsteps were quiet across the carpet. Standing outside the reinforced steel door, I wasn't sure whether to check on her or not. I hoped she'd be asleep.

When I unbolted it and turned the locks, the door swung back. She was still lying in the exact same place I'd left her in, curled up on her side with her eyes closed

I ventured in. She didn't stir, but it couldn't have been comfortable for her lying like that with her hands cuffed behind her back. I walked around and squatted down. I unlocked the cuffs and slipped them into my pocket.

A whimper cut through the silence. I brushed her hair back from her face. Her cheeks were wet. A very small part of me felt responsible for her misery.

Avery didn't know why her parents needed to die. To her, I was just the guy who'd taken away her loved ones. Now she didn't have anyone else but me.

I didn't think. I just did. Picking her up, I walked backwards until I was up against the wall. I sat down with her in my lap and cradled her to my chest.

"Shhh," I whispered, stroking her hair when she whimpered again.

Her fingers curled around my t-shirt, gripping it with her fist. She was so fucking small in my arms. I knew she was about twenty years old. She certainly looked and felt all woman, yet she was still so small compared to me.

And here I was being a fucking idiot. I'd never offered anyone comfort before or held someone because they needed a hug. That just wasn't me.

It was like some part of me knew what Avery needed right now was someone to take care of her. That if I wanted to make her mine, I had to make her need me. No matter my sick

Betrayal

attraction to the girl, I still had to carry out my plan. I needed her for that.

Avery shifted in my grasp. I looked down at her. Her eyes were open. For a moment, we just stared at each other. Tears split down her cheeks unheeded. Then Avery did something I didn't expect. She let go of my t-shirt, placed her hand right above my heart, buried her face in my chest and sobbed. I sat there, stroking her hair. I let her cry on me without saying a word.

Her skin was icy to the touch. Given I'd left her on the concrete floor in nothing but her underwear, it wasn't a surprise. She needed to get warm again.

I pulled out the key from my pocket and unlocked the manacle around her ankle. I stood with her in my arms. She didn't raise her head when I carried her out into the hall and along to the bathroom. I set her down on the edge of the bath before putting the plug in and turning on the taps.

Only then did she look at me. Her eyes roamed across my face and down to my arms. She bit her lip. It was the first time she'd seen me in anything but a shirt. I knew she was staring at the intricate designs snaking up from my wrists. It had taken years to have my entire torso and arms marked in ink, but it was a badge of honour for me. They told the story of my life. Except no one would be able to decipher their meaning without context.

Curiosity burnt in her doe eyes, but I knew she wouldn't ask me about them.

"If you need to… uh… go, then go," I said, indicating the loo behind me.

She stood up on shaky legs and walked towards it. My back was to her so she didn't have to worry about me watching. She sat back on the bath when she was done, her eyes on me again.

"Why are you doing this for me?" she asked.

"You're cold. Can't have you getting sick."

I took her injured hand and peeled off the bandage. Her knuckles looked better than they had done yesterday. It was lucky she hadn't hurt herself worse.

When the water was high enough, I shut off the taps. I walked away a few paces to give her some privacy.

"Um, Aiden, can... can you help me, please? I can't undo my bra."

When I turned back, her face was bright red. The way she said my name made my dick hard. For fuck's sake. That was the last thing I needed.

"What's wrong with you?"

"My arms, it hurts too much what with them having been cuffed behind my back all night."

I moved closer to her.

"Turn around then."

She did as I asked. I could see goosebumps all over her skin. Taking a breath, I unhooked her bra. My fingers trailed upwards, pushing down the strap on her left shoulder. She put her hands up, cupping the bra to her breasts. I stared down at her cleavage as I pulled down the strap on her right shoulder. My fingers brushed down her arms, coming to rest on her waist. The urge to tug her against me grew until it was almost unbearable.

"I don't want to get my hair wet," she whispered.

I brushed her hair away from her ear, leaning down closer.

"No?"

She swallowed.

"It's not like you'd have a hairdryer lying around."

I smiled as I trailed my fingers along her shoulder. She trembled and fuck, did I want her. Here she was, almost naked in front of me and no matter how much she hated me, she was affected too. Her breath came faster, her teeth making indents on her bottom lip.

"Wait there."

Girls I'd had in my flat in the past sometimes left things behind. I most likely had a hairband for her somewhere. I dug through the bathroom cabinet above the sink, finding my prey. I stalked back over to Avery, resuming my position behind her. I carefully gathered her hair up and tied it back for her.

"Do you need anything else?" I asked, resting my hands on her shoulders, kneading them slightly with my fingers.

I felt her relax so I continued. She let out a little moan.

"Do you like that? You're all tense," I whispered in her ear, stepping closer so my chest was almost touching her back.

I didn't think she'd answer me, but she nodded. She arched into my touch when I dug my fingers harder into her shoulders.

What the fuck was I doing right now?

This was going to end badly if I didn't stop, but my fucking common sense had fled. Being close to her, touching her skin made all my senses come alive. It was fucking lucky I was wearing shorts because my hardon was raging out of control. I teetered on the edge of pressing her into me. We were only inches apart. Those inches felt like miles.

"You should get in before the water gets cold," I said.

"O… Okay."

Her neck was flushed. Even the tips of her ears were red. She stepped forward and I let my hands drop. Her arms fell to her sides and her bra dropped to the floor. I couldn't fucking move. She hooked her fingers into her underwear, bending down slightly as she took off the last piece of her clothing.

Fuck. Fuck.

Her pert behind was like a fucking beacon. My cock twitched, wanting to be nestled between her cheeks. I almost groaned before I tore my eyes away.

She stepped into the bath and sunk into the water, covering herself with her arms. I moved away, putting the toilet lid down and sitting on it.

"For what it's worth, I never intended for you to see what I did to them," I said, wanting to break the tense silence between us.

"I know."

She didn't look at me as she sunk lower in the water until only her head was above the surface. I wasn't going to look because I knew if I did, nothing would stop me getting in that bath with her. And as fucked up as I was, I would never, ever fuck a girl against her will. That would put me on the same level as the sick fucks I was trying to destroy.

"Is it helping?"

"The bath? Yes."

I couldn't think of what else to say to her. It wasn't like I really knew anything about the girl other than what her uncle had told me and what I'd seen in the tabloids.

Betrayal

I stood up, walking over and picking up her discarded clothes. I made to leave, but her voice stopped me.

"Where are you going?"

I didn't turn around.

"To get you something else to wear. I suggest you stay there until I get back."

I walked out and away into the kitchen. I checked the labels on her bra and other clothes, making a note of her size before dumping them and the clothes I'd taken off her yesterday in the washing machine. I'd get her some new stuff because she couldn't exactly stay here and only have one set of clothing. I couldn't go and fetch stuff from her place. The police would be all over that and no one knew I had her. It had to stay that way.

I went to my bedroom and selected one of my plain white t-shirts and a clean pair of boxers. I wasn't sure what else to put her in, so it would have to do.

When I returned to the bathroom, she hadn't moved. I sat back down on the toilet seat and dumped the clothes next to me.

"You'll have to tell me what you need and I'll get it for you."

"What?" she asked, turning to me.

"You know, the girl shit you might need."

"Why would you get me stuff?"

I shook my head. She didn't get it.

"I told you before, you're mine. That means I take care of you and give you all the things you need."

I didn't stop to think about what things other than possessions she might need from me and whether I could really give her everything.

"You didn't really explain that part."

"You just haven't been listening. You will learn to rely on me and only me. Until then, you're going to stay in that cell."

She didn't reply. I watched her fidget in the water under my gaze. At least she wasn't fighting me. That would be a battle she'd lose and I was pretty sure she'd worked that out.

Now, I just had to combat the war going on in her head. She didn't want to submit to me, but she would. Just so long as I didn't keep touching her, things would be okay.

I looked away when she grabbed one of the bottles of shower gel from the side of the bath. I really needed to get her back in the cell so I could take care of myself. It was the only way I'd get rid of my burning need to rip her out the bathtub, bend her over the side of it and fuck her senseless.

Sick fuck. Sick in the head.

Wanting her was so wrong.

"Can I have a towel... please?"

I got up, snagging a clean one from the shelf and held it up for her. I closed my eyes when she got out and took it from me. I walked away, getting the clothes I'd brought her off the floor. I kept my back to her as she put them on.

She put a hand on my arm, to get my attention. My skin prickled from the direct contact. My sick need for her grew. Fuck.

"Come on," I said, pulling my arm from her grasp.

Betrayal

Her eyes flashed with confusion, but she followed me from the room. I didn't take her into the cell. We walked into the kitchen.

"Go sit down at the table."

She did as I asked. It was still dark outside, but with it being winter, the sun wouldn't rise properly for a few hours or so.

I got my box of medical supplies and bandaged her hand again. She watched me without saying a word. Her doe eyes spoke volumes. Grateful I'd taken care of her.

I packed up the supplies and got up. I pulled out some breakfast stuff from the fridge and set about making a protein shake for myself and eggs on toast for her. I still wasn't sure what she ate, but we could broach that subject later.

I thrust the plate under her nose when I was done, leaning back against the counter with my glass.

She ate in silence with me watching her. My t-shirt swamped her small frame, but it didn't stop her tits sticking out. Her nipples were hard against the fabric. Fuck me if I didn't want to bite them until she begged me to stop. Shaking myself, I downed my protein shake and dumped the glass in the dishwasher. She stood with her plate and did the same.

I didn't speak as I led her back into the cell and chained her up again.

"Can I have the light on, please?" she asked as she sat against the wall.

"If you want," I replied, walking away to the door. "Have a list of things you need ready for when I come see you again."

"Aiden?"

"Hmm?"

"Thank you."

I almost turned around to look at her, but I couldn't. Whatever reason she had for thanking me, it didn't matter. I turned the light on for her before I shut the door. This time I didn't lock it. Wasn't much point when I'd chained her up.

I walked away to my bedroom. It was time I took care of some things, including my raging hardon which had plagued me since she'd spoken my name out loud for the first time.

That girl had a lot of shit to answer for.

A heck of a lot of shit.

Chapter Five

Avery

I felt like the days were merging into one another. My sense of time was all messed up. I had no idea how long it had been since he'd taken me. Time alone in the cell did things to me. Somehow, I began to look forward to when he'd open the door. Even though we didn't talk much, having another human around me was comforting.

My hand had healed up with his care. The evidence I'd split my knuckles was all but gone. I wondered how he knew basic first aid. Asking him anything about himself was impossible. He'd likely jump down my throat.

Aiden had got me the few things I'd asked him for. Girl shit as he put it. Simple things like deodorant, a hairdryer, my favourite shampoo and conditioner. I didn't want to push my luck.

I was glad I didn't have to ask him to get me tampons. I no longer got periods with the birth control I was on. It would've been a seriously embarrassing conversation. Things were already weird after that day he'd let me cry on his chest.

I tried not to read too much into it. Especially not what happened afterwards.

I shook myself. I had to forget about how incredible his fingers felt when he'd massaged my shoulders. How much I wanted his fingers in other places. Places I really shouldn't ever want the man who'd killed my parents to touch me.

I hit my head against the wall behind me several times. Not particularly hard, but just enough to dislodge the thought from my head. I really needed to get a grip. This cell was seriously getting to me. The lack of human contact felt so isolating.

I wondered if Gert had gone on our holiday without me. I couldn't imagine how her and James felt, knowing I was missing. And then there was Peter. The guy I'd just sort of started seeing. It wasn't serious. We hadn't slept together yet, but he was nice. In comparison to the man who had me now, Peter was a puppy dog.

He was in one of my classes so I'd known him for almost two years, but he'd only just worked up the courage to ask me out. I would've said yes if he'd asked me in our first year. He was cute in a geeky sort of way, but I liked that he was a proper gentleman. Unlike a certain individual who made my blood pound for many reasons. Fuck my traitorous body for feeling that way about him. I needed to get that man out of my brain, but I couldn't. He was always there because I was always waiting for him to come see me.

Crazy. Fucking crazy. I was totally losing it.

I just had to try to focus my mind on other things. I remembered what James had said when I told him about my first date with Peter.

"About time you went out with someone who wasn't a complete cunt."

James didn't mince words and liked to swear, a lot. My heart ached. I missed him. His ridiculous crooked grin. His blue eyes sparking with amusement whenever Gert said something funny. The boy was a legend and never failed to cheer me up. I could really do with that now. Anything would be better than being on my own. Anything except Aiden. And he was all I had.

I whacked my head against the wall again, but this time it was a little too hard. I winced, rubbing the back of it.

"What is wrong with me?" I said aloud. "Why does everything always come back around to him? I'm so stupid."

Idiot. Talking to yourself now.

I closed my eyes, imagining Peter's face instead. His messy dark hair, green eyes blinking behind his glasses and the way he smiled when he looked at me. The first time he'd kissed me, it had been terribly awkward. We'd both been nervous. Stupid really. It wasn't like either of us were virgins. I think it was more down to the fact that we already knew each other pretty well as friends.

Who knew what he thought with me being gone? I was supposed to meet him the day after my dinner with my parents. I guessed everyone knew they were dead by now. It wasn't like my family and the company could keep that hidden long. And there was no way Aiden would've left anything linking him to the crime scene. I might not know much about the man, but I knew for sure he'd know how to get away with murder.

Fucking Aiden again. The amount of space he took up in my head was intolerable. I was curious about him. About what reasoning he had for killing my parents. Why he really needed me alive. Why he wanted me to learn to rely on him. Obey him. And not least of all, what the hell the tattoos on his arms meant. He'd only allowed me to see them that one time, but the images had burnt into my brain. I'd be able to draw them if he gave me a pen and paper.

Down his left arm, he had several skulls and roses along with some text which I hadn't been able to make out. It was his right arm that fascinated me. On his bicep was a bird in a cage and wrapping around his forearm, a chain. There were other things, but those two stood out to me. I wanted to know what the caged bird meant. To be honest, I wanted to know what all of it meant. Some part of me wanted to understand him.

And as if he knew I was thinking about him, the door to my cell swung open. I blinked. First, he dumped a bucket in the corner of the room and left. When he returned, he had a plastic bag with him. He set it down next to me along with a large bottle of water. He'd fed me breakfast not long ago so I wasn't expecting him.

"I have to go out and I don't know when I'll be back. There should be enough to keep you going," he said.

He'd been out during the day before. I mean I knew he had to have gone out, but this was the first time he'd actually come and informed me.

"Oh."

"If I could trust you, I'd let you out into the flat, but I don't yet."

"You think I'd try to leave?"

He cocked an eyebrow.

"Wouldn't you?"

Betrayal

I shrugged.

"Probably."

Something told me escaping him wasn't ever going to be an option. And at this point, I wasn't really sure I wanted to. Despite my deteriorating mental state and the isolation, being here was easy. I knew I'd see him three times a day. He stood outside when I went to the bathroom instead of coming in with me now. I was beginning to rely on the man staring down at me no matter how hard I tried not to. Rely on the routine he'd given me. It was the only thing keeping me sane.

"Well then."

There wasn't really anything I could say to that. He turned and left, shutting the door behind him. For the first time in what I thought might be two weeks but could be longer, he locked it. I was trapped in his concrete cell and he wasn't here any longer. I tried not to think too hard on that fact.

The first few hours were okay. I thought about Gert, James and Peter. Then it became harder to forget Aiden wasn't just outside. He'd left me snacks and sandwiches. I ate a little when I got hungry and got desperate enough that I had to go in the bucket.

How long had he been gone? I lost all sense of time, beginning to lose my grip on reality. I kept hearing the locks turning in my head but the door never opened. I thought I heard his deep voice whispering in my ear.

"Avery. Avery. Avery."

I whipped my head around but there was nothing. The cell was empty. I couldn't take it any longer. Marching over to the door, I banged on it over and over.

"Aiden, please, please, I can't deal with this anymore. I promise I'll be good. I promise. Just let me out. I don't want to be alone anymore."

Tears fell down my cheeks.

"Aiden. Please. I... I need you."

The moment those words left my lips, I collapsed on the floor. They were the truth. I did need him. It wasn't just to end this torment in the cell. I looked forward to seeing him. My beautiful avenging angel.

"I need you," I sobbed, burying my face in my hands. "I need you."

When I saw him, I forgot my parents were dead by his hands. All I saw was him. All that hard muscle beneath his clothes which I'd felt pressed up against me when he'd pinned me to the wall. The self-assured way he carried himself. The deadly look in his eyes. Those silver eyes which haunted my every waking moment and even my dreams. Aiden was all of that and so much more. And I was the stupid girl who couldn't look away.

"Avery."

"Please, Aiden, come back to me."

I crawled away from the door. The locks rang in my ears. I peered at it, but it didn't open.

Was I having a mental breakdown?

Had I finally snapped?

I was definitely hearing things that weren't really there.

"Avery, you are mine. Mine."

I put my hands over my ears. It had to stop. All of it.

I saw feet in front of me. I looked up and there was my father.

Betrayal

"Dad?"

"My little angel. I've missed you. Daddy is home now."

His voice sounded disjointed. I didn't understand how he was here. He was supposed to be dead. I saw him die.

"You're not real."

"Don't you want to see me, sweetie?"

"No. No, you're not real. You can't be."

"Avery, why didn't you save me? Why didn't you stop him?"

No. This couldn't be happening. I couldn't have done anything to stop Aiden. No. His eyes looked exactly like my dad's with those little crinkles in the corners.

"You're not real! Not real. Please, Aiden. I need Aiden."

"Aiden killed me. How can you want the man who killed me?"

I put my hands over my eyes. I was hallucinating my own father. This could not be happening.

"Stop. Please stop. Aiden, make it stop."

"Aiden isn't here, angel. Aiden can't save you. Look at me, baby, look at me."

"No. He can. He can. I need him," I sobbed. "I need him."

I was fucking crazy. All of this was a sick twisted dream and I couldn't get out of it. Was I asleep or was this just guilt? Either way, I needed the stupid vision of my father to go away. He was messing me up even more. I couldn't take this.

"Look at me, Avery."

I slowly removed my hands from my eyes. Right between his eyes, a hole started to form, blood pouring out of the wound. I screamed, scrambling backwards until I hit the wall. Lifeless eyes stared back at me.

"Why didn't you save me?" my father said one last time before he collapsed on the floor.

I huddled my knees up to my chest and buried my face in them, sobbing. It wasn't real. Nothing was real anymore

All I could think about was Aiden coming back and finding me like this. A mess. No longer able to distinguish between a hallucination and reality.

Is this what he wanted?

Did he want to break me this much?

Seeing my father had well and truly fucked me up.

Why did I even care what Aiden might think?

He caused this. He killed my family. I should be angry with him, except I wasn't. It didn't matter if that made me insane. All I wanted right now was him. He was real. I'd find my way back to reality for him.

Whether hours had passed or not, I didn't know. I peered out from my knees, but I was alone again. My dad wasn't on the floor. I almost cried in relief.

Hauling myself up to sitting position, I dragged the bag with the snacks Aiden had left to me. The big Cadbury's caramel bar stared at me. I'd told him it was my favourite chocolate.

I ripped open the packet and ate three squares in quick succession. The sugar hit my system immediately, spreading through my veins. I sighed at the simple pleasure.

Before I knew it, I'd consumed half the bar and instead, I felt sick. I shoved it away from me, putting a hand over my mouth.

Idiot. Why did you eat it so fast?
Stupid. Fucked up. Crazy. Losing it.

Betrayal

I looked around the room. The single bulb illuminated all the corners. Nothing was lurking. No more hallucinations.

That's when I heard the locks turning again. I put my hands on my ears.

No. No. Not that again.

The door swung back. I stared up at the figure there.

Aiden.

I scrambled to my feet as he took a few steps towards me. Was it really him? I wasn't seeing things again, was I? Who cared. All I knew was I needed him.

Him.

"Are… are you real?" I whispered.

He frowned, taking in the mess of wrappers on the floor. "Are you okay?"

That deep voice rumbled through me. I knew that sound. It could only mean one thing.

I launched forward and barrelled my way into his chest, wrapping my arms around his solid back. I clung to him like a leech.

"You're real. You have to be real," I mumbled.

"Avery, what the fuck?"

"I kept seeing things. Hearing things. But you, you're real. I can feel you. I thought you'd never come back. Don't leave me again, please. I can't face it."

I didn't care I was rambling nonsense to him. His heart thudded against his chest. The chest that moved with every breath he took.

"Please, Aiden. I don't want to be alone anymore. I don't want to see my dad again. I don't. I can't."

He grabbed my shoulders and tore me away from him, staring down at me with those steel grey eyes which sent my heart into overdrive.

"What is wrong with you?"

"Are you angry with me? I'm sorry. I'm so sorry. I didn't mean to do anything wrong. Please, just please don't leave me alone."

He frowned further, searching my face.

"Is this some kind of act? Because it's not fucking funny if it is. Do you think I'm going to fall for bullshit like this?"

Tears welled in my eyes. He didn't believe me. What could I do to make him see? How could he think this was an act?

"No, please. I'm serious. I saw my dad die again, right in front of me. I don't fucking know what is real or not. I can't deal with this. I need… I need you to believe me. I…I…I need you. Please."

I sounded so pathetic. Hot, wet tears dripped down my face. Begging the man who'd murdered my parents was just fucked up.

I fell to my knees, putting my hands out.

"I'm sorry. I'm sorry. Please believe me. I will do anything. I just need you."

I bowed my head to my chest.

"Please," I whispered. "I'm yours."

Those were the words which well and truly sealed my fate. Seconds seemed to tick by so slowly, but I didn't move. I felt his hand cup my face, his thumb running along my bottom lip.

"Come here," he said, his voice gentle.

Betrayal

When I raised my head, he was sitting in front of me. He dropped his hand. He let me crawl into his lap and held me to his chest. I breathed him in. He smelt faintly of cedarwood and pine.

"Tell me what you saw."

"I kept hearing the locks on the door turning. And your voice in my ear. I saw my dad. He kept asking why I didn't save him. I kept telling him he wasn't real. All I wanted was to see you because I know you're real. He asked me why I wanted the man who killed him. He said you couldn't save me. Then I saw the bullet in his head again and he collapsed on the floor. I was so scared. I know it wasn't real, but it felt real."

Aiden clutched me closer, stroking my hair.

"I've got you now, Avery. You don't have to be scared."

The fear I'd felt leaked out of my body. My limbs no longer felt tense. Aiden's presence calmed me, soothed me. He rested his cheek against the top of my head. I closed my eyes, my hand curling around his neck and threading in the short hair at the back of his head.

"You're okay now," he murmured. "You're safe with me."

And the fucked up part?

That was a lie I wanted to believe.

I would never be safe with Aiden.

Not now.

Not ever.

Chapter Six

Aiden

I'd broken her without even really trying. Keeping her in that cell had done the work for me. I hadn't realised when I'd left to go deal with what Chuck wanted, she'd completely lose her mind. Hallucinating her own father's death all over again. Shit. That would fuck anyone up, especially what she'd imagined he'd said to her.

Her father was right. I wouldn't save her. I planned on ruining her entirely. Yet, here and now, I just held her because she needed me. She'd said it herself.

I didn't like seeing her like this. Scared. Terrified. This wasn't the girl who challenged me and told me to go to hell.

"Are you hungry?" I asked her.

"Yes."

She looked up at me, her eyes still wet with tears. Fucking doe eyes. I couldn't resist them. And a part of me didn't even want to.

"Come on, you can have a shower and I'll make dinner, okay?"

She nodded, pulling away from me. I shifted, pulling the keys out of my pocket and unlocked her ankle manacle. I took her hand and led her into the bathroom.

I could clean up her cell later when I'd put her to bed. The thought of having her in my bed did things to me, but I was pretty sure if I left her alone for too long, she'd freak out again. I couldn't have that. Pushing her further wouldn't get me anywhere.

"Are you going to be okay in here without me?"

"Just leave the door open," she replied.

I nodded, walking out and away into the kitchen. I pulled out a bunch of stuff from the fridge and cupboards. Avery wasn't picky, which made things easier.

As I chopped vegetables, my mind wandered back to when I'd seen Chuck earlier. I'd gone to his office after he called me last night to say he had things for me to take care of. I'd heard from him a couple of times over the past three weeks.

The police had released details of Mitchell and Kathleen's deaths and Avery's disappearance to the press. They had no leads and no clue where to start when it came to finding Chuck's niece.

There was nothing but speculation all over the internet. Some people said she might be ransomed. Some people thought she'd killed her own parents and others that she'd run away. Stupid really.

It was just as well I'd kept her away from all of this. She didn't need to read that shit about herself. Especially not now when she was in such a fragile state. The one I was about to exploit for my own benefit.

Betrayal

Chuck had been sitting behind his desk when I walked in. He looked like Mitchell except younger with lighter hair. There was a strong resemblance between him and Avery.

"Thank fuck," he said, looking up at me. "It's been crazy around here for weeks. No one knows how to deal with Mitch being gone."

I nodded, sitting down on a chair in front of him. Chaos was exactly what I wanted.

"I've got some leads I need following up."

"Leads…?"

"Well, people who haven't been paying their way to be exact."

"I see."

"Business can't just come to a standstill. The board is looking after the company until Avery is found and I'm stuck dealing with the other side of things as usual."

The other side being their underhanded dealings. There were many sides to Daniels Holdings. So many sides the public didn't see. The fact that anyone thought they were a reputable property business was testament to their ability to keep secrets and silence anyone who threatened to talk. It helped that they had so many powerful people in their pockets.

Shaw Associates dealt with the legal side of their property business. A shit hot solicitors firm run by Frazier Shaw, Mitchell's best friend and the man who made sure none of their dirty secrets came to light. That fucker needed to be torn down too. Him and his snivelling little son, Tristan.

Fucking prick was about as stuck up as a little rich boy could get. He was sick in the head. Worst of all, they had always intended for him to marry Avery so he could run the business by her side. Made me sick to think of Tristan touching her. No one was allowed to touch her except me. No other man would ever get close enough to Avery again. I wasn't going to sleep with her, but she was still mine.

I ignored the voice in my head telling me it was idiotic to believe I wouldn't give in to temptation and bury my cock deep inside her tight pussy.

"So, you need me to shake down some doors."

"Precisely. The little maggots can't be allowed to take advantage of the delicate situation the company is in. A show of strength if you will."

"Consider it done."

"I always know I can count on you."

I bit the inside of my cheek to keep from smiling. Chuck was so confident in that knowledge, he wouldn't see it coming when I stabbed him in the back. They all should've known better considering what they'd done to me, but I'd been good at deceiving them all. Too good.

"Anything else?"

"No. Just wish I knew where the fuck my niece was. Everything would be easier if we had her to show a unified front. Still, things could always be worse."

Oh, they could and they would be. Soon. I just had to bide my time and let this play out.

"I'm sure she'll turn up soon."

I'd left after that, taking the names he'd given me and paying a few people a visit. It'd taken longer than anticipated. A few of them failed to understand their place. I'd had to show

Betrayal

them. With my fists. Just one of the many things I did for Chuck and his sick family business.

I shook myself, staring down at the meal I'd prepared. I hoped it would make her happy. I'd left her some pyjamas outside the bathroom door.

I turned, finding her standing in the kitchen, staring at me with wide eyes.

"I can fix you a drink if you want," I said.

She came over to me. Her hair was still damp, but she'd tied it up. I'd make sure she dried it before I put her to bed. I snagged a hand around her waist and pulled her into me, resting my chin on the top of her head. She clung to me. Avery needed soft right now. Something tangible to hold onto.

"What kind of drink?"

"What do you like?"

"You'll say they're girl drinks."

I snorted.

"Well, do you drink gin and tonic?"

She nodded against my chest.

"That's sort of girly, but I'll let you off."

She turned her head, looking down at the two plates on the counter.

"That looks good."

It wasn't particularly fancy. Sticky sesame chicken with stir fry vegetables and rice. A healthier version than what you might get from a takeaway. I wasn't one for eating crap.

"We should really eat it before it gets cold."

She pulled away from me and took the plates to the table whilst I fixed her a drink. I snagged a beer from the fridge and popped the cap off with the bottle opener. Setting the drinks down, I sat with her. She was quiet for the first five minutes. Fiddling with her glass, she looked up at me.

"Aiden… Will you tell me what's happening in the outside world?"

"What do you want to know?"

"How is… I mean things must be all over the place."

I took a swig from my beer before setting it down and leaning back.

"They are. It's all over the news, as are you."

"What do they think happened to me?"

"All they know is you're missing."

She looked down at her plate.

"Your uncle has people looking for you."

Her doe eyes met mine again, her expression hardening.

"Uncle Charlie? I bet he's pissed off more than anything else. How do you know about what he's doing?"

I frowned. It didn't sound like she had any love for Chuck.

"What makes you think he's pissed off?"

"He hates that my dad's Will made sure I would inherit the company and their money in the event of his death. The board signed off on it. Nothing he can do about it from a legal standpoint. So ergo, he kind of hates me, but I don't care. He's a dick."

I smiled, unable to help myself. If Avery hated her uncle, then it would make things easier.

"What did he ever do to you?"

Her eyes flashed with pain for a moment.

"I don't want to talk about it," she muttered. "And you didn't tell me how you know my uncle."

Betrayal

I made a note to make sure I found out what had gone on between Chuck and her. If he'd done anything to hurt her, I'd seriously consider putting a bullet in the fucker's head right now. I knew he had some sick perversions. His death needed to be drawn out.

I wished I could've drawn out Mitchell and Kathleen's deaths, but I'd had to settle for quick and painless. The only person who'd been hurt was the girl in front of me.

"I know everyone in your family."

She stared at me with confusion written all over her face.

"Even the ones from my great aunt's side?"

"Even them."

Her great aunt, Matilda, was dead just like her grandfather, Nicholas Daniels. Her daughter and two sons were alive. The men, Troy and Arthur, were just as deeply involved as Mitchell and Chuck. The sick family business.

"How?"

"I think you know enough, for now, Avery."

I was done with her questions. She wasn't ready for the truth. Not after her little breakdown earlier. I couldn't shatter her illusions about her parents and the rest of her family just yet.

She looked as though she might argue for a moment, but she picked up her fork and started eating again. I did the same.

I could feel her eyes on me every so often. I wondered what she was thinking. How she'd processed what I told her.

She set her knife and fork down when she was done. I'd long finished and was sipping my beer.

"I'm tired," she whispered.

"Finish your drink and you can go to bed."

"Are you going to put me back in the cell?"

"No."

Her brow furrowed, but she didn't ask me where I'd put her instead. I wasn't sure what she'd think when she discovered I intended her to sleep in my bed. With me. I needed to keep an eye on her. It was the only way.

I stood up and gathered the plates. Pulling open the dishwasher, I stacked all the dirty dishes and took her glass when she was done.

"Can I have some water, please? To go to bed with, I mean."

"The glasses are in the cupboard above the sink."

I watched her select one and pour herself some water. She held it to her chest and looked at me with expectation written all over her face. I took her by the arm and walked out. She followed me into my bedroom. Her eyes went wide as she took in where we were. I took her glass from her and set it on the bedside table on the right-hand side of the bed.

"Go brush your teeth, dry your hair and come back here, understand?" I said.

She nodded slowly before shuffling back out the way we'd come. I pulled back the covers for her before stalking out the room. I went back into the cell, picking up all the discarded chocolate wrappers and everything else she'd left all over the floor, stuffing them back into the bag before I picked up the bucket. I left it outside the bathroom door because she was still in there and dumped the bag in the kitchen to deal with in the morning.

Stalking back down the hall, I snagged my laptop from the sofa in the living room where I'd left it. I still had things to do.

Betrayal

I found the bucket was gone when I walked back out into the hall. She'd dealt with it. Good girl.

Avery was standing in the middle of the room when I got back. Her eyes darted around, taking in her surroundings.

On one side, I had big built-in cupboards behind sliding doors. I'd put the clothes I'd bought her in one of them. My king size bed took up most of the back wall. A huge window with the curtains drawn on the left-hand side. The walls were deep blue and the furniture black. The headboard on my bed was welded metal. Perfect for handcuffs, chains and rope, which I most definitely should not be thinking about right now. Not when she was about to get in my bed.

"You sleep here," I said, pointing at where I'd drawn the covers back.

"Um… with you?"

"Yes with me."

A blush crept up her neck and face, all the way to the tips of her ears.

"You did tell me you didn't want to be alone, did you not?"

She nodded.

"I'm not going to bite, Avery. Just get in bed."

She shuffled over to it and crawled in, settling the covers over herself. She hadn't had a bed in three weeks.

I left my laptop on my side of the bed before going over to the cupboards. I unbuttoned my shirt and pulled it off. I had a t-shirt on underneath. I dumped the shirt in the washing basket before unbuckling my belt. I took off my trousers before tugging on a pair of shorts. I sat on the end of the bed to take my socks off, which went in the basket too.

I eyed Avery who was still huddled under the covers, not looking at me. Picking up the laptop, I leant against the headboard with my pillows tucked up behind me and set about getting some work done.

An hour later, I was sick of looking at lines of code so I turned it off and dumped my laptop on the floor beside the bed. Pulling the covers back, I got in and lay down, switching off the lamp which I'd left on.

Despite the size of the bed putting space between us, I could feel the heat radiating off her. And I was drawn to it. Drawn to her.

"Are you asleep?" I asked.

"No," she replied.

"What's wrong?"

"It feels weird being in a bed. I don't even know how long it's been."

"Three weeks."

It didn't matter to me if she knew how long it had been or not. I imagined her sense of time was a little skewed.

"It feels like longer."

"Come here."

I wasn't sure why I said that, but she needed to rest. It took a minute before she shifted towards me.

"Turn around," I told her.

She did as I asked, but yelped when I tugged her against my front, wrapping my arm around her waist. Her whole body went rigid.

"What are you doing?" she squeaked.

"What does it look like?"

Betrayal

She didn't reply. It was pretty obvious what I was doing. Fucking holding her so she could relax and go to sleep. Except this was making it increasingly difficult for me to think straight. Her arse was right up against my crotch, making my cock twitch.

"Relax," I whispered in her ear. "You said you needed me, Avery. I'm giving you what you asked for."

A moment later, she wriggled against me before settling down. That wriggling was the last fucking straw. My cock went ramrod straight. Neither of us said anything, but I knew she could feel it pressing into her behind. Everything about this was torture. Having her so close. The way her hair smelt of coconut. Her subtle curves moulding to my body in a way no other woman had. It wasn't as though I held women like this. I'd certainly fucked them in this position before, but cuddling wasn't something I did.

Avery's breathing didn't settle down, if anything it came faster. My thumb trailed a circle around her stomach. She shifted again, my cock digging further into her.

Fuck.

I wanted to pull her shorts down and bury my cock in her. Never had I felt such a desperate need for another person in my life.

I buried my face in her neck, trying to tamp down on the urges coursing through me.

"Aiden," she whispered.

"Hmm?"

"I… I can't sleep."

"Why not?"

She shifted. This time I realised she was pressing back against me.

What the fuck?

Avery wasn't going to verbally acknowledge that my cock was digging into her arse. The tension between us was palpable. I wanted to see her face, see her expression. I needed it. Needed to know it wasn't just me.

I grabbed her by the waist and forced her to turn around. Her eyes met mine as I dragged her against me. I pressed myself between her legs, not caring that I'd trapped one underneath me. I could feel her heat on my cock through our clothes.

Her doe eyes were wide in the low light streaming in from a gap in the curtain. Her lips parted but she didn't make a sound. Her tits were pressed up against my chest, her nipples pebbled. Fuck I wanted to touch them, but I wouldn't.

I gripped her hip and ground into her, pressing my dick against her pussy. She didn't tell me to stop. Her hand snaked around my back. Avery fucking wanted me as much as I wanted her. I saw it in her eyes as we stared at each other.

I moved again. Avery began to match my rhythm, her hand moving to clutch my waist. Neither of us said anything. I wanted her to come. I needed her to. The sick part of me wanted to prove she was really mine. To prove I commanded her body and she wanted only me.

Me in her head.

Me between her legs.

Avery was fucking mine.

My cock was so hard and her heat drove me fucking crazy. I was in two minds about ripping her clothes off so I could fuck her properly. If I did that, who knew if either of us could come back from it. I couldn't give in to that temptation. Dry humping her was already a stupid idea to begin with. Stopping would be impossible.

My name left her lips, almost masked by a groan. That fucking sent me right over the edge. I pressed harder into her.

"Come for me, Avery," I growled. "Fucking come on my cock."

Her eyes didn't leave mine. She bit down on her lip, her fingers digging into my waist.

"I want to hear you," I told her.

She released her lip, bucking against me as she moaned.

"Aiden," she breathed. "Harder."

I ground into her, the pressure between us reaching boiling point. Her cry of pleasure echoed around my skull. She rocked against me, her body trembling all over. The sight of her coming on me was like fucking magic. She was beautiful. So fucking beautiful.

She panted when she came down from her high. I could feel her heart hammering in her chest where it was pressed against mine. I wasn't fucking done with her yet. And it seemed she wasn't done with me either. She pressed herself against me. My dick got harder, pulsating wildly. I needed to come so fucking bad. I needed her.

I ground harder and faster until I felt the familiar tug that signalled I was on the edge. I pulled away from her, rolling over and grabbing the tissues off the bedside table. Whipping out my cock, I managed to catch the hot spurts in the tissues rather than coming in my shorts like a horny teenager.

Cleaning up, I moved away and chucked the tissues in the bin before crawling back into bed next to her. I flipped her over and tugged her back against my front again. Her breathing became soft and steady. She was asleep.

I'd had a long day and having her close soothed me. Her steady heartbeat thudding against her chest lulled me into a dreamless sleep.

Chapter Seven

Avery

The sunlight streamed in through the gap in the curtains. I woke up disoriented and confused. I was too hot. Opening my eyes, I found my limbs tangled up with Aiden's. He was still asleep. I could tell by his steady breathing.

Fucking hell. Last night. Last fucking night. The memory made my face burn. I couldn't believe I'd actually encouraged it. Wanted it. Wanted him. Feeling his cock digging into my bum made me lose all my stupid common sense.

It hadn't been enough. Even though I'd come so hard I thought I was going to pass out. No. The sick, sick part of me wanted Aiden to fuck me for real. Wanted him to tear my clothes off.

Touch me.

Kiss me.

Bite me.

Fuck me.

I stifled a groan. How could I? Especially to Peter. We'd never had the conversation about exclusivity, but it still wasn't right. Aiden was the man who'd murdered my parents. I couldn't afford to forget that. Not even when I'd told him I was his. I hated that it was true.

When I felt him shift against me, I knew he was awake. His free hand ran down my side and lower until he'd cupped my bum. I froze, stiffening.

"Did you sleep okay?" he murmured.

"Yes."

He raised his head, staring down at me with a frown.

"What's wrong with you?"

"What do you mean?"

"You're tense."

I spluttered, unable to form words. How could I say anything when I'd dry humped his dick last night like it was going out of business?

"Don't bullshit me right now, Avery."

"I can't. This, I don't even know what the fuck this is, but I can't."

His brow furrowed further.

"Can't what?"

"What happened between us last night. That. I can't do that."

His eyes flashed with anger.

"I wasn't fucking asking you to do anything. Do you think just because we helped each other out that it meant something? Let me be clear. It didn't."

Except I knew he was lying. It meant a whole fucking great deal of things. Things neither of us wanted to admit.

Betrayal

He tore away from me, stalking out of the bed. Pulling open one of the sliding doors of his cupboards, he pointed at it.

"Your stuff is in there. Get dressed and meet me in the kitchen."

He pulled a few things out of his own cupboard before storming out of the room. Holy shit. I'd really pissed him off. A part of me wanted to run after him and take back what I'd said. The idiotic part of me. The other part was angry.

How fucking dare he say that to me? Meaningless? I'd show him meaningless. He fucking well wanted me as much as I wanted him. I remembered the way he'd said my name. Told me to come on his cock.

I jumped out of bed and dressed, leaving my pyjamas folded neatly on the pillow. It was time I gave that man a piece of my mind.

Walking into the kitchen, I found him fully dressed with a glass of his protein shake in his hand.

"What happened wasn't meaningless," I said. "You can't just pretend nothing is going on when it suits you."

He didn't turn around, but his back stiffened.

"Can't I? You seemed to be doing it."

"What's that supposed to mean?"

"It means I shouldn't have believed the fucking scared girl act you pulled on me yesterday."

I froze, my limbs locking up. It hadn't been an act at all. I was still half terrified I'd see my dad again. And still entirely grateful to the man in front of me for comforting me when I needed it.

"I told you the truth. Do you seriously think I'd make shit like that up? I'm not a fucking masochist, Aiden. I didn't want to have hallucinations of my own father which by the way is entirely your fault that I even saw him die in the first place."

He turned to me very slowly. Grey eyes full of unrepressed violence. That gaze rendered me completely unable to say another word.

"Your father fucking deserved it. In fact, I wish I'd fucking made it worse for him. So don't you start with who's to blame here. If anyone is responsible, it's him and the rest of your sick fucking family."

What the hell had they done to him to make him hate us so much? Did my 'sick family' as he'd called it include me?

Did he hate me?

The thought of it made my heart stop. I didn't want Aiden to hate me. I wanted him to know me. To see me without the Daniels name attached. Just me. Avery.

"What did they do to you?" I whispered. "I don't understand."

"You don't need to understand."

All my need to challenge him fled. Having all his anger directed at me hurt. It fucking hurt. My chest felt tight and my gut twisted.

"Do you…?"

"Do I what?"

I flinched at his tone. All the coldness I'd seen him display the first time we'd met was back.

"Do you hate me?" My voice was so small and timid, so unlike me in every way.

"Why would you ask me that?"

Betrayal

"Because you act like you do sometimes. Like right now. And yet last night… I know you didn't hate me then."

My heart thudded in my ears. The way he looked at me chilled me to the bone. I couldn't take it. I was still all kinds of fucked up after yesterday. This argument wasn't helping anyone, least of all me.

"I don't…" His expression didn't soften, but he looked away from me. "You piss me off, but I don't hate you."

It was all I needed to hear. I closed the distance between us before he could stop me and wrapped my arms around his back.

"I'm sorry."

He put the glass down on the counter and held me, his hand tangling in my hair as he pressed my head onto his chest. Tension radiated from his body, but he hadn't pushed me away. I could only take that as a positive sign. And fuck did I need him to hold me. The fucking idiot I was needed Aiden like air.

"For what?"

"For making you angry."

"I'm not… angry with you. Frustrated would be more accurate."

"I'm sorry for that too."

"You seem to be apologising a lot to me."

"I keep breaking your rules."

He clutched me tighter. I tried and failed not to be affected by his presence around me.

"You can make it up to me."

"How?"

"You know how to cook, don't you?"

"Yes."

"Make me dinner tonight and perhaps I'll think about letting this slide."

It was something I could do with ease. Did that mean he wasn't going to put me back in the cell? I wanted to ask but pushing him any further was a bad idea.

"Okay. I can do that."

He gently pried me off him, setting his hands on my shoulders as he stared down at me. His eyes were no longer as hard as steel. I didn't really want him to let go of me. Wrapped up in his arms is where I felt safe. Completely stupid of me to ever think Aiden provided me with a place to hide from my memories. Hide from the reality of my situation. I was losing myself to him. I could feel it and it killed me.

Something about Aiden was so fucking heartrendingly beautiful and so broken at the same time, it had me in knots. I wanted to be the girl he needed to survive whatever it was that happened to him. To fix him. It was so fucked up. I couldn't fix a man like Aiden, but it wouldn't stop me trying.

"Get yourself breakfast, then you can stay in my bedroom today."

"You're not putting me in the cell?"

"Did you want to go back?"

"No. I really, really don't want to go back in there."

The thought of hallucinating my dad again made me shiver. The cell would only bring that shit back on.

"I don't need you going batshit crazy on me again, so for now, you're allowed out, but only where I say you go. Clear?"

I nodded. I'd pretty much agree to anything to stay out of those four walls. He pushed me towards the fridge. I opened it, looking through the contents to work out what I could make him later. An idea formed in my head.

"Aiden…"

"Hmm?"

"Will you get some things for me for tonight if I give you a list?"

"I suppose so."

I knew he liked to eat healthy meals. I'd got used to it in the weeks I'd been with him. Not that eating healthy bothered me or anything. He certainly knew how to cook. Aiden took care of me and returning the favour only seemed fair.

When I closed the fridge after grabbing the milk, he stood next to me with his phone.

"Type it for me," he said.

It was the first time I'd seen a phone in weeks. He watched me as I noted down what I thought I needed. Handing it back to him, I felt a stab of sadness. I wanted to talk to my friends. Just to know they were okay. He wouldn't let me do that. I knew asking was futile.

I made myself some tea and cereal with him watching my every movement. Unnerving, but I understood he still didn't really trust me. In all honesty, I could hardly blame him. We were still practically strangers even if we'd dry humped the fuck out of each other in his bed last night. The thought of it made my face burn all over again.

As if pulled by the thread of my thoughts, he walked over to me, put a hand under my chin and forced my face up towards him. He appraised me for the longest moment without speaking and when he did, I really wished I was anywhere else but right there with him.

"If you keep blushing like that every time you think about what I did to you last night, then I'm not going to be responsible for my actions." He ran his thumb over my bottom lip. "Tell me, Avery, if it's not meaningless, then what is it?"

"What's what?"

He leant down, his lips brushing against my ear.

"This thing between us."

I swallowed as his fingers ran down my throat and brushed across my collarbone.

He just acknowledged it. So it wasn't just me.

"I don't know."

His teeth grazed over my earlobe causing me to jerk in his hold.

"I suggest you work that out fast before you do something you later regret."

What? Like letting him fuck me? That was almost inevitable at this point. He knew it. I knew it. It wasn't a question of if. It was a question of when. When would we be stupid enough to fall into bed together and ruin everything. That's if he even fucked me in his bed. I had images of him pressing me up against the kitchen counter, bending me over the kitchen table.

His mouth was so fucking close to mine I could hardly breathe. If Aiden kissed me, I would be done. Nothing would save me. He'd successfully strip me of everything and really fucking own every part of me. And I was so fucked up for wanting that. Wanting that when I had a boy waiting for me. A boy who cared about me. A boy who wasn't a part of this sick fucked up game between Aiden and me.

Betrayal

This was a game to him. He wanted to use me for something. It's why he wanted to break down all my walls and have me at his mercy. I wasn't stupid enough to think that he didn't have an ulterior motive for any of it. The small part of me that still cared enough about myself knew those things. She was very quickly being drowned out by my insatiable need to know Aiden. Know him and understand him. Understand why he hated my family. Why he felt the need to murder my parents.

He straightened abruptly, letting go of me. My face was on fire and my pulse raced out of control.

"Are you done? I have things to get on with."

"Yes," I whispered.

He pulled me up from the chair and forced me out of the room without letting me clean up my breakfast things.

What was the rush?

Was he as affected by me as I was him?

When we got to his bedroom, he let go of me.

"When I go out, this door is going to be locked. I suggest you use the bathroom before I leave."

"Aiden…"

"What?"

"Would you be willing to give me some paper and a pen? Pencils would be better, but I'll take what I can get."

He frowned.

"Why would you want that?"

"I draw. It's my thing. It's why I am… was doing architecture at Uni."

I'd already missed three weeks of classes. It was unlikely Aiden would ever let me go back and even if he did, I'd have issues catching up. I wasn't sure how I'd ever reintegrate back into my real life if this ever ended. It was a big if.

He didn't answer me. He just left the room. I went over to his bed and sat down on the end. I was sick of being left to my own thoughts all the time. I needed something. Something to help me hold onto my rapidly disintegrating sanity.

A few minutes later, he returned with a stack of paper, pens and pencils for me. He dumped them next to me along with a book for me to lean the pages on.

"Is that enough to keep you going?" he asked.

"Yes, thank you."

"You can thank me by behaving yourself whilst I'm out."

I hadn't been planning on doing anything to further incur his wrath. Now I could sit and draw, I'd be okay. At least it would help me focus.

"I can still thank you when you give me something," I muttered.

"Don't think this is an act of kindness on my part. I'm not kind or nice."

He could say that all he wanted, but he'd shown me he could be nice to me. He held me not because he wanted to but because he knew I needed it. Aiden felt something for me that wasn't a part of his plans. It might grate on him, but it was the truth. Just as I felt things for him. Things I didn't want to feel at all.

"I know that."

He left me alone. I wasn't sure where he'd gone, but it didn't matter. I picked up the things he'd given me, stuffed the pillows up against the headboard and sat against them in the middle of his bed. It was nice to finally have somewhere to sit that wasn't a cold concrete floor.

I put a couple of sheets of paper on the book, thought for a moment, picked up the pencil and started to draw.

Aiden came in to tell me he was leaving at some point. I hot-footed it to the bathroom and was back on his bed sketching again before long. I barely heard the lock click on the door as he left. I got lost in my own world. Finding my imagination brimming with things that needed to be let out.

I didn't really notice it getting dark nor the door opening. I looked up when the lamp by the bedside illuminated my drawing. Aiden stood next to the bed looking down at the drawing I was working on. It was of the city skyline outside his bedroom window. I hadn't closed the curtain so I could look out at it.

He picked up the discarded pages before I had a chance to stop him, looking through them one by one until he landed on something. His eyes widened a touch. I put the book down with my drawing and shuffled over, peeking around his hands. Fuck. He was not supposed to see that.

"This is…" he started but closed his mouth the next second.

"You," I finished for him.

His suit was perfectly formed over his solid body and behind him were two huge black feathered wings. In his hand was a gun. His expression was cold.

My beautiful, dark, avenging angel.

Just as I'd seen him the first day we met.

I wished I had some colours so I could fill in the rest of the details. I'd have made his eyes grey and highlighted the feathers in his wings a little more.

"Is this how you see me?"

I looked down at my hands.

"I guess so."

"I didn't know you were so talented."

I raised my head to him. His eyes were still on the drawing. It was a very rough sketch to me. If I had more materials, I'd have drawn it on a bigger scale and really brought out all his finer details.

"You didn't ask. I can do better than that, but I'd need my sketchbook and supplies."

He looked at me then, his grey eyes assessing me for a moment.

"Why?"

"Why what?"

"This." He pointed at the drawing. "Why?"

"Why did I draw you like that?"

He nodded once. I took the drawing from him, running my fingers over the wings.

"It's how I saw you when we met the first time. It's stupid really."

"You saw me as an… angel?"

"An avenging angel. I don't know what I was thinking. It just seemed appropriate at the time."

He smiled a little, but it was haunted.

"I take it your family didn't encourage this."

"Not really. Architecture was a compromise."

Betrayal

It wasn't that I didn't enjoy it. It was just a lot of work that didn't necessarily involve me being creative.

"I won't stop you drawing."

"You won't?"

"No." He looked away. "I got you what you asked for. It's on the counter."

"Oh, right. Dinner."

I hadn't exactly forgotten. It'd just been pushed to the back of my mind. I put the drawing down and hopped off the bed. I walked towards the door, turning to find him staring down at the pages scattered across the bed. Who knew what Aiden really thought about me drawing him in the way I had. I knew better than to ask.

I left him to it, going into the kitchen and getting started. It took a little while, but when I was done, the kitchen smelt amazing and I was ravenous. Still, I was nervous. What if this wasn't enough?

I placed the dishes down on the table. When I looked up, he was standing in the doorway.

"Um… I was just going to come find you," I said, leaning back against the table.

He came into the room and stood before me. He'd changed into a plain t-shirt and shorts. It hugged his muscles and my mouth went dry. Why the fuck did he have to look so beautiful all the time? The intricate patterns of his tattoos were stark on his tanned skin. I wanted to trace my fingers over them. Have him explain each one.

"Something smelt nice…"

I shifted away from the table, showing him what I'd made. Steak fajitas complete with all the trimmings. I'd made the guacamole and salsa from scratch. I had a thing about Mexican food, but I was hoping Aiden would like it too.

I was perfectly aware just how fucked up me trying to please the man who'd taken me and held me against my will was. Nothing about this situation was anything other than completely twisted.

"I hope it's okay," I mumbled.

Aiden reached out, grabbing me by the waist and pulling me into him. He tipped my head up with his other hand.

"I'm sure it's more than okay."

My breath caught. The way he looked at me sent shivers down my spine. And his touch scorched my skin.

Get a grip.

"I don't want it to get cold."

He let go of me and moved away to sit down. It took me a second to put my head straight on again before I joined him. Aiden being close to me gave me all kinds of feelings and urges. I really couldn't think about how much I wanted a repeat of last night so desperately it made me ache. How much I craved him on a level I didn't really understand.

"Who taught you to cook?" he asked after we'd both served ourselves and were digging in.

"Um… my mum mostly, but I used to bake with Esme, my nanny."

"You bake?"

I shrugged. Not so much these days, but I wasn't bad at it.

"I used to. Why? I didn't think you'd be into desserts."

"I can be partial to something sweet… on occasion."

Betrayal

The mischievous glint in his eye and his suggestive tone told me he wasn't talking about puddings. It sent heat right down to my core. I squeezed my legs together.

Holy fucking hell. Not helping, Aiden, not one fucking bit.

This wasn't going anywhere good. I couldn't. I just fucking couldn't do this shit with him.

"If you were going to have a pudding, what would it be?"

"Cheesecake, but it can't be some fancy one."

"So, like a baked one?"

He nodded, taking another bite from his fajita.

"I can make that, maybe… if you wanted."

He eyed me but didn't respond. The rest of the meal was silent. I didn't really mind because at least he hadn't made any more suggestive statements towards me. Still, it didn't help me get to know him. Know the man who'd trapped me but who I didn't know if I wanted to actually leave if I could.

I'd washed up as I went, so there wasn't much to do other than put the plates in the dishwasher when we were done. He sent me to bed, telling me he'd be along soon.

I lay there in the dark after I'd gotten ready for bed, staring up at the ceiling. Knowing he would be here any moment made it impossible for me to sleep.

I'd tidied up my drawings and left them on the bedside table, but I noted the drawing of him was missing. It didn't much matter because I could recreate it easily, but knowing Aiden had my drawing of him made me nervous. What did he even want with it?

He didn't turn on the lights when he came in. After listening to him move around the room, I felt the bed dip slightly beside me. I could feel him. And I wanted him.

How the fuck was I ever meant to keep my resolve not to do anything else with him when my body ached for his touch? Ached so much, I couldn't stop myself from shuffling over to him. He let me curl up against his side and wrapped his arm around me.

"Can't sleep again?" he murmured.

"No."

His fingers traced a line down my arm. I trembled.

"You pleased me today. I think I want to reward you for that."

Wait, what? Reward me?

I didn't really do anything other than make him dinner and try not to piss him off any further like I had done this morning.

He turned, facing me, grey eyes glinting. His fingers ran down my throat and lower, brushing over the side of my breast. I froze.

"Do you think you deserve a reward?"

Fuck knows how I was supposed to answer that. I could hardly breathe as his fingers traced a line around the bottom of my breast.

"Do you want me to touch you?"

All the air felt like it'd been sucked out the room.

"Because I think you do."

He edged closer, leaning down towards me so our eyes were level.

"Tell me I'm wrong."

If I could unstick my tongue from the roof of my mouth, I might have answered him.

"Tell me you don't want me, Avery."

I couldn't. I'd be lying and lying to him would never end well for me. His face came ever closer until our breath mingled together.

"Tell me to stop."

"Aiden, please…" I whispered.

"Tell me."

His lips brushed against mine with the barest of touches and I was utterly fucking lost. A wave of desire shot down my stomach, ending up right in my core where it pulsated with need.

And that's when Aiden's phone rang, the noise cutting through the air, startling both of us.

Chapter Eight

Aiden

Whoever the fuck was calling me could go fuck themselves. I probably should be thanking them for reminding me I should not be trying to fuck Avery, but I couldn't find it in me to be remotely grateful. Not when she was so fucking close to giving into me.

"Stay there and don't say a fucking word," I growled at her.

I turned and reached for my stupid motherfucking phone. When I saw the caller display, I literally wanted to punch the fucker in the face.

"What?"

It was lucky he was used to me answering the phone to him like that.

"I need you to follow up on a lead for me."

"Right now? I'm busy, Chuck."

"Yes, right now."

Avery stiffened next to me. I hadn't forgotten about her issues with her uncle. Ones I would make her tell me sooner rather than later.

"Is it a lead or do you just need me to go beat some fucker up?"

"Really, Aiden? Do you have to put it in such terms?"

"Just fucking tell me what you need."

I was seriously not in the mood for his shit. My dick was so hard, I thought it might fucking explode and I had Avery fucking wet and wanting next to me. I didn't have to touch her pussy to know she was wet for me. She couldn't fucking hide it. Her body screamed at me. Begged me. Needed me. Just like mine needed hers.

"The police interviewed my niece's little friends, including the boy she was seeing."

The world fucking stopped. I stared at Avery. She was seeing someone. Was it serious? Why the fuck hadn't she told me? Was this why she told me she couldn't this morning? Fuck. I was so angry at the thought of anyone touching Avery but me. I was going to rip the little shit's head off.

Mine. She's fucking mine.

"He said she was supposed to be having dinner with Mitch and Kath the night they died. They found her phone at the penthouse. They think whoever killed her parents took her."

"What?"

Fuck. I'd left her phone at her parent's place. It wasn't on her. I hadn't had time to find it because I had to get out of there before the CCTV came back on.

I had to do something about this. They still wouldn't tie it back to me, but I couldn't take chances. Not when I hadn't made sure Avery was on my fucking side. I needed more time with her. I had to stop thinking with my dick and start thinking with my head. That meant not getting into situations like this. Where we wanted each other so fucking much it hurt.

"I know, fucked up, right?"

"I take it your little informant in the force squealed then?"

It was the only way he'd know any of this. The police hadn't released many details to the public.

"Of course, but he won't say any more. I need information. If we don't find her soon, things are going to get complicated."

"Did you stop to think that maybe she doesn't want to be found?"

I shot Avery a warning look. Her eyes were wide, but her mouth remained shut.

"Perhaps. Little upstart never wanted to be a part of the company. Mitch pushed her into agreeing. I don't claim to get along with my niece. She's too fucking innocent of our world, but she did confide something to me when she was drunk at the annual Christmas do last year. She said, 'Uncle Charlie, I wanted him to give the company to you because I don't want it. I don't want to be a part of this family's legacy. I hate it. I hate all the expectations. Dad forced me to sign those documents. He said he would cut me off if I didn't.' I remember it like it was yesterday. I think that's the first time she realised her dad wasn't Mr Nice Guy. Things had been strained between them since, not that anyone else would have guessed. Got to put on a show for the public."

Chuck didn't know it, but he'd just given me more leverage on her than I could've hoped to get by myself. If she had an inkling there was a darker side to her father, maybe she'd believe me when I told her who he'd really been behind his well-constructed mask.

"He was always good at bullshitting."

Chuck laughed.

"Mitch was the best at it. Shame really. Too many fucking enemies to count. Don't suppose I'll ever find out who took him out. Who the fuck cares anyway? The fuzz will spend a lifetime trying to work it out. Whoever it was knew what they were doing. The important thing is finding Avery even if she doesn't want to be found."

There was no love lost between the brothers. And Avery wouldn't be found until I decided she would. Until I decided she was ready to do what I needed her to. Plans began to form in the back of my mind. How to fix this mess.

"Are you going to tell me what you need from me or not?"

"Well, you can't go and beat up a pig, but you can go and lean on his boyfriend for me."

"Now I know you've lost your mind. I told you I won't deal with police or anyone related to them."

"I didn't tell you to hurt him."

Chuck was really fucking pushing his luck here.

"Get someone else to do it."

"As if I can trust anyone else with this information."

I almost smiled. He still really had no idea. I didn't have much of a choice but to go deal with this for him. If I continued to say no, he'd get suspicious. I couldn't have that.

"Just fucking text me the details. You owe me for this."

"Don't worry, you'll be well compensated."

Betrayal

He hung up. I almost threw my phone against the wall. Everything about that conversation had thrown me one curveball after another.

I didn't look at Avery as I got up and stalked over to my cupboards. I didn't have time for this. All I fucking wanted was to lie next to that damn girl and hold her close. Last night was the first time in fuck knows how long I didn't dream.

"Aiden?"

"What?" I snapped. I shouldn't have but my temper was frayed.

"Are you leaving?"

"I have to go do something. You need to go to sleep."

Pulling out what I needed, I turned to her. She looked so small and scared huddled under the covers. The sight of it broke something deep inside me. I was such a fucking arsehole. I'd made her need me. I was fucking with her head. I had to do it, but it didn't make me feel any less of a fucked up piece of shit for dragging her into all of this.

"Okay," she whispered.

"Avery..."

"It's okay."

It wasn't fucking okay. I dumped my stuff on the bed and crawled over her. She stared up at me with those doe eyes which haunted my every waking moment.

"We need to talk about some things, but it can wait until morning. I need you to go to sleep for me," I said, trying to keep my tone soft.

We needed to talk about a lot of shit, not least of all why she'd kept the fact that she had a boyfriend from me. If she cared so much about him, why the fuck did she let me touch her?

"I can try."

"Good."

I brushed her hair from her face. Fuck, she was beautiful. I leant down, pressing my forehead to hers for a moment. I wanted to kiss her. So fucking much. And I never wanted to kiss anyone. She wasn't just anyone. Avery was mine.

"Is my uncle trying to find me?"

"Yes."

"You won't let him, right?"

"No."

"Is it really fucked up that I hope I never see him again?"

If he'd done what I suspected, then it wasn't fucked up at all.

"Will you tell me what happened between you?"

I needed to know. It might change things. It might make my need to silence the fucker for good easier.

"Maybe."

My phone buzzed on the bed.

"I need to go."

She nodded. It took a considerable effort on my part to tear myself away from her. I dressed quickly. Before I left, I leant down and brushed my lips against her forehead. She stared at me with no small amount of confusion in her eyes.

I strode out of the room, locking the door behind me because if I didn't go right then, I would've got in that bed with her, ripped her clothes off and made sure she knew exactly what it meant to be owned by me. Fuck the consequences. Fuck the future. Fuck everything. In those moments, it'd just be me and her. Every touch would cement my hold on her and every moment would bind us together in this fucked up mess.

And that's exactly why I couldn't fuck her. Binding myself to her was out of the question. I couldn't let her have any power over me. That would mean ruin for both of us. Avery would tear me apart. I was already broken enough as it was. My only solution was not to give in. Not to let us consume each other. And it was going to be the hardest fucking thing I'd ever do.

I tugged on my jacket and grabbed my helmet before I left the flat. Time was of the essence. I needed to get this done fast.

As soon as I walked in the club, the pounding bass assaulted my senses. Fucking clubs. It was a mess of sweaty bodies grinding together. It wasn't hard to spot my prey behind the bar. The bright pink hair gave him away instantly. Plus, he was the only male.

I stalked over to the bar and leant against it. His eyes fell on me and he frowned. I was well aware I wasn't the normal type of clientele you'd get in a place like this.

"You're definitely not here for a drink," he said to me.

"No. Anthony, right?"

"I fucking knew it. I take it you're here about Ethan."

I was surprised he knew, but perhaps his boyfriend talked about his work more than he should. Considering he'd blabbed to the Daniels, perhaps it wasn't so surprising after all.

"I'm not here to harm you. I just need more information about the investigation."

Anthony raised an eyebrow. Sceptical little fuck.

"I told him not to get involved with them, but he didn't listen to me. The money isn't worth this shit. Look, if I get you what you need, will they leave him alone?"

"I can't make those sorts of promises."

Once you got involved with the Daniels, you rarely got out unscathed or alive.

"But you can get them to back off? Ethan loves his job and I don't want him losing it over this shit with that missing girl."

"I'll make sure they don't bother you again."

"What about Ethan?"

I shrugged. Not much I could do for his idiot boyfriend really. That was up to Chuck.

"He made his own bed."

Anthony looked away, expression sour.

"I know you're right."

At least he wasn't stupid. I pitied him really. Wasn't his fault his boyfriend fell for the Daniels company line.

"So, you get me what I need, I keep off your case, but I also want something else. This is personal and not to do with them."

Anthony bit his lip.

"What?"

"I'll tell you when you get what I need. Got a pen?"

Betrayal

He shuffled away, grabbing some receipt paper and a pen which he handed to me. I wrote down a number for him. It was a burner phone so it wouldn't trace back to me. I was still working out what I was going to do about the police's new line of investigation into Avery's disappearance. Anthony might just prove to be key in making sure they stopped looking for her.

"Send me a text when you have it. We'll arrange a meet. Don't forget I need everything. Both investigations or the deal is off and I won't give a fuck if they leave you in an alley."

"Fine. The things you do for love."

The crazy thing? I knew exactly what he was talking about.

"Stay out of trouble."

I left the club, not sparing Anthony a second glance. I pulled out my phone and dialled Chuck's number.

"Is it done?"

"The boyfriend will get us what we need if we leave him alone. The pig is fair game, but I suggest you don't take him out just yet."

"Noted. Mitch was always better at this shit. Smooth talking bastard. I can barely get them to give me anything. It's all 'we're still investigating', should get a fucking move on if you ask me."

"As I said, I doubt she wants to be found."

"I'm beginning to agree with you. I'm fed up of fielding calls from her friends. I've fucking had it with that girl and her antics. If she wasn't so important, then I'd say fuck it. Anyway, Frazier had some work for you if you're interested, otherwise, I'll give it to John."

One thing I never did was work for Frazier motherfucking Shaw. He was nothing but trouble. I might have sunk low enough to integrate myself into the Daniels clan, but Shaw was a sick cunt. Worse than Mitchell. Much worse than Chuck.

"I don't know why you bother asking me."

"You're the best, but whatever. John always gets it done. I'll be in touch."

I got back on my bike which I'd left not too far away and jammed my helmet on. The ride home would give me time to think. Mostly about what I was going to do with Avery and my ridiculous need to own her completely. We needed to talk. There was no question about it. And that talk had to not escalate into an argument or fucking.

She obeyed me in some things, but that girl had a temper on her. So did I. The combination was deadly. There was always the lingering threat of the cell. She didn't want to go back there. It was my leverage if things got heated.

The reality was I had no fucking idea how to unravel the tangled mess between us. She was meant to be a tool for me to use in my vendetta against her family and all the sick fucks involved with their dirty dealings. Avery had become more than that. So much more to me than I ever wanted her to be.

She no longer reminded me of Mitchell even though she looked like him. Avery was her own person and she wasn't anything like the rest of her family.

And her fucking drawing of me? My heart almost stopped dead in my chest. It was beautiful but haunting. Mostly because I wasn't sure what the fuck to think of her depicting me as an angel. I was no fucking saint. I was a bastard through and through. And I certainly made no apologies for it.

Betrayal

I don't know why I took her drawing and pinned it up in my office. That was most definitely the one place she was never allowed. I just needed the reminder. That she thought about me when I wasn't there. That she saw me as something more than the sick, fucked up man who killed her parents. Avery had seen me. The real me inside when she drew that. The darkness that consumed me. The hatred in my heart and the need to destroy those who had ruined me.

That she'd even thought to look made me wonder how she really felt about me. She'd told me she was mine but was it because I'd broken her and made her reliant on me? Or had it started before then? Had she realised it when she saw me the first time? That I would come to own her.

Who fucking knew? It wasn't like I could ask her outright anyway.

I slowed as I reached my building, driving down into the underground car park and pulling up in my space. I took the lift up to my floor before discarding my jacket and helmet in the hall when I let myself in. I stripped down to a t-shirt and boxers before I went into the bedroom.

Avery was hugging the duvet to her chest, her dark hair spread across the pillow. She didn't stir when I got in the bed.

Shifting closer to her, I moved her hair before wrapping my arm around her waist. She turned in my embrace and curled up against my chest. Her breathing was still steady. Fast asleep.

Fuck. I was done for at this rate. She was so fragile and small. And fuck if I didn't want to protect her. That was the thing. I couldn't. I couldn't protect her from the truth.

The truth about her family.

The truth about their company.
And most of all…
The truth about me.

Chapter Nine

Avery

Aiden was awake before me. When I opened my eyes, he was staring down at me. Those beautiful grey eyes full of emotions I didn't understand. My heart thumped against my ribcage. I hadn't heard him come in last night. I'd fallen asleep not long after he left.

The bed sheets smelt of him. Distinctly Aiden and it helped me forget he wasn't there.

"Hi," I said.

"You're disrupting my routine."

"What?"

He rolled me over onto my back and pinned me to the bed with his body. I felt like the air had been ripped out of my lungs.

"My routine."

He curled a lock of my hair around his finger.

"I run first thing, but with you here, all I want to do is stay in bed."

"Why…?"

It was a stupid question to ask since the answer was clear, but he'd caught me off guard and I'd only just woken up. He let go of my hair. I found my legs pressed open the next moment as he settled between them. I felt him, rock hard and pulsating against me. He didn't have to say anything. He stayed because he wanted me. And I was done pretending I didn't want him too.

I knew it was wrong. He'd murdered my parents, kidnapped me and kept me locked up. He wanted to use me in his own personal war against my family. None of it mattered. Not when it was me and him alone together in his bed with barely anything between us.

So I was done hiding.

"Aiden, either you want me or you don't. This back and forth between us isn't fair."

"Life isn't fair." His hand crept up and wrapped around my neck. "Tell me why you think it's okay to keep things from me."

What?

What did he think I was keeping from him?

He confused me so much. I never knew what to expect. His moods were so interchangeable.

"What do you mean?"

"Did you think I wouldn't find out about your boyfriend?"

What the fuck? What boyfriend? Wait…

"Who? Peter?"

"Is that his name?"

"He's not my boyfriend. We never had that conversation."

Betrayal

His eyes brimmed with barely concealed anger. Why the hell did the thought of me having a boyfriend rile him up so much?

"Has he fucked you?"

"What? No. What the hell, Aiden? Where is this coming from? I don't know who told you about him nor why you think I'd keep it from you if I did have a boyfriend. I'm not stupid."

Who the fuck had told him about my private life? I'd been so careful not to let onto the media that I was seeing Peter. He didn't deserve that kind of attention. I would never go public with anyone unless it was serious. I might feel bad about this shit with Aiden when I hadn't had a chance to talk to Peter, but I wasn't doing anything wrong either, relatively speaking at least.

"Then why the fuck did he tell the police you are together?"

Peter told them that?

He really shouldn't have. It wasn't for him to make assumptions about the two of us. I liked him, but he wasn't... Aiden. My heart sank. Even if Peter was waiting for me, it no longer mattered because I wasn't going back to my old life. Not now. Not ever. Aiden wouldn't let me and if I was being honest with myself, I had no desire to either.

"He what? My uncle told you this, didn't he? I'm not in a relationship with anyone. I haven't even had a real boyfriend before so don't start shit with me about this."

Aiden reeled back slightly, letting go of my throat.

"What?"

"What part didn't you understand?"

Anger simmered in my veins. I didn't like accusations being flung at me.

"What do you mean you've never had a boyfriend before? You're not a…"

"Not a what? A virgin? No, definitely not."

"Who the fuck have you been with?"

"What kind of question is that? I don't ask you about who you've slept with. Seriously, what is with you?"

I shoved at his chest. He moved a little which allowed me to scramble out from underneath him and tear out of the bed. I glared at him.

"Where do you get off accusing me of shit first thing in the morning?"

The next moment, he was out of the bed and in my face. He grabbed me by the arms and held me in place.

"You are fucking mine, Avery. Mine. No one else can touch you. No one else can have you. No one. Mine."

"Oh, so what you're going to be all fucking possessive and shit just because I've got a past? Screw you."

I tried to get away from him, but his grip on me was so tight, it almost hurt.

"Get off me."

"No."

"I don't know what you want from me, Aiden. One minute you're locking me up, the next comforting me, then you're trying to fuck me… or not. And now, I don't even know what this is. What do you want? Do you want me to tell you I'm yours? I already fucking said that. I have been yours from the moment you walked into my life and fucked it up. What else do I have to do to prove it to you? I. Am. Yours."

Betrayal

Steel eyes stared down at me. Disarming me on every level. Aiden had a way of making me so angry yet one look from him had it flying out the window. I just wanted him to make some semblance of sense or at least be consistent in the way he treated me.

"Tell me how many."

"Three."

I knew what the fuck he was asking. I wasn't going to tell him who they were, but if he was going to be such a prick about this, I had to give him something.

"Let me make something clear to you now. If anyone else tries to put their dick in you, I will put a bullet in their head."

That sentence pierced right through my irritation. Why the fuck would he resort to killing someone if they tried anything with me?

"Why because only you're allowed to do that?"

I wished I'd kept my mouth shut. I wished I'd never got angry with him.

Aiden leant down until he was right up in my face.

"Say that again."

I shook my head. His expression terrified me. Cold. Deadly. Heartless. He grabbed my face roughly.

"Say it again, Avery."

"No."

"Is that what you want? Do you want me to fuck you? Should you really want that from the man who shot your parents?"

That question cut me to the core. No. I shouldn't want him to fuck me, but I did. He couldn't say a damn thing either because he wanted to fuck me too.

"Answer me."

I shook my head.

"Is that no, you don't want me to fuck you or no, you don't want me to answer me?"

"Aiden, please," I whimpered.

"Fucking answer me, Avery."

"Stop it."

"Are you too fucking scared to admit it? Admit how fucked up you wanting me is."

I couldn't fight back tears. I hated him. I hated him so much, but I needed him. I'd lost everything to him. This was a battle and I had no hope of winning against the man who stole my life. There was no doubt Aiden would continue to take from me until I was nothing but his puppet. Or maybe he just wanted me to be his fuck toy now. Either way, I knew I'd give in.

The funny thing about it?

I didn't care.

My life wasn't my own any longer. What was the point in fighting it? I was tired. The last three weeks had taken a toll on me emotionally.

"So what if I do? It's just as fucked up as you wanting me too."

He looked down at my mouth.

"You're too fucking innocent, you know that? You couldn't handle what I want. I don't do vanilla. I don't do sweet."

He backed me up until I was against the wall. He pinned me there with only his gaze and his hands either side of me, caging me in. Leaning down, his breath danced across my ear.

Betrayal

"If I fucked you, Avery, you wouldn't know what hit you. I'd tear down all your walls, all your fucking defences and I'd wreck you."

He pulled back and stared at me. The way he said it made my chest constrict and my body flood with heat. Even though I knew he would make good on that promise, it didn't stop me wanting him all the same. The insane, fucked up part of me wanted him to wreck me entirely so I wouldn't have to feel any more. So I wouldn't have to be so conflicted by my emotions and loyalties. At that moment, all I wanted to be was Aiden's. Consequences be damned.

"I want you to wreck me," I whispered. "I want you."

The tension between us overflowed. Neither of us could move. My words hung in the air. The thin line between what I should do and what I wanted to do was about a hundred miles behind me. I jumped head first into a fucking pit of insanity and I didn't care.

The look in Aiden's eyes shifted. And I knew immediately he wasn't going to fuck me right then. He grabbed my arm and tugged me from the room. When I saw where we were going, I completely lost it. I tried to pull my arm from his grasp and kicked out at him.

"No, no, no, Aiden, please. Don't. I don't want to go back in there. Please."

He didn't respond. Opening the door, he threw me inside and before I had a chance to scramble back to my feet, it slammed shut. The locks turned, the sound echoing around my skull. Even in the dark, I knew where that fucking door was. I threw myself at it, hitting it with my fists.

"Aiden, let me out. Don't do this. Please. Let me out. Aiden. Please. Aiden."

He'd put me in the cell again. The one place he knew I hated.

"Aiden, please. I'm begging you. Don't put me through this again. I can't do it. I can't. Please."

I pounded the door until I had no energy left. Sliding down it, I sobbed.

"I hate you. I hate everything about you. You make me hate myself. I hate how I feel about you. I hate wanting you. I hate needing you. Aiden, please, stop hurting me like this. You don't need to break me anymore. I'm already yours. I'll do what you want me to. I don't even know what it is, but I'll do it. Please, I'll do anything. Please. Aiden."

I had nothing left. There was no point to this any longer. My life felt worthless. I felt like nothing. Nothing and nobody. The darkness crept into my skull, rattling my brain with thoughts of what happened last time he left me in here alone.

"Aiden, let me out," I whimpered.

The locks turned in my brain. I knew it was a trick of the mind. Aiden wasn't letting me out anytime soon. I'd pushed him. I didn't know why me giving him my body would cause this reaction when it was clear he wanted me. Was he struggling with his attraction to me? It was fucked up we wanted each other, sure, but it didn't warrant me being thrown in the cell.

"Of all the things you've done to me, Aiden, this is the worst. You know what will happen if you leave me in here. I'm already broken. Don't you see that? Why do you want to hurt me further? You told me you didn't hate me. I feel like you do now. You hate me because you want me, don't you? You think I don't see who you are. Reality check, Aiden, I see you. I know you're hurting and stupid me wants to help you. Stupid, idiotic girl."

It didn't matter if he could hear me or not. I could be talking to thin air for all I cared. I just had to get my thoughts out. Had to say something to fill the silence. The silence which clawed at me and made me want to scream.

I closed my eyes and all I could see was my parents. My parents staring back at me with bullet holes in their heads. Then I really did scream. I screamed and tried to tear my face off because the visions were still there when I opened my eyes.

"Stop. Go away. No. You're not real."

"Why didn't you save us?" they both said to me.

"I couldn't. No. Stop."

"Why did you let him take us away, sweet angel?"

I buried my head in my knees. They wouldn't go away. I could still see them in the corners of my eyes.

"Avery, look at us, baby girl. You can stop him. Avenge us."

"No. I won't. I won't do it."

"He took us from you. Take his life. Avenge us, baby."

What the hell was happening to me?

"No. I need him and he needs me."

"He doesn't need anyone. He doesn't want you."

Lies. Aiden did need me. He needed me to help him. If he didn't, then he would've killed me too. The fact I was even trying to justify Aiden's behaviour to the parents I was hallucinating, the parents that weren't even real made everything worse.

"You're not real. You're not real. You're not real."

"Baby girl, we are real. We're here. Avenge us. Take his life."

"Not real. Not real. Not real."

I crawled away from the door and huddled in the corner of the room, rocking back and forth.

"Not real. None of this is real."

"Avenge us. Avenge us, Avery. Avenge us."

"No. No. You're not real. None of it is real. I can't see you. I can't hear you."

Done. I was just done. Even though I hated Aiden for putting me back in here, when he let me out, I'd fall at his feet and beg him to forgive me for whatever it was I'd done.

I'd beg him to keep me with him.

I'd do anything for him

Because the sick, stupid, broken girl I was needed the man who'd killed her parents.

Needed him to care of her.

Needed him to hold her.

Needed him like she needed air.

And she would go to the ends of the earth for him because that's what you did when you cared about someone as much as this sick, stupid, broken girl cared for Aiden.

"Please don't leave me again. Please stay with me. Please, Aiden. Please."

Chapter Ten

Aiden

I really felt like the world's most fucked up piece of shit. I sat against the cell door with my head in my hands. I heard everything she said. Every word echoed around my skull. All of it shattered me. I knew she was hallucinating again when she screamed. And when she'd said, "I need him and he needs me," it broke me further. I couldn't fucking cope with it. My need for her.

She deserved far better than me. Too fucking innocent. When she said she wanted me, I just couldn't do it. She didn't know what she wanted. Not really. I'd made her need me and took away her choice. Her decisions weren't made with clarity. So I couldn't do it. I had to put her in the cell not because she deserved it, but to save myself from her.

It was wrong on so many levels. Putting her back in there only brought her more pain and misery. It was like she said, I was hurting her further. It wasn't cruel to be kind. It was self-preservation. I was a fucking arsehole.

What am I doing to you, Avery? What the fuck am I doing?

The silence was worse than her screaming. I wanted to open the door. To make sure she hadn't hurt herself. I didn't go in. The thought of seeing her broken. Watching her deteriorate further, that fucking killed. Everything inside me had been dead for so long. Avery made me feel again. And the force of those feelings made everything so fucking complicated.

She stroked my hair with such a delicate hand. I stared up into the grey eyes which mirrored mine. The only part of her I had in me. The rest, who knew. She never talked about him.

"I'm so proud of you, my little man. You're doing so well at school and Tina says you're making friends."

"When are you coming home?" I asked.

"Soon, sweetheart. Mummy is getting us a new home. It'll be just you and me. Would you like that?"

The bruise around her eye was stark, but she smiled down at me.

"Yes. Will I have my own room?"

"Of course, my darling angel."

"Can I have green and blue walls?"

"I'll paint them for you myself."

I wrapped my hands around her legs, only just coming up to her stomach.

"Mummy, will we always be together?"

"I hope so, my angel."

She pulled away and squatted down to my level, putting her hands on my shoulders.

Betrayal

"You be a good boy for Tina, okay? I promise I'll see you soon. Mummy loves you so much."

I could see tears welling in her eyes, but I didn't know why she was crying. She gathered me up in her arms, kissing the top of my head.

"My beautiful boy."

"I promise I'll be good. I love you, Mummy."

She held me for the longest time, stroking my hair and murmuring to me.

"My sweet boy. My angel."

When she let go, she wiped her eyes, wincing as she touched her bruised face. She kissed my forehead one more time before she rose.

"Take care of him," she said to Tina who was standing behind us.

"Of course, Miss Lockhart," Tina replied.

And then she walked away, leaving me alone with Tina.

Shaking, I stood. The memory clung to me, tearing my insides to shreds. I knew they'd find a way to haunt me again. Now they had no control over my dreams because I had Avery there to chase that darkness away.

Fuck this.

I got up and walked away from the cell. I went to my office, unlocked the door and strode in. I stood there, staring at Avery's drawing pinned to my noticeboard.

My angel.

Thinking of her made my head hurt. And thinking of the girl who'd depicted me as her avenging angel tugged at the organ I swore I'd never breathe life into again. I had to fix myself before it was too late.

I ran for an hour. My muscles burnt from the pace I set, but I didn't care. The pain reminded me of what I needed to do. Gave me the strength to go through with it. She was going to hate me even more. Hate me for showing her the truth. That was okay. She could hate me all she wanted. She'd still do what I asked of her. She'd comply.

After showering and dressing when I got back, I prepared what I had to. This would only be the start. She needed to be told in small, manageable pieces until she finally understood. Understood the horror of the people who had given her life.

I unlocked the cell door. I knew the light would hurt her eyes, so I didn't switch it on. She was in the corner, her head buried in her knees. I walked over until I stood before her.

"Daniels."

She raised her head slowly, looking up at me with no small amount of fear and hatred. It was quickly overtaken by relief. She opened her mouth to speak and began to reach for me, but I put a hand up.

"No. You won't get anything from me until you've seen what you need to see."

She closed her mouth, her eyes filling with tears. I knew what I was doing. It fucking cut me, but I had no choice. If I comforted her now, it wouldn't help her later. It wouldn't help me either.

Betrayal

"Do you need the loo?" I asked.

She nodded.

"Go and return here to me when you're done. Do you understand?"

"Yes," she whispered.

Avery tried to get to her feet, but she struggled. I put a hand out to her, which she took, and helped her up. Instead of letting go, I guided her from the room and left her at the bathroom door. I went into the kitchen and poured her some water. She'd not had anything since she'd woken up. I'd feed her, but only after this.

Avery was standing by the cell door when I returned. I gave her the glass before pointing to the room. She took a large gulp before staring at me.

"Why?" she asked.

"Move. I won't tell you again."

Her eyes flashed with pain. I knew I was hurting her with my behaviour. Fucking piece of shit. Couldn't be helped. She'd understand why it had to be in there after and she'd fucking thank me for it.

She walked in, every step slow and cautious. I followed her, taking the glass from her hand and replacing it with a tablet.

"What you're going to see will help you understand. It is not for the faint-hearted. Do not look away. This is the truth of what you were born into."

Her hands trembled, but she pressed play on the video. It was taken from security footage.

Her father, her uncle and their cousin, Troy, were all stood around a desk in Mitchell's office, staring at something on the computer screen.

"He really is one sick fuck," Chuck said.

"No less than the bitch deserves for stepping out of line," Mitchell replied. "Silly cow thought she could escape us."

The three of them laughed.

"You're a sick cunt, Mitch," Troy said.

"He's the sick cunt," Mitchell said, pointing at the screen.

It was clear on the screen there were two people naked, but what they were doing was hard to make out.

"Well, at least now you know what we do to girls who step out of line," Chuck said, looking at Troy.

"The family business. They make us rich men. Our property is most profitable," Mitchell said, a grin apparent on his face.

They laughed again. Chuck looked back at the screen and scrunched up his face.

"Even I think he's wrong in the head. Who gets turned on by that?"

"Frazier clearly."

"Sick fuck," Troy chimed in.

"Sick fuck indeed."

The video ended. Avery stared down at the blank screen with confusion on her face.

"Play the next video."

I didn't want to see this again, but she had to understand. Had to see what the men in her world did to people. And she

Betrayal

would understand why Frazier Shaw was not a man you messed with.

Avery hit play and her face went white as a sheet. It was a clip of what her father, her uncle and her father's cousin had been watching.

I didn't want her to see the whole thing because it was so sickening, it made me throw up the first time I'd seen it.

⚜

A naked girl tied up with leather straps and rope. Her body was covered in bruises. She was on her knees, staring up at Frazier.

"So, little girl, I heard you tried to escape us? Did anyone ever tell you that running away never solves anything?"

"No, please, sir, please. I'm sorry. I'm sorry."

"Sorry isn't good enough."

He picked up a ball gag from the table beside him. The table which held various torture implements. Her eyes went wide with fear.

Frazier approached her. She closed her mouth, shaking her head. He grabbed her face, forcing her mouth open again.

"Say ahhh."

He stuck it in her mouth and tightened the straps around her head. He picked up a drill next, pressing his finger down and making it whirl.

Tears fell down the girls face as Frazier kicked her down onto her back. He knelt beside her and held her leg steady.

"I'm going to make you bleed, little girl. Bleed all over me and then I'm going to fuck you until you bleed some more."

He lowered the drill to her leg.

The video cut off. Avery put a hand to her mouth. She didn't look at me as she shoved the tablet back in my hand before fleeing the cell. I followed her as she ran to the bathroom.

I set the tablet and the glass of water down on the side of the bath. She fell to her knees and threw up in the loo. I pulled her hair away from her face. She didn't have much in her stomach, so it was mainly water, spit and bile. It's why I hadn't let her eat first.

When she was spent, she put her head on the seat and tears fell down her cheeks.

"Why did you make me watch that?" she whispered.

"You know why."

"I don't. You made me face my nightmares again and now this. Did they mean what I think they did? Does my family deal in human trafficking?"

"Yes, but it's more complicated than that."

"Why was she being… punished?"

"She threatened to go to the police. She even got away from where she was kept."

"Is she still alive now?"

I wasn't sure why she was asking these questions, but the truth was more important than keeping her in the dark.

"No, she's not. She killed herself not long after that happened."

"When did it happen?"

"Ten years ago."

Betrayal

She let out a wracking gasp before dissolving into quiet sobs. I moved away, picking up a face cloth from the sink. Wetting it and wringing it out, I brought it back over to her. I squatted down and tugged her away from the toilet. She let me wipe her face and clean her up.

When she looked at me after I was done, her eyes were haunted and full of pain and sorrow.

"Do you want me to hold you?" I asked.

"I hate you."

"You can hate me, but I'm all you have now."

"Is this why you hate my family?"

"One of the many reasons."

She didn't say anything, just put out her arms to me. I tugged her into mine and held her close, stroking her hair.

"I hate you, Aiden," she whispered. "So why do I still need you when all you do is hurt me?"

"The truth hurts."

"Why are you doing this to me?"

"Because you are going to help me destroy them."

"How can you be so sure of that?"

"You won't be able to live with the knowledge of what they've done and not do something about it. Only when you know the whole truth, you'll understand."

She clutched me tighter, wetting my t-shirt with her tears.

"My life is built on a lie. If that's who they really are then I don't know them at all."

The pitiful note in her voice ground into me, making it impossible not to feel something for her. Fuck. I hated how lost and lonely she was. I hated how responsible for her I felt.

"How do I make it stop? The pain. My heart hurts. I'm bleeding for someone I didn't even know. All of my memories of him feel tarnished."

Him. Her father. Mitchell.

I wished I could make it go away for her, but she needed to feel. To feel so she could learn to hate them. To hate them like I did. Then she could do what I needed her to. Help me destroy them. Only then would I ever set her free. That's if I even could.

Avery was mine in the most fundamental way a person could be. She'd surrendered herself to me over and over again. Despite what I'd done and shown to her, I knew she'd still let me in. She'd let me touch her in the ways I shouldn't. And she'd let me fuck her. Because Avery wanted and needed me.

"You focus on what you have here and now."

"But all I have is you."

"I told you I'll look after you. Give you what you need."

Even though I hadn't been doing a very good job of it. I'd have to try harder for her.

"What I need is not to feel. I'm fed up of being cooped up and alone. I don't want to fight with you anymore. I'm so tired. I just want to give in. I'm sorry. I'm sorry if it's wrong to want you. I'm sorry for whatever I did to make you angry with me."

Fuck. Fuck. Fuck. This girl. Avery. She hates me and wants me. And I fucking wanted her too. She was wrong about me hating her. I didn't hate her. Her family? Yes, but her? Not at all. I couldn't. Avery hadn't done anything wrong. She'd just been in the wrong place at the wrong time. And she was paying for that when it hadn't been her fault.

"I'm not angry with you."

"Will you forgive me?"

"There's nothing to forgive."

"But I broke the rules again."

"Fuck the rules, Avery. You and I don't need rules. Not when you're mine already."

Her fingers traced a line down my spine. I fought against my instinct to stop her. Or was it that I wanted to lean into her touch? Who fucking knew.

"Yours. At your mercy. Under your control. That's what you want from me, isn't it?"

"Yes."

And so much fucking more. I wanted her mine on every level. Her body. Her mind. Her fucking soul.

"You have that already. I won't run from you. I won't tell anyone what happened."

She pulled away and looked up at me, her eyes still watery.

"Our secret, Aiden. What happened is our secret. Yours and mine."

She placed her hand on my heart. I covered it with my own. The fragile girl in my lap was stronger than she knew. And now I knew she'd fight for me. There was still a long way to go before she knew everything, but Avery would be my secret weapon.

And the rest of the Daniels clan wouldn't know what hit them until it was too late.

Chapter Eleven

Avery

Aiden held me for the longest time. I felt sick by what I'd seen. I recognised the man in the second video. My father's best friend, Frazier. I'd always felt there was something off about him and now I knew why. I couldn't begin to imagine what else that girl had to endure or any of the other girls they kept. I was scared to ask Aiden about the real extent of it all.

I could only be glad he didn't show me everything. Those short clips had been enough. I never knew. They'd hidden it all from me. I only really had an inkling something wasn't perfect about my dad when he'd laid down the law about the company to me. I didn't want it. I had no real interest in the property business. He threatened to cut me off from not only my inheritance but my entire family. So I signed the papers and agreed to study architecture.

Now, what I didn't understand was why he was so adamant about me running the business. How could he have expected to keep the other side of it from me forever?

I burrowed myself further into Aiden's chest. Even though I was angry with him for showing me those things and putting me back in the cell, I still wanted his arms around me. I still wanted to feel his solid chest against mine. And I would keep the truth about what he'd done to my parents from ever seeing the light of day. As fucked up and stupid as that was.

"You haven't eaten. I'm going to make you something and then you need to rest," he murmured.

"Are you going to leave me alone?"

"No."

He helped me off the floor and led me to the kitchen. I watched him cook for me. The way his muscles moved as he shifted around the kitchen with ease. The concentration on his face. His beautiful face and those lonely grey eyes. And his mouth. I wanted to know what his lips felt like against mine.

I'd given up berating myself for craving him. What was the point? My attraction to him was as real as the need to breathe. He already knew I'd say yes if he wanted it. Wanted me. Naked. In his bed. Just the two of us. Alone.

I'd do anything he asked just to have him close. To feel his skin against mine. To know these feelings were mutual and real.

He'd told me he didn't do vanilla. I never once thought sex with him would be anything but brutal and unforgiving. He wasn't the type for sweet sentiment or gentleness.

Aiden didn't do sex. Aiden fucked. Of that I was sure.

My face felt hot the instant I thought about him tying me to his bed. Of being taken without mercy or restraint. Why I was even thinking about all this after what I'd just seen, I had no idea. It hit me then. Why he'd made me watch it in the cell.

Betrayal

"You didn't want me to associate those videos with anything outside of the cell," I said.

"No. That's the only place I'll show you the truth. This is your home now whether you've agreed to it or not."

My home. Was it really? It didn't feel like it. This was all Aiden and not me. I didn't have anything of my own here.

He brought over a plate and a mug of tea. Toast, eggs, beans, bacon, tomatoes and mushrooms. For himself, just another one of his protein shakes. He sat with me whilst I ate. Neither of us spoke.

"Thank you," I said when I was done.

He shrugged and put my plate and mug in the dishwasher. Taking my hand, he led me back into his bedroom and encouraged me to get into bed. He didn't leave. He sat up in the bed and let me lay my head in his lap.

"When you wake up, I want you to do something for me," he said.

"What is it?"

"I'll tell you later."

He stroked my hair, the motion soothing and his touch gentle.

"How long have they been doing that?"

"Your family? Longer than anyone cares to remember."

"You mean it started before the company was even created?"

"Yes. From what I gather, it was started to help them appear more legitimate, but the reality is, your family has traded in people for hundreds of years. However, what is happening now is your grandfather's legacy."

"My dad and Uncle Charlie never called him, father. It was always Nick. I never understood it. He was very cold towards them, but not me. I was his beloved granddaughter for some reason. I never did anything they wanted, but that never mattered to him."

Aiden looked down at me.

"What do you mean you never did what they wanted?"

"They expected me to be like all the other rich kids my age. Wanting expensive clothes, falling out of clubs at three in the morning, stealing their alcohol stash, having wild parties, but none of that seemed fun to me. I preferred quiet nights in with James and Gert watching old movies or drawing."

His other hand rested in his lap. I reached out and entwined my fingers with his. I thought he might pull away, but he didn't.

"And how did they take that? Their only daughter being a good kid."

"Not well. Mum kind of understood, but Dad? Not so much. Expectations in my family are high. I never lived up to the Daniels name. Sure, I've been photographed when I tried to be what they wanted, but it's all so fake. It's not the real me. The one who wants to be left alone to make art rather than be the heiress to a billion-pound company that I'm realising is not all it seems."

He didn't reply immediately. His fingers tangled in my hair, running down my neck.

"Would you like it if I bought you supplies so you can draw more? You'd have to show me what you need."

I turned my head up towards him. His expression was neutral.

Betrayal

"You'd do that for me?"

"If it's what you need to be happier here, then yes."

Did he want me to be happy here? I wasn't sure I knew what happiness was anymore. I'd be happy if he continued treating me like this rather than resorting to the cold, heartless Aiden who terrified me to my very core. The one who'd thrown me back in the cell earlier.

"Am I allowed to say thank you?"

That brought a smile to his lips. When he genuinely smiled, it made my heart ache.

"You're allowed."

"Can I ask you something?"

"It depends on what it is."

"What does this say?"

I pointed at the tattoo on his arm. The text I couldn't decipher.

"It's Latin. *Nemo Sine Vitio Est*. It means no one is without fault."

The fact he'd even explained it surprised me. So much so, I didn't want to press him any further. To ask why that phrase specifically. It was true. Everyone was at fault for something in this world. I just wanted to know what it meant to him.

"All my tattoos are by the same artist," he continued. "I don't trust anyone else."

"They're very talented."

"He is. Perhaps one day I'll allow you to meet him."

That made my heart stop. Aiden allowing me to meet someone in his life. It seemed surreal, but he'd said it. Did I mean something to him? Today had brought on too many revelations. Ones about my family and ones about him.

I ran my fingers over the words down his inner arm. I wasn't sure when he'd decided to allow me to touch him, but I never wanted to stop. Aiden felt so real. Such a tangible thing in my life when all else had been torn away.

I ached for him. Craved him. Desired him. The thoughts from earlier blared in my head. The strong, self-assured man who owned me, claiming me as his. Branding himself into my skin. Cementing us together so deep, neither of us would be able to function without the other.

I felt the pulsating need in my stomach and lower. My body simply reacted to his like it was starving for his presence. His touch. It needed his fingers. His mouth. His cock. It didn't want anyone else.

Correction.

I didn't want anyone else. I couldn't use my body's reaction to him as an excuse or a justification. I had to own what I wanted.

None of the guys I'd been with made me wet with a simple look. Not even when I'd kissed Peter. But Aiden did. When his eyes were molten with lust, I responded. Just like I was responding now to having him close with thoughts of what he would do to me running through my head.

He'd told me to rest, but how could I with all that whirling around my brain?

I couldn't wait for Aiden to sort his crap out and make up his mind. Taking matters into my own hands was an awful idea, but my need overcame my common sense.

I moved, shifting up the bed and straddled him. Aiden's eyes went wide.

"Avery, what are you—"

Betrayal

I put my fingers over his lips.

"Don't say anything."

I took his hand, pulled it between us and pressed it to me.

"Touch me. I'm not asking you to fuck me. I need to feel something else other than pain and heartbreak. So please touch me."

I pulled both my hands away from him and put them up to show him I wasn't going to do anything else. His eyes fell to where I'd pressed his hand against my pussy. Seconds ticked by without either of us moving.

His fingers crept beneath my shorts and brushed over my underwear, right over my already sensitive nub. I shuddered.

"Fuck, how wet are you?" he muttered.

His eyes flicked back to mine, burning with heat. His free hand curled around the back of my neck and he dragged me towards him, pressing my forehead to his. He stroked me. My lips parted. Jolts ran up my spine. I let my hands fall to my sides.

"Is this what you want?" he asked, his voice a little hoarse.

"Yes, please don't stop."

"I want to see you come again. You look so fucking beautiful when you come."

I thought I'd misheard him for a moment. Aiden thought I was beautiful. Holy fuck. He increased the pressure and pace. I groaned. His thumb ran circles around my neck. His eyes kept mine, the intensity of his gaze sending me spiralling higher.

"I want to hear my name on your lips when you come."

"Aiden."

"That's it. Say it again."

"Aiden, make me come."

He growled. The sound vibrated through me. There was nothing but me and Aiden. I forgot about the situation we were in. I forgot about what I'd seen today. Aiden eclipsed it all. He was the sun, the sky, the moon and the earth. The pressure inside me intensified. It built and built, coursing through my body.

"Fuck."

"Come for me, Avery. Say my name."

I shattered. Spots formed in my vision. And I cried out his name as my body shook and trembled against him. I tried to breathe oxygen into my lungs, but I was drowning in the sensations he elicited. Waves and waves crashed over me until I all but collapsed against him.

He let go of my neck and my head fell on his shoulder. He pulled me against his chest, stroking a hand down my spine.

"You should rest," he murmured.

"Mmm, thank you," I whispered.

I closed my eyes and drifted off, lulled to sleep by the sound of his breathing and his heart thumping against my chest.

When I woke up, I was alone, the covers tucked around me. The light was fading. Had I slept the afternoon away? I got up and tried the door. It opened. I crept along to the bathroom.

When I came out, I wondered where he was.

"Aiden?"

Betrayal

"In here."

The sound came from down the hall. I followed it and found him in his living room. A place I hadn't been before. He sat on a huge, worn leather sofa with his legs kicked up on the coffee table. It had big windows looking over the city. I was struck for a moment by it. I knew we were still in London, but I didn't realise just how close to the centre we were.

"Come."

I looked at him. He waved me over with his hand. He had his laptop with him. Walking over and sitting down, I found myself nervous after what happened before I fell asleep. He wrapped an arm around my shoulder and pulled me into him. It seemed Aiden was content not to let it change anything, but I couldn't help but respond to his touch. A feeling of contentment washed over me. Safety. I shouldn't let him be my safe place, but he was.

"Did you sleep okay?"

"Yes, thank you."

I looked over at what he was doing. It was lines and lines of text. Weird text that didn't make sense to me.

"It's code," he said. "It's what I normally do for your family, making sure their systems aren't hacked into and such things like that."

"But they make you hurt people too."

"Yes."

"How do you know how to do all of this anyway?"

He smiled and ruffled my hair.

"I was in the army for six years. Military intelligence, but I learnt a lot of things on the side. Never had a tour of duty. Didn't stop me going down the firing range."

That made far more sense than anything else he'd told me about himself. Aiden's flat was so neat and tidy. All his stuff in perfect order down to the way he folded clothes, including mine.

I dreaded to think what his real reaction was when I'd scattered all my drawings all over his bed. Did it bother him that I'm not the neatest of people? He always seems to be picking up after me. Perhaps I should make more of an effort.

"How old are you and how long have you been working for my family?"

"You're in a very inquisitive mood."

"How can I not be?"

"Twenty-eight. Worked for your family for four years, but I've known them a lot longer than that."

So he was eight years my senior. Probably why I saw him as all man, unlike the boys I'd been around before. My cousins were of a similar age to me, so it wasn't as though I hung out with many people older than me.

"You said you wanted me to do something for you."

"Yes. I need you to go pick out some clothes because we're going away for a few days."

I looked up at him. What did he mean we were going away?

"What? Why?"

"You told me you're fed up of being cooped up in the flat. I thought you'd be happy."

"I am… I just didn't expect you to actually let me outside."

"I have my reasons. It's not all just for your benefit."

I didn't ask what that meant. I was just happy we were leaving. Perhaps it would allow me to forget about what he'd shown me about my family and the awful hallucinations I had

Betrayal

in the cell. I couldn't forget what they'd asked me to do. Avenge them. It's just now I knew my father wasn't worth avenging. I couldn't see him in the same light any longer. Not after the way he'd laughed about that girl's torture. I would never like my uncle and cousin Troy was a bit of a creep, but my dad? It was the opposite of the man I knew.

It wasn't so much I wasn't aware Aiden was trying to manipulate my views, but I couldn't refute what I'd seen. I imagined it's why he gave me evidence rather than just telling me. If he hadn't, I doubt I'd have believed a word he said.

"Are we going today?"

"Yes. I was waiting for you to wake up."

I pulled away from him and got up. He smiled at me before I left the room. I got dressed and picked out enough clothes to last me a week along with my toiletries, setting them out on the bed. Aiden came in a few minutes later and packed it alongside his own stuff without saying anything.

He pulled a box out of the cupboard and handed it to me. I opened it finding a brand new pair of black and white Vans inside.

"I got you these when I bought you clothes, but you haven't had any need for them until now," he said with a shrug.

He'd asked me what kind of things I'd wear weeks ago. I only found out the extent of his shopping spree when he'd let me out of the cell. Definitely hadn't spared any expense outfitting me. I hadn't worn much of it yet.

I took them out of the box and laced them properly. They fit perfectly when I put them on.

"I never did thank you for getting me all this."

His eyes roamed over me and down to my feet. I'd put on a pair of jeans, a plain black t-shirt and a cardigan. A smile appeared on his lips.

"Something about a girl in trainers."

Before I could reply, he picked up the bag and indicated with his head I should follow him. When we reached the front door, he pulled a jacket off the hook and handed it to me before taking his own. The one he'd given me matched his. Leather.

"It's getting cold out now," he said.

I shrugged it on and followed him out the front door, which he locked behind us. It felt weird to leave his flat. I never thought I'd see anything outside those walls again.

We took the lift down to the underground car park. I found myself staring at a black Jag. Aiden opened the boot and stashed the bag before coming around and opening the passenger side for me.

"Are you going to get in or gawk at it?" he asked.

"It's pretty."

He rolled his eyes. I slid in and got comfy in the leather seat, putting my seatbelt on. He got in the driver seat and started the car. The low hum of the engine vibrated through me. He revved it, looking over at me with a grin.

"Are you showing off?" I asked.

"Perhaps a little. Just wait until I get you on the back of my bike."

I baulked at the suggestion. I'd never been on a motorbike before. He pointed over at it sitting next to the car. It was huge and terrifying.

"Um, there is no way I'm going on that with you."

Betrayal

"We'll see."

He screeched out of the car park causing me to fly back in my seat. The streets of London whizzed past us as Aiden took the back roads until we were finally out of the city and on the M25. He put some indie rock on. I sat back and watched the cars driving along next to us. It didn't much matter where he was taking me. I was happy to be out of the flat.

I must've drifted off because I jolted awake when Aiden opened the car door and ducked his head inside. He gave me a half smile

"How can you still be tired?" he asked.

I yawned, stretching a little. My neck felt stiff from falling asleep with my face smashed against the window.

"I don't know."

He helped me out the car. I was a little unsteady on my feet, still in a bit of a daze. Rather than waiting for me to get my bearings, Aiden swept me off my feet and carried me into the small cottage. I clutched his neck.

"Hey, I can walk."

"Really? You were about to fall over."

He set me down on the sofa. It was open plan with a kitchen and dining table in the corner. There were two doors off the room. I assumed the bathroom and bedroom.

"It's late, but we still should eat."

Clearly, he'd stopped on the way and got some food in as two bags sat on the kitchen counter.

"Where are we?"

"Near the Devon moors and before you ask, I own this place."

"You own it?"

He shrugged.

"I have a few places."

My family dealt in property. I shouldn't be surprised by this, but I was a little. He'd be well compensated for what he did for them.

"Why here?"

"Because it's far enough away from London."

He said no more as he started to sort us out dinner. I sat quietly, watching him. I was always entranced by the way Aiden moved with such precision. It was as if each step was calculated carefully.

"Do you like what you see?"

I jumped at the sound of his voice.

"What?"

"You're watching me."

My face felt hot immediately. He'd caught me staring. Fuck. What the hell was wrong with me? I had no answer for him. I looked down at my hands, suddenly very interested in my fingernails. I heard him chuckling and I swear my face burnt hotter.

Note to self: do not stare at the man who wants to use you in his personal war like you want him to tear your clothes off and give you the ride of your life.

We didn't say much to each other when Aiden served up dinner. I felt awkward and he seemed lost in his own thoughts. I wanted to ask him what we were really doing here, but I knew he wouldn't answer me.

I washed up when we were done as the cottage didn't have a dishwasher.

Betrayal

Aiden left me alone and took a shower. I could've walked out the door, but I didn't. What would be the point when he'd just chase me down and haul me back. Then I'd be in serious trouble. No. I wouldn't leave Aiden. Not now because this stupid girl had got a case of the feelings for the man who'd killed her parents. Feelings she really didn't understand.

I went into the bedroom, which Aiden had pointed out, and found our stuff on top of the desk near the bed. I guess we'd be sharing again. I wasn't quite sure what else I expected. Aiden seemed to want me close.

Changing into pyjamas, I got in bed. How I was still tired was beyond me. I snuggled into the covers, feeling their warmth encompass me.

A moment later, the door to the bedroom opened and in the low light, I could see he was towelling off his hair. He'd put a t-shirt and boxers on. My mouth watered at the sight of him and my insides clenched.

Would this ever end? My desperate attraction to him was beginning to be a curse. It was only this morning when we'd fought with each other over Peter and I'd admitted I wanted him to fuck me. It felt like longer.

He pottered around the room for a moment before he crawled in beside me. My fingers itched. My body suddenly felt on high alert. The air in my lungs didn't seem like it was enough to sustain me any longer. I had no idea what it felt like to be tortured, but this was making my brain hurt. He'd already pleasured me earlier, so why did I still need more? Why wouldn't these cravings go away?

His hands snaked around my hips and he tugged me against him. I felt his cock digging into me. His heart hammered against my back. Heat radiated off him, seeping into me.

"Fuck, I want you, Avery," he growled.

"What?"

"I want you so fucking much, but you and I can't have each other."

His words tore at me. Can't we? Why did something so wrong feel so right?

His fingers danced over my stomach.

"What happened to me being yours?" I whispered.

"You are, but that changes nothing. There's still so much you don't know. Still so much you don't understand. I won't have all of you until you know and you can't make a choice until then. So you and I can't have each other."

He placed delicate kisses to my neck. I shuddered against him. Fucking hell.

"You won't like what I want you to do for me. You'll hate me even more than you do now."

"Aiden…"

"You'll have to choose when you know. Me or them. There is no in between."

My heart broke. There was more to what he'd shown me today. So much more. My loyalty to my family would be eroded piece by piece until it scattered like dust in the wind. Would it be enough for me to throw away everything for the man pressed to my back?

Instead of answering, I let Aiden hold me. He didn't try to touch me further and I didn't encourage him. I was too wrapped up in my own indecision.

No matter what I felt for Aiden.

Betrayal

I wasn't sure if he and I would be enough.
I wasn't sure if I could go against everything I knew.
I wasn't sure of anything at all.

Chapter Twelve

Aiden

She hadn't said anything.

She hadn't fucking said anything.

I wanted to damn well crawl inside her mind and rip out her thoughts. I needed to know what she fucking felt about what I said last night. I wasn't sure why I'd said it. There was this need inside me I couldn't deny any longer. After she told me she wanted me to wreck her, it'd played on my mind.

There was a huge difference in knowing someone wanted you and them telling you that was the case. I needed her to know she wasn't alone in feeling things she shouldn't. In wanting a person she should never seek to have.

Avery had severely fucked with my head. Dug her way inside my fucking mind and made a permanent place for herself. The more I learnt about her, the more I realised she was the exact opposite of what I expected. She didn't share the arrogance of her family. There was a humbleness to her. She wanted a quiet life. And really, if I was to be honest, that's what I wanted too. I'd been fighting since I was a child and I was growing tired. I wanted this war with the Daniels to be over. They'd already stolen so much of my life.

She didn't speak when we sat and had breakfast together. She wouldn't even look at me. It unnerved me because it wasn't like her. If she wasn't going to acknowledge anything then fine. I'd just get down to business and the real reason I'd brought her here.

"There's something I need you to do for me."

She looked up, her eyes not quite meeting mine.

"What?"

"We're going to take a walk and you're going to make a video for me."

That got her attention. Her brow furrowed.

"A video?"

"Yes. So we can clear up a little misunderstanding with the police."

She put her fork down and really looked at me.

"What exactly are you after, Aiden?"

"I want you to tell them to stop looking for you because you don't want to be found and I want you to tell that boy to stop waiting for you."

The blood drained from her face.

"You… want what?"

"You see, he went and told them you were meant to be at your parents and because they found your phone there, they assume the killer took you."

"You want me to lie for you."

She already knew I wanted that from day one.

Looking down at her hands, she fidgeted in her seat.

Betrayal

"I will tell them to stop looking for me if that's what you need. And I'll tell Peter on one condition even though I would rather have a conversation with him."

"What's your condition?"

If I had my way, she'd never talk to that boy ever again. She was mine. And she fucking knew that.

Fuck. I was such an arsehole. I wouldn't sleep with her even though it's what we both wanted but I wouldn't let anyone else have her.

"Let me say something to James and Gert so they don't worry about me."

Her friends. Right. I didn't care if she did that. It'd make it more believable anyway.

"Fine."

"How exactly are you going to give this to them?"

"I have ways and means. It's not for you to worry about. Just play your part."

She looked away, staring back down at her plate. Picking up the fork, she started eating again. I didn't like this sudden distance. Yesterday, she'd been happy to talk to me and asked me to touch her. Fuck. When I made her come, it drove me crazy. I was so close to pushing her clothes aside so I could sink into her heat. I wanted her pussy clenching around my cock when she came.

Now, she'd closed herself off from me. I wanted to be honest with her, but that honesty had come at a cost. All of this was impossible. Denying what we wanted from each other. Denying there was something real and tangible between us. It went beyond families and revenge.

If things were different, we could've been two people who found solace in each other. Instead, we were on opposite sides of the same coin. She was still a Daniels — and me? I was just the fucked up guy who killed her parents and stole her away from her life.

"Should we go then?"

I looked at her. She'd finished and already washed the dishes whilst I'd been lost in thought. I stood up abruptly.

"Yes."

We both wrapped up because it was chilly outside. I slipped a small camera into my jacket pocket before we left. I led her along the track I'd driven down yesterday evening and on to one of the many footpaths in the area. Our breath was visible in the late morning air. Avery dug her hands in her pockets, looking around the fields surrounding us.

"It's not far," I said.

She didn't reply. I just planned to take her to a wooded area nearby. Somewhere out of the way where they'd have trouble working out where we'd filmed it. I was sure they would still look for her, but my other plans would make it difficult.

This was a gamble. Sometimes you had to take risks in order to reap the rewards. My reward would be the police backing off and giving me more time to bring Avery around. It was only a few more weeks till Christmas and I needed her ready for the new year.

I wasn't sure how she'd take it. Being forced to spend what should be a family holiday with me, away from everything she knew. I'd tell her soon. And for her sake, I'd try to give her some semblance of normality. If she wanted a tree and decorations, I'd do it.

I hadn't really celebrated Christmas since I'd left the army. I'd always spent it with Ben, my tattoo artist's family. Things had changed when we'd gone back to civilian life. I'd become so focused on taking down the Daniels, we only saw each other during inking sessions. It'd been six months. Ben understood. It wasn't as though his life hadn't changed either.

"You're quiet today," I said, needing to break the silence between us.

"Just have a lot on my mind."

I didn't have to ask what. Yesterday had been difficult for her. I hadn't made it easier on her either.

"Do you want to talk about it?"

"I don't know what to say. It wouldn't change anything even if I did. What you say goes so there's no point."

What the fuck was that supposed to mean? I tried to give her things within my power when she asked for them.

"Let's just not do this, Aiden. I told you I don't want to fight with you any longer."

"Do what exactly?"

"Did you even listen? Don't push me, please. I can't deal with any more."

I stopped, grabbed her arm and forced her to look at me.

"Deal with what?"

"Please, stop."

"No. What is wrong with you today?"

She tried to wriggle away from me, but I wouldn't let her. Irritation flared in her eyes.

"What's wrong? You're making me do something I don't want to do."

"That's not it."

I wasn't fooled. She was bothered by something else.

"Fine. I'm pissed off with you. I can't take this blowing hot and cold business. For fuck's sake, Aiden, you keep pulling me close and pushing me away in the next breath. I barely even know how to process the fact that my whole life has been built on a lie and then I have you messing with my head. I can't do it. I can't. Stop pushing me. I'm already fucking broken and all you're doing is making it worse. So just fucking stop."

I released her because I felt like she'd just slapped me in the face with her words. She stormed away from me, her breath coming fast and her fists clenching and unclenching at her sides. Even when she was angry, she was perfect.

Fucking hell. Having all that thrown back at me made my blood pound. And the sick part? My cock demanded my attention. It throbbed uncomfortably. Angry and upset Avery was hot. She might be timid on occasion, but her temper made me want to teach her a lesson.

I strode towards her, taking her by the arm and tugging her along next to me.

"What are you doing? Let go of me."

"No."

"Aiden!"

I ignored her tone and her struggle to stop me in my tracks. We weren't far from the woods now. No one would be about so I could do what I wanted with her. And Avery couldn't do a damn thing to stop me. I dragged her into the trees when we reached them.

Betrayal

"Stop. Please, let go."

"I told you there weren't rules any more, but you still have to obey me. And right now, you're going to do what I say or it'll be fucking worse for you."

"Aiden, stop it."

When we were far enough in, I shoved her stomach first into a large oak tree and held her there. My mouth was right next to her ear.

"What are you doing?"

"I'm teaching you a fucking lesson."

I kept an elbow at her back and tugged her hips towards me. I knew this angle would be uncomfortable for her, but I didn't care. My cock pressing against her behind almost made me groan. I kicked her legs open and ground into her. Her gasp echoed around my skull.

"You think you can talk to me like that, Avery? News flash, you can't. You don't get to tell me how to treat you. This isn't a fucking game. You are mine and because of that, you're going to get down on your fucking knees in front of me. Do you understand?"

She whimpered. I ground into her again.

"Don't make me repeat myself. Do you fucking understand?"

"Yes."

I released her, stepping back. She turned around slowly. Her eyes were watery, but she did as I told her. She got down on her knees in the dirt. I really wasn't thinking straight, but at that moment, I didn't care. My need to make sure she understood her place outweighed everything else. My fucking feelings towards her be fucking damned. Everything else was insignificant.

I cupped her chin, forcing her face up towards me.

"What do you think I want you to do?"

She swallowed.

"I don't know."

"Oh, I think you do."

I tugged her face towards me, pressing it against my thigh. My cock twitched in anticipation.

"Aiden, don't do this," she whispered.

"Tell me what I want."

There was silence for a long moment.

"You… You want me to… don't make me say it, please. I don't want to do this with you. Not like this."

"You don't have a fucking choice. Tell me what I want."

Her hand wrapped around my leg.

"You want me to take your cock out and suck you off until you come down my throat."

Hearing her say those words only made my need worse. Fuck. I wanted more than that, but I'd already made up my mind. We weren't going to fuck unless she picked me.

"Good girl."

I stroked her hair. She was going to look so beautiful with her lips wrapped around me.

She reached up and unbuckled my belt. Pulling away from my leg, she unbuttoned my jeans and unzipped the fly. Her fingers brushed over my cock. Fuck her touch was heavenly. I let her tug my jeans down slightly, just enough to give her access to me.

Betrayal

"Aiden," she whispered. "I'm not very experienced in this. I don't want to do it wrong."

If it had been any other time, I would've told her to stop because of how fucking innocent she was. It was too late for that. I needed my cock in her mouth. I needed to come so fucking much, it burnt. Nothing else would do. It had to be in her.

"Stop stalling."

"I'm serious."

"Avery, take my cock out right now and wrap your fucking lips around it. If you're doing it wrong, I'll fucking tell you."

She hooked her fingers into my boxers and pulled them down. My cock sprung free. Her eyes went wide. I wanted to shove her down on it, but I needed her to do it. Needed her to accept it was going to happen.

She reached up and held my cock in her hand. Her fingers barely fit around it because she was so fucking small. I jerked in her hold. Her touch was so fucking soft and delicate.

She rose up further on her knees and swallowed. When she finally wrapped her lips around the head of my cock, I groaned. Her mouth was hot and wet. So fucking delicious.

My fingers threaded in her hair. The urge to force her into taking more hammered in my chest.

"That's it," I grunted. "Suck me, Avery. Fucking show me how much you want to make me come."

She did just that. She moved, bobbing her head up and down with long, drawn out strokes, taking more of me. Her fingers worked me from the base. Her other hand rested on my thigh, fingers digging in slightly.

Fuck. Her mouth was unlike anything else. No one had touched me in a way that was so innocent yet so fucking magic. Perhaps it was because she was so inexperienced. I didn't care. All my focus was on my cock buried in her sweet, wet, hot mouth.

My fingers kneaded her scalp. Her pace increased. I grunted, feeling my climax building. Fuck it was too soon. I wanted to draw it out but I didn't want to stop her.

"Fuck. Fuck, your mouth. Don't fucking stop. More, fuck, Avery, more."

I couldn't help it. I was losing control and she was dragging me down with her. My cock hit the back of her mouth. She'd only managed about half my length. Her lips were stretched obscenely around my cock. It made me twitch.

Her eyes met mine. There was no anger or hatred in them. No. Avery looked at me with no small amount of desire flickering in the depths of those doe eyes. Doe fucking eyes.

"Is this turning you on? Are you wet for me?"

She pulled away, releasing me and taking a few deep breaths.

"Yes."

"Good. When you've made me come, I'm going to shove you against that tree and you're going to let me feel just how fucking wet you are."

She said nothing, merely looked at me with acceptance. Then she took me in her mouth and I lost all fucking ability for rational thought. My cock hit the back of her mouth again, but she didn't stop there. She took more, letting me sink deep into her throat. I didn't want her to gag on my cock. That wasn't hot.

Betrayal

She wouldn't allow me to pull away. She just kept taking it until she couldn't anymore. Two fucking thirds of my cock and it was so tight I could hardly fucking breathe.

Avery let me fuck her throat without complaint. My balls tightened and I was about ready to fucking blow. I pulled back slightly as the sensation built until I couldn't fucking hold on. Hot, sticky streams erupted from me. I grunted, continuing to fuck her mouth as it washed over me. Intense and fucking wonderful. The release so much sweeter because it was in her. Because she'd fucking given it to me.

To her credit, she swallowed every last drop I gave her. I wasn't angry with her any longer. She'd been good and done what I asked even if she hadn't really wanted to at first. Lesson fucking learnt. Obey me and you won't fucking get in trouble.

"Put my cock away then get up," I said.

I wanted to tell her how fucking amazing she'd been, but it would ruin the effectiveness of my lesson.

Her hands shook as she adjusted my clothes, zipped my jeans back up and re-buckled my belt. Then she stood, looking at me with wide eyes. She was waiting for what came next. I pointed at the tree. She moved and stood before it.

I stalked towards her, pressing her against the bark. I ran a hand down her side. Her body trembled.

"Do you want my touch, Avery?"

"Yes."

"Tell me how much you want it."

"I want you, Aiden. I need your hands on me. I need you to feel how much I want you."

"Where do you want my hands?"

Her eyes flickered with longing.

"My… I want you to touch my clit."

Fuck. If she wasn't careful, she was going to breathe life back into my cock and then we'd have a problem.

"Mmm, do you deserve that?"

"Please, I don't, but I want you so much. Having your cock in my mouth made me so wet."

I flicked open the button on her jeans. We both knew I couldn't stop myself touching her. It was fucking inevitable we'd end up like this. I rested my forehead against hers.

"Please, Aiden."

Her plea broke through the last fucking ounce of my control. I tugged open the zip on her jeans and shoved my hand inside her underwear. She wasn't fucking joking about how wet she was. My cock jerked as soon as my fingers ran over her fucking delectable pussy. She moaned. The sound like fucking music to my ears.

"Do you want me to fuck you with my fingers, Avery? Fuck you until you come."

"Please."

"Then I need something from you first."

Her breath dusted across my face. I could feel her pulsating against me. I stroked my fingers across her clit. Fuck, she felt incredible.

"What?"

"Your fucking submission. Do you understand? I want you to promise me you'll never let another man touch you again because you're fucking mine. I own you."

"I promise, Aiden. I'm yours. No one else can have me. No one. I promise."

Betrayal

The fact she didn't hesitate to make that promise almost broke through all my fucking resolve. Fuck I wanted to rip her clothes off and shove her down on her hands and knees and fuck her.

"What will happen if someone tries to touch you or put their dick in you?"

"You'll put a bullet in their head."

"You remembered."

"I remember everything you tell me."

Good girl.

Now I'd extracted what I needed, I'd give her what she wanted. I sunk two fingers into her pussy. Fuck she was so tight. She cried out, her body bucking against me. My thumb swept over her clit as I thrust my fingers inside her. I wasn't gentle about it. I wanted her to feel it. To know she was fucking mine and I would never give her mercy.

"This is just a taste of what I'm going to do to you when I fuck you."

"Aiden," she moaned. "Don't stop."

"I have no fucking intention of stopping. I want you to come all over my fingers."

Her eyes glazed over as she stared at me. Her heart pounded in her chest, her breathing completely erratic. And she looked so fucking beautiful.

I didn't let up in pace. She bucked and trembled against me, crying out. Her fingers dug into my waist where she'd gripped me.

There was nothing but me and her. Avery was the fucking sun and I was drowning in her submission. I fucking craved her. Seeing her so lost in me and what I was doing to her fed me. It brought me back to fucking life after all these years of feeling nothing but pure fucking hatred for those who had wronged me.

"Mine, fucking tell me you're mine."

"I'm yours," she breathed. "Yours, Aiden."

I felt her pussy clench around my fingers. Her eyes rolled back in her head and I knew she was on the precipice. One last thrust and she came undone. She couldn't hold back a scream. It caused the birds above us to scatter and shattered the peace of the silent forest.

When she slumped against the tree with her eyes closed, I stroked her face with my free hand. She leant into my touch.

"I'm going to take you back now. What we were going to do can wait until tomorrow."

She nodded. She wasn't in any state to make a believable video after this and in all honesty, neither was I. I needed to get a fucking grip. This was never meant to happen. I wasn't supposed to lose control.

"Come on, I'll give you a piggyback."

She opened her eyes and smiled at me. Radiant, just like she was.

"I can walk."

"You don't look like you can."

I pulled away from her. She zipped her jeans back up and I bent down so she could get on my back. She hesitated for a few moments but climbed on. I hooked my arms around her legs and set off back towards the cottage.

Today had been a fucking disaster.

No matter how good it felt to be inside her mouth and have her come all over my fingers, it was a fucking mistake.

Betrayal

Avery might be mine but I couldn't become hers.
Not now.
Not fucking ever.

Chapter Thirteen

Avery

I couldn't think about anything other than what happened in the forest yesterday. I stared at the ceiling as I lay in bed, not wanting to get up. Aiden had gone out for a run, so I was alone, but he'd locked all the doors and windows in the cottage. I wasn't planning on getting up until he got back.

The brutal way he'd handled me should've made me want to run away. Instead, it turned me on to the point of insanity. I questioned whether it turned me on because it was Aiden or because I liked it rough. Was it a combination of both?

I'd never explored the boundaries when it came to sex before. Innocent is what Aiden had described me as. He was right. My sexual conquests were limited to three.

The first time was a drunken fumble when I'd been sixteen with a guy I met on holiday in Jamaica. I don't even remember his name.

The second, George, one of the popular boys at school, had been a mistake. He only slept with me so he could brag about having fucked Mitchell Daniels' daughter. A small mercy my dad never got word of it because James punched George in the face for spreading shit about me.

And the third… James himself. The only male I felt close to who wasn't part of my family. Gert didn't know. In fact, no one knew except the two of us. Not something you go around blurting out. It became a way for us to let off steam up until I started seeing Peter. Families with expectations meant we both felt like the weight of the world was on our shoulders. We understood each other in a way Gert couldn't. She didn't have rich parents like us.

A sudden wave of sadness hit me. I missed them, but James especially. And I could never, ever tell Aiden. How would I even explain it? I loved James, but not in a romantic way. Did it even matter? Whatever Aiden and I were doing with each other wasn't exactly love or romantic. More like raw and animalistic. Two people who needed to possess each other with a desperation that bordered on madness.

I wanted to explore the side of me Aiden had brought out. I wanted to know the girl who needed to submit to him in every way possible.

The front door banged. Aiden was back. I shot out of bed and opened the door. He was covered in a sheen of sweat and holy fuck did he look hot as hell. His t-shirt clung to his muscles, moulding to his body.

His steel eyes roamed over me. I remembered what it felt like to have him in my mouth and the look in his eye as he came down my throat.

"We're going out after I've showered so eat something," he said before he strode into the bathroom.

Betrayal

He'd barely spoken to me after what happened. And for the first time, he didn't hold me when we went to bed. I didn't know how to take that. Something was off with him and it had everything to do with the forest. Did he regret it? Because I didn't. No. I wanted more. I needed more.

I got dressed and made myself some food. I didn't pay much attention when he moved from the bathroom to the bedroom. And when he came out, he looked pissed off.

"Shoes and coat on now and this time, we are going to film this video. Understood?"

I slipped off my chair and did as he said. Disobeying and arguing with him had only brought punishment. Admittedly I liked the lesson he dealt yesterday, but something about Aiden still terrified me. I didn't want him to put me back in the cell when we returned to London. Staying in his good graces meant obeying.

We walked for a long time. He didn't take me back to the woods. Instead, we found an empty field, still wet from the early morning dew. He pulled a small camera out of his pocket and handed it to me.

"In order to make this believable, it has to be filmed by your hand and you need to be fucking careful of what you say."

"I know what you expect of me, Aiden."

"Good."

I'd thought long and hard about what to say. I didn't want to disappoint Aiden. This was important. I held the camera up and pressed the button to record.

"Hello, my name is Avery Charlotte Daniels, but you probably know that. I know I've been gone for a while and for that I can only apologise. You see, when I discovered my parents were dead, the news hit hard. I didn't want to be in the world any longer. So I disappeared instead. I'm sorry for making you worry about me. I'm sending you this message because I want you to stop looking for me. When I'm ready, I'll come home and face the world, but for now, please know I'm safe."

I paused, taking a breath as tears pricked at my eyes. The next part made me equal parts nervous and sick.

"Uncle Charlie, I know the company is in safe hands with you. To the boy I cared for, I'm sorry. I never meant to hurt you, but what we had was never meant to be. I hope you find someone who loves you in the way you deserve. Gert, I miss you and I'm sorry for being a shit friend by disappearing on you like this. And James, don't let them give you too much shit, you know who I mean. Whatever happens, I love you always."

I waved at the camera before I stopped the recording.

"There, happy now?" I asked, looking at Aiden.

His expression left me in no doubt he was the complete opposite of happy.

"Give me the camera."

I walked over and handed it to him. He stuffed it in his pocket before taking my arm and dragging me back the way we'd come.

"Hey… I can walk by myself."

"Do not test my patience, Avery."

"What have I done wrong now? I did what you asked, didn't I?"

Betrayal

He stopped, causing me to stumble. It was lucky he was holding on to me so I didn't fall over.

"Done wrong? Who fucking said you did anything wrong?"

Aiden's eyes were cold and full of repressed rage.

"Then why are you angry? Is… Is it because of what I said to James in the video?"

His nostrils flared, eyes growing darker. And I tried to take a step back.

"It's fucking everything you do. Every fucking moment with you is fucking torture, do you know that?"

I shook my head, unable to quite comprehend what he'd just admitted to me. What did that mean?

He dragged me against him, crushing me to his chest before burying his face in my hair.

"Aiden, I don't understand."

"My whole life I've hated your family and everyone involved with them. I hate them so much, it's hardwired into my blood. But then you came along, so fucking innocent and so unlike them on every level. And no matter what I fucking do, I can't keep you at arm's length when I should. I fucking should be able to. You have to stop pushing me too."

I wrapped my arms around his back, clutching him. My heart ached. I had no idea how much I made him suffer.

"I want to hate you so much, but I can't," he continued. "I just fucking can't. So tomorrow, we're going back to London. I'm going to make sure the police see this video and we're going to talk about your family properly."

"Okay," I said, my words muffled by his chest.

I felt in that moment if I said anything about his confession, things would escalate further. Too exhausted to deal with any more conflict between us.

We pulled away from each other. Aiden did the unexpected. He took my hand, entwining our fingers together. He didn't drag me along with him. We walked at a steady pace.

When we got back to the cottage, he put a film on for me. Some stupid action flick, but I actually got to do something other than stare at the wall, so I didn't complain. And he let me curl up with my head in his lap as he stroked my hair.

I felt for those few moments like things had gone back to normal, but I knew when we returned to London, things would never be normal again.

A quiet calm descended over the two of us on the way back to London. We stopped once because I was desperate for the loo, but the rest of the journey was silent, peaceful almost. As if Aiden and I had left the part of us banded in sorrow behind in Dorset. The illusion would be shattered soon. The truth would always cut through our desires. I knew that. The truth of who he was and what I'd been born into were iron bars holding us back from each other.

Too many secrets.

The truth would hurt.

Me.

Him.

And everything around us.

Betrayal

Returning to the flat made me wonder if Aiden would ever let me out again. He said he needed me to help him destroy my family. Did that mean he'd send me back out into the world when he successfully made me flip sides? How was he so sure I would? My feelings for him didn't outweigh the rest, did they?

The questions nagged at me. I had a headache. Aiden disappeared into a locked room an hour ago and hadn't emerged.

I had free roam of the flat now. I stood in the living room, staring out the window. The city loomed like a dark presence around my heart. The city holding secrets and lies hidden beneath its surface. Was I about to step into the darkness? Would I ever be able to see the sunlight again when I learnt the truth?

"I have to go out."

His voice startled me. I looked back at him. In his hands was his laptop.

"There are some things you need to see."

"More videos?"

"No. Just information. You can make your own mind up about it. Don't try going on the internet. I turned it off. There is nothing here you can use to speak to the outside world. Understood?"

Trying to speak to anyone was the last thing I'd been thinking about. Didn't he trust me after I made the video for him? I supposed he had to take precautions.

"I get it."

He placed the laptop on the coffee table.

"I want you to go through what I've left open on there before I get back. I haven't doctored any of it, but if you don't trust me, that's fine. I can't force you to believe any of it."

I didn't think Aiden would do anything but show me the truth. Stupid fucked up girl. Trusting him. My feelings clearly clouded my judgement. Feelings I could neither turn off nor change. Aiden eclipsed everything. The fucked up broken man in front of me. I saw him. He saw me. Behind all the walls we built up to survive.

"I'll be back late."

"Okay."

He came around the sofa and stood before me. Taking my hand, he brought it to his lips and kissed my knuckles. I wished it was my lips. They tingled in anticipation. When Aiden finally kissed me, we would be lost. Nothing would stand between us. The tidal wave would crash over our souls, binding us together and we'd burn for each other. Destroy each other. All in pursuit of one thing. To silence the ache we both felt inside. To soothe the broken parts of our hearts.

Perhaps it was that knowledge which kept us apart. Which kept the wall up in place so we didn't drown in each other.

"Don't miss me too much."

His tone was teasing but his eyes spoke volumes.

Don't be scared.

Face the truth.

Do it for me.

Choose me.

Fight for me.

I wanted to. So fucking much.

"I'll try."

My tone was just as light.

I want you.
I need you.
I will try to fight for you.
For us.

He let go of my hand and walked out of the room.

Would there ever be an us? Or would it just be me falling at his feet and giving him my all?

Could Aiden ever be mine?

I shook myself. Thinking about the future was futile. I didn't know what future he had in store for me. What I could do is educate myself about my family.

What had he left for me?

I sat down on the sofa and picked up the laptop. Tucking my legs up, I settled down with it. The first thing on the screen was a spreadsheet of some kind. There were a lot of figures. I read the headings.

Name. Payments in. Projects. Girls.

I scanned down the list. I recognised some of the names of the businesses. Each line showed a payment they'd made to an offshore account. Some of them corresponded to building projects and developments, some of them had girls names against them and others, both.

It dawned on me. I knew some of those developments. They'd been handled by our company. I felt sick. So sick. How could this be true? Had they really been accepting bribes? And the girls names? That part made no sense to me.

I checked the other documents Aiden left for me to look at. It soon became clear what girls meant. Girls owned by my family. Loaned out to their clients. I put my hand to my mouth. It noted they were gifts. The length of time they spent with a client depended on the sum of money donated. Donated? It wasn't a fucking donation. Payoffs. Bribes.

Oh fuck.

Was this how we'd got so rich? Dirty money?

It was too much. All too fucking much. Our fortune tainted. My inheritance. I didn't want it. None of it. Not if it came from this. An empire built on lies, sex trafficking and bribery. Worst of all, Aiden told me my family bought and sold people for longer than Daniels Holdings had existed. It could only mean one thing.

Slavery.

My heart couldn't take it. My fucking soul burnt.

Anger.

Betrayal.

Disgust.

Sorrow.

Pain.

Waves and waves crashed over me until I felt like my body hurt all over and my mind wanted to shut down. Tears dripped down my cheeks.

I placed the laptop back on the coffee table. Its screen sat unblinking at me. Taunting me with the reality that my family were scum.

Greedy fucking scum.

I stood on shaky legs and made my way into the bedroom. I picked up a pencil, paper and the book Aiden left me. I took it over to the rug on the floor, sat down and started to draw.

Images of brutalised girls. Of men sitting in their gilded offices, laughing at the misfortune of others. Of fallen angels.

Betrayal

Of people in chains. Of violence and destruction poured out from my hand onto the pages. Pages and pages of drawings until they littered the floor and covered the bed. I drew until my fingers throbbed.

My soul shattered to a million fucking tiny pieces on the floor.

I crawled under the covers, not caring about the paper everywhere. Aiden's scent surrounded me. Soothing my aching heart.

I cried until I could cry no more.

And I fell asleep when exhaustion finally settled over me.

Chapter Fourteen

Aiden

I had too much to do. Those couple of days we spent away. The bliss I'd experienced having her submit to me. It was all fucking gone. I shut it out, buried it in the deepest part of me. Only there could it remain, nestled against my fucking useless organ beating in my chest. The one chaining me to misery and loathing. For her sake and for mine, it had to disappear.

I'd admitted too many things. Given her too many insights into my complicated soul. And worst of all, I'd lost control of myself in her. It couldn't happen again.

My fucking weak point. That's what she was. Unhinging me. Tearing me apart. Making me feel. Feelings weren't welcome in the hellhole that was my soul. Not when they tangled themselves up with memories.

Memories.

Screams. More screams echoed through the flat. Tears ran tracks down my cheeks.

"*Stop, please. Please.*"

I crept along the hallway.

"*Stop. It hurts. Please, not there.*"

Louder. The screaming, crying, pain. It hurt my ears.

"*Take it darlin',*" *a gruff voice I'd never heard before grunted.*

"*Stop.*"

"*You missed me, didn't you?*"

His voice was accented. American.

"*No, please.*"

I peered around the doorframe. All I could see was a man with light brown hair, his back to me. In front of him, on hands and knees, she stared straight ahead. They were both naked. I could see exactly what he was doing.

"*You always miss me. You can't think about anyone but me because of what I gave you.*"

"*He's nothing like you.*"

He slammed into her. It wasn't the place I saw other men doing this to her.

"*Don't lie darlin'. Every time you look at our son, you see me.*"

My hand flew to my mouth. I backed away. Unable to listen any further. I ran. I ran back to my room, crawled into my bed and put my hands over my ears.

The man with my mother.

The man hurting her.

That man was my father.

Betrayal

I took a breath. One fucking long breath. I sat in the car, trying to ignore how much that fucking night broke something so deep inside me. So many memories. So much pain. Nothing to fill the void.

Nothing but her, a voice whispered to me.

No. I couldn't let her have that power over me.

They were getting worse. The flashbacks. With her in my bed, I no longer dreamt, but having them invade my waking moments crippled me. Especially that one. It might not be the worst, but it was up there on the scale of fucked up things in my life. I could take down the Daniels empire. But that man, the one who gave me life. He was untouchable.

I slammed my hand down on the steering wheel. I locked my thoughts back up and shoved them in the pit of darkness where they festered. They belonged there.

Time for business.

I got out of the car, locked it and strode towards the cafe where I'd agreed to have this little meeting. If he reneged on our deal, he would pay the ultimate price.

It was four in the afternoon, but already dusk had fallen. Sat at a table near the back, pink hair glinting in the low light, Anthony fidgeted. I took a seat opposite him.

"Oh, you came," he said.

"A deal is a deal."

"Do you want anything?"

I shook my head. He took something out his shirt pocket and slid it across to me. A memory stick.

"Everything I could find is there. Both investigations, just like you asked."

I slid it off the table and tucked it into my jeans pocket. He took a sip of his coffee, eyes darting around.

"I take it you didn't tell him."

"Whatever you think, I'm not stupid."

"Unlike your boyfriend. You should really be more careful about who you get involved with."

He glared at me but didn't retaliate. I took out my own little task for him and dropped it next to his hand. Another memory stick. Next, I handed him a folded piece of paper.

"I expect you to destroy this when you're done."

I pointed at the paper.

"What is it?"

"Strict instructions. Follow them to the letter. I will know if you don't. Trust me, I'm worse than the Daniels to people who double cross me."

He put his hands up.

"Hey, I'll do it. You don't need to threaten me."

"Wasn't a threat. It was a promise."

"Honey, you really need to chill."

I rolled my eyes. 'Chilling' was not something I could afford.

"So, what do I do with this after?"

He tapped the memory stick.

"You destroy it too. Leave no trace. Understood?"

"None of this will lead back to me, will it?"

"As long as you follow the instructions, no."

I made sure everything I did was untraceable. That included this. If he fucked up, it would be on him. It's why I even involved a third party in the first place.

"What exactly is on this?"

"You'll know soon enough."

I got up, giving him a cold smile.

"Don't disappoint me, Anthony."

I left the cafe, turning back once to find him reading the instructions I'd given him. Gamble. Huge gamble. Had to be this way so she'd stay mine. Mine. A part of me wished I'd never laid eyes on her and the other, the fucking other wanted to bow to the connection between us. Give in.

I wouldn't. All my fucking plans would go up in fucking flames. How could I make her do what she needed to if I let her in? Hardening myself, I got back in the car and drove home. The journey did nothing to calm the storm. I hadn't allowed myself to think how she might feel about what I'd left for her to look at. As strong as she was, I kept breaking her further. Telling her the truth was a necessary evil.

I let myself in the front door, kicked off my shoes, hung up my coat and prowled through the flat. I fired off a quick text to Chuck to let him know I had the information he wanted.

Avery wasn't in the kitchen or bathroom. In the living room, the laptop was left out on the coffee table. Had she seen it? Seen the evidence of her family fortune and the lies it had been built on?

When I opened the door to the bedroom, I stood in the doorway for the longest moment. Paper littered the room, covering the bed and almost every available inch of floor space. I looked at the nearest piece. A drawing of a man sitting at a desk, a sick smile on his face with piles of money surrounding him. The desk was sitting on top of a pile of bodies. Dead bodies.

The next drawing was of angels falling from the sky, their wings disintegrating around them. I picked up another one. A girl tied up with a black eye and cuts across her body.

What the fuck?

The last one I dared to look at almost fucking broke me. A man, tattoos snaking up his arms, staring down at a girl at his feet. She'd ripped her heart out of her chest and was offering it up to him. They looked distinctly like me and her. I had no fucking clue what the hell it meant until I read the caption she'd written in neat handwriting below it.

I've torn my soul out to fight by your side.

Did she really want to destroy her family with me? Had it been enough? She still didn't have the full story.

It cut me. I wasn't here to help her deal with it. Those drawings. They were her way of letting out her emotions.

I approached the bed and pulled the covers off her head. She looked so fucking innocent and small. So fucking precious.

"Avery?"

I brushed her hair from her face. She didn't stir.

"Avery, wake up."

I shook her, careful to be gentle. Her eyes fluttered open. She blinked.

"Aiden," she whispered.

Her hand clamped around my arm.

"You saw."

"I'm sorry about the mess."

I sat down on the bed.

"Don't worry, it's nothing. Are you okay?"

Betrayal

For once I didn't fucking care about how untidy the room was. Normally it'd have bothered me, but she was my main concern.

"No, I'm not."

"Come here."

I put my arms out to her. Before she had a chance to move, I heard the buzzer for my door. Who the fuck was that? Her eyes darted toward the bedroom door. I wanted to fucking hold her, but it'd have to wait now.

"I have to get that."

She nodded. I slipped from the room. When I saw through the small screen who it was, I cursed.

"Chuck, why the fuck are you here?" I said, pressing down on the intercom.

"I have someone for you to deal with."

"Are you insane? You know you can't bring people here without talking to me first."

"This is personal, Aiden."

"Fine, wait there. I'll be down in a few."

There was no fucking way he was coming up here when I had Avery freaked out over what she'd learnt. Chuck couldn't find her. I was so fucking close to getting the police off the scent.

I strode back to the bedroom. She sat up in bed, her hair cascading down her back. Lost and lonely. Fuck. She needed me and I couldn't fucking be there for her.

"I have to go deal with something."

"Oh okay."

"When it's done, I'll make us dinner and we can talk or watch a film. Whatever you want."

She nodded. Fucking hell. Her doe eyes killed me.

"Do you just need a hug?"

Her eyes watered and her fingers curled around the covers.

"Fuck, Avery, come here."

She climbed off the bed and shuffled over to me. I gathered her up in my arms and held her. Chuck was waiting for me, but I could give her a minute.

"I'll be okay until you get back," she whispered.

I let her go. She squeezed my arm before stepping back.

"And I'll clean this up."

She indicated the scattered drawings. I nodded and left. I couldn't fucking talk to her about those right now. Especially not the one that depicted us.

Shoving my feet into trainers, I left the flat and rode down in the lift to the basement car park. Chuck leant on his car several feet away.

"Nice of you to join me," he said.

"Where are they?"

He shoved off the car and went around to the boot, opening it. Inside lay a man on his side with a hood over his head.

"What exactly do you want from him?" I asked.

"He has information about Avery."

My skin prickled. How could anyone have information about Avery? I'd been careful. So fucking careful.

"He does?"

"The bartender at Galaxy overheard him bragging. He called me, naturally."

Betrayal

Galaxy was a bar in central London owned by the company. The employees were very loyal. I hated the place. Full of suits and gold diggers.

"And?"

"He won't talk. I thought you could persuade him."

I peered at the man. For my own fucking sake, I needed to know. I pulled him up slightly by his shirt.

"What the fuck do you know about Avery Daniels?"

"N…N…Nothing," he whimpered.

"Don't bullshit me. I don't want to hurt you, but I will."

"My cousin said he saw her in a motorway service station this morning. That's all I know. I swear."

"Which one?"

"I don't know. He wouldn't tell me."

This guy was an idiot, but it still concerned me enough that I couldn't just let him go yet.

"You give us your cousin's details and we'll let you walk."

"Yes, yes, it's in my phone. In my pocket."

I made him tell me the pin code and found out exactly who his cousin was.

"Ring him and get him to tell you."

"Yes, yes."

I put the phone to his ear. He spoke to his cousin for several long minutes before saying goodbye.

"He said the Reading services on the M4."

I almost fucking thanked the man. We hadn't driven that way. I could breathe again. I shoved him back down in the boot and slammed it shut.

"I'll look into it for you," I said to Chuck.

"Well, that was easier than expected. Anyway, you said you had the info from the police investigations? Let's go look through it."

Oh, fuck no. Chuck couldn't come upstairs with me. And I hadn't been through the stuff Anthony had given me yet.

"I've got stuff to do and you need to drop that guy off somewhere because he's not coming upstairs. Best not kill him."

"I insist."

The look in his eyes said he wasn't taking no for an answer. *Fucking Chuck.*

"Drop him off first, then we'll go through it."

He shrugged.

"Fair enough."

He got back in the car. My fucking heart slammed against my ribcage at a hundred miles an hour. I'd bought myself enough time to hide Avery and fucking pray she'd stay where I told her to.

Chuck drove off and I got back in the lift. As soon as I was back in the flat, I went straight to find her. She'd piled up the drawings on top of the bedside table and was sitting in the middle of the bed tapping her fingers on the cover.

"Avery, I need you to listen to me very carefully."

She looked up at me, brow furrowing.

"What is it?"

"I need you to make sure you gather up all the drawings and things in the flat and put them in your cupboard."

She slipped off the bed.

"Okay… Aiden, what's wrong?"

"Just do it then come back here."

Betrayal

She left the room, but not without shooting me a questioning look. I needed her to hurry. Who knew how long Chuck would be. Armed with all her pictures, she came back into the room and added them to the pile before putting them in the wardrobe.

"I don't want to do this, but I need you to hide in there for me."

"You need what?"

"Hide, Avery. In the cupboard."

"Why?"

I ran a hand through my hair. This was not how I envisioned this evening going.

"Because your uncle is going to be here any minute and he can't find you."

Her face went deathly pale.

"Charlie?"

"Yes."

"But Aiden…"

"Avery, don't. I'm asking you to stay out of sight. You don't need me to tell you what happens if he finds you."

This would test everything between us. Every fucking thing. If Avery was really mine, she'd do as I said. She'd stay hidden. She walked towards me. Her doe eyes filled with fear. Taking my hand, she placed it on her cheek.

"I want you to trust me," she whispered.

"Do this and maybe I will."

"Don't you know I'd do anything for you?"

My heart stuttered in my chest.

"Anything?"

"I am yours. You command. I obey. That's how this works, doesn't it?"

Fuck. She had no idea how much self-control I had to exert right then. I wanted to crush her to me. Kiss her until she fucking drowned.

"This isn't a command. It's a request. A request that you stay in here. Stay hidden until he's gone. I'll understand if you can't do that."

She reached up and ran her hand over my arm where underneath my shirt lay the tattoo of a songbird in a gilded cage. The only representation of my mother I had. One day I might explain it to her, but not now.

"Do you know why they called me Avery?"

"No."

"Before Mum married Dad, she used to have an aviary where she kept injured birds and nursed them back to health. He refused to name me after a bird, so Avery was their compromise. I guess I'm one of her broken birds now."

Broken bird. Fuck. She wasn't a fucking broken bird. She wasn't the bird in a gilded cage either. Avery was strong and I would fucking well show her just how much. But not now.

The buzzer sounded.

We'd run out of time.

"You're not broken. You're just hurting. There's no going back if you stay hidden, you know that?"

"There was no going back from the moment you took me."

She turned away from me and climbed in the cupboard, nestling herself on the floor underneath her hanging clothes.

Betrayal

I closed the door, sealing her away in the dark. I could only hope it wouldn't remind her of the cell.

I went out to the intercom and buzzed Chuck in. I kicked her shoes under mine and hid her coat before I paced the hallway, waiting for him to come up in the lift.

When he knocked, I let him in.

"So, did you have a nice few days away?" he asked as we walked through into my living room.

"Yes."

I'd told him I had to leave the city for a couple of days, but not where I went.

"I hope the little prick has got what we need. If it's stuff we already know, then it's useless."

I grabbed the laptop from the coffee table and got rid of the evidence Avery had left open on there before Chuck had a chance to see.

"Want a drink?" I asked.

"Got any brandy?"

"Aren't you driving?"

"So?"

I shrugged.

"You know I don't drink brandy."

"Well, whatever else you might have will do. Just make sure it's strong."

I rolled my eyes and carried the laptop through into the kitchen. I pulled out the memory stick Anthony had given me and plugged it in. I fixed Chuck a drink. Whisky. He'd appreciate that.

I took the glass and the laptop back through into the living room. He'd made himself at home on my sofa. Arrogant piece of shit. I hated having him here.

"Here," I said, handing him the glass before sitting down.

I set the laptop on the coffee table and began going through the documents on the memory stick. I handed it to Chuck since he cared more about this than I did. He looked them over whilst sipping his whisky.

"Damn, this is good shit."

"It should be, wasn't cheap."

Chuck smirked before turning back to the laptop. I really didn't know why he insisted on going through this here. I could've got him the files tomorrow.

"You know, Aiden, you've been very cagey recently."

"Have I?"

Where the fuck was this going?

"Mmm, ever since Mitch died."

I shrugged. He pointed to something on the screen.

"I didn't think the little fuck would come up with the goods, but here we are. Crime scene photos and everything."

I didn't need to look at them. I'd been there, but I indulged Chuck anyway. The satisfaction of seeing Mitchell and Kathleen dead calmed me. I'd taken away their lives after what they'd done to me. To me fucking personally.

"You know who'd get off on seeing this shit? Fucking Frazier, the dirty bastard. He has a thing about blood."

Why'd he have to go bring up that sick shit? I knew all about his sickening desires.

"Does he now?"

"Fucking sicko likes to torture woman. I'm surprised his wife doesn't know. Perhaps she's like Kath was. She liked watching Mitch."

And that's exactly why both Avery's parents had to die. Because her mother was just as sick in the fucking head as her father.

"I wouldn't know."

"No, of course not. Frazier went apeshit when Mitch died. Never seen someone so incensed. He is on the fucking warpath."

Exactly why I stayed out of his way. As much as I wanted Frazier Shaw dead and in the fucking grave, he was a key player in this game. The game I was playing to win. Win or die. He'd get his comeuppance soon enough.

"It's all shit. The whole fucking thing."

"Damn right it is."

Chuck handed the laptop back to me and sipped his whisky. I set the files to transfer on to my laptop. When they were done, I pulled the stick and tossed it to him. He pocketed it.

"Well, I shan't take up more of your time."

He knocked back the whisky and popped the glass on the coffee table, standing.

"I'm going to ask you something, Aiden, and I want you to answer me honestly."

I tensed. Was this about me being cagey?

"You don't happen to know who killed my brother, do you? You and I both know your past dealings with my family and I wouldn't want that to get in the way of our little arrangement."

I kept my expression neutral even though my heart slammed against my chest and sweat beaded at the back of my neck.

"Why would I know? The first time I met your brother was when you introduced us last year and I only saw him once after that."

Chuck eyed me for several long moments, then he smiled.

"I thought not, but it never hurts to ask. Anyway, I can see myself out."

I clenched my fists as he walked away down the hall. I watched him, making sure he left and didn't fucking pry into my flat any further.

When the front door slammed, I bolted from the room. I ripped open the cupboard door in the bedroom and there she was.

"Is he gone?" she asked.

I pulled her up out of the cupboard and crushed her to me. She hadn't come out. She'd stayed.

Fuck. Avery. Fuck.

The relief I felt crashed over me, melting my broken soul into a puddle at her feet.

"Aiden? Is he gone?"

"Yes. Yes, he's fucking gone and you're still here."

"Did you forget I don't like my uncle?"

"No, but you could've come out and then this would've been over. He'd have known it was me all along."

"I told you I'd keep your secrets."

She had. And I'd believed her to an extent. She'd proven right then she was willing to stay with me even though she could've exposed everything.

Betrayal

I stroked her hair. So beautiful. So fragile. So strong. And all mine. Her arms banded around my back.

"I don't want to leave you," she said. "I'm staying of my own free will."

I was losing.

Losing myself to her.

And the connection we forged the day she'd walked into my life.

Chapter Fifteen

Avery

I didn't feel like talking about the things I'd found out about my family. I shoved those emotions in a hole and locked them up. The pain was too real. Too visceral.

"Aiden, you're squishing me."

He let me go, his eyes wild with too many emotions to decipher. Leaving his arms always tore at my heart.

Stupid girl. You just sealed your fate. Stupid, stupid girl.

I sat in the cupboard, waiting. Indecision plagued me. When it came down to it, I couldn't leave. I picked a side. I picked Aiden. The man who gave me such a complex array of emotions, I could barely get them straight in my head.

Aiden could help me make this right. Help me change the course of history.

Stop my family. End the abuse. Abuse of power. Abuse of people.

Their greed. A sickness. A curse.

"We need to talk about your family. What you learnt, what you saw, that's not everything," he said.

So I wasn't getting out of a conversation with him about it.

Great.

"What else could there possibly be?"

"It goes beyond money and girls. They know powerful people. People who rely on their services and keeping each other's secrets."

"What services?"

"You saw the video. Do you think that's normal? Trust me, there's more. Playing out their sick fantasies in exchange for silence. In exchange for underhand business dealings."

My stomach dropped. What I'd seen Frazier do. I never wanted to see anything else like it.

"They're monsters."

He gave me a sad smile.

"And you think I'm not one too?"

"Do you take women, rape them, force them to do unspeakable things, mutilate them?"

His eyes flashed with pain.

"No. Those aren't the only things that make people monsters."

"Then what makes you a monster?"

"I killed your parents for a start and I took you."

In my eyes, it didn't necessarily make him a monster. Not anymore. Not now I knew what my dad had been involved in. What he'd allowed. Perhaps the fact he'd taken me and broken my fucking mind made him a shit person. That didn't seem to matter to me any longer. I'd sort of forgiven him for it as fucked up as that was.

"And what else?"

"You wouldn't want to know."

"Try me."

"Some things are better left unsaid."

I crossed my arms over my chest.

"Then I say you're not a monster."

He reached out, cupping my face.

"You don't know the things I want to do to you."

The air felt too hot. The molten silver of his eyes made my insides pool. I'd seen how he looked at me the day he'd handcuffed me in the cell. Restraints made him hard. Submission and total control. That's what Aiden wanted. Needed. I knew it deep within my bones. And I wanted it too.

The day in the forest opened my eyes to a lot of things. Even though I'd fought him at first, when I'd submitted, I felt a sense of freedom. Of belonging. I'd given into my instincts. I needed to obey him and have him take control.

"I have some idea."

"Are you sure about that?"

"Am I sure? No. Am I scared of what I think you want? No."

He dropped his hand.

"You don't know what you're saying."

I fucking did. I knew my own mind and it was time he learnt that too.

"You might not want to talk about what happened in the forest, but you need to understand something."

His eyes flashed and he took a step back from me.

"Avery…"

"No. I'm not letting you get out of this. Yes, I'm fucking innocent and inexperienced, but that doesn't mean shit."

My blood pounded in my ears. I clenched my fists. How did this man manage to drive me fucking crazy and yet all I wanted was to fall at his feet and beg him to take me?

"I wanted to hate you for forcing me. I wanted to, but I couldn't. You know why? Because I'm fucking yours. I've been struggling to accept it this whole time, but that day, I finally understood. You need my submission and I need to give it to you. In return, you gave me freedom for the first time in my life. I felt free. And then you shut me out. I thought I understood, but instead, you made me feel like what we did was wrong. That I was fucking wrong for wanting that with you."

Aiden just stared at me. He wasn't exactly expressionless, but I couldn't read a thing either. Why did we keep fighting with each other over this? Wouldn't it just be easier if we gave in? It's what we both wanted. He knew it. I knew it. Fighting exhausted me. Fighting had no point to it.

He turned away from me.

My heart constricted. My legs almost buckled. Except I couldn't fall apart.

He walked over to the bed, squatted down and pulled out a padlocked storage box. He turned the dials until it clicked. Discarding the padlock, he opened it and stood up.

"This is the truth of what I want from you," he said, his voice so quiet, I strained to hear it.

I approached him with caution in my steps. Did I really want my suspicions confirmed? I stopped next to him.

Betrayal

When I looked down at what was in the box, my pulse kicked up a notch. There were more than just handcuffs. Ropes, chains and silk bindings lay nestled together.

Aiden shifted on his feet, moving to stand behind me. He rested his chin on my shoulder and held my waist lightly in his hands, his thumbs running circles across my t-shirt.

It wasn't so much the restraints I recognised which bothered me. It was the other things in the box. It wasn't whips or crops or any of the other stuff I expected. None of it was about pain. It was about control. And there was something else. Something which made me tense up. Aiden wanted to take me in the one place I'd never given anyone. That much was clear.

"Does this repulse you?" he asked.

I pointed down at the ropes and chains.

"Those, no. I expected those."

His fingers ran down my sides.

"The rest scares you."

"I don't even know what half of this is, Aiden. But no, I'm not scared about most of it."

"What exactly are you afraid of?"

Could I even bring that up? If I was going to do this with him, then I had to find a way to accept what he needed. I could do the submission thing. I could let him take control. Tie me up and be at his mercy. The other thing? I had no idea.

My face felt too hot. I knew my cheeks were burning.

"Do you really want to…"

"Want to what?"

I couldn't say it. The word just wouldn't come out. I took his hand and guided it behind me, rested it on my bum.

"Fuck me here?"

I heard him let out a breath. He didn't move his hand.

"Yes."

I almost choked. The last thing I'd ever expected. And my inexperience when it came to sex showed. Stupid naïve girl wanting to play with the adults.

"Aiden, I can accept all the other things."

"But you won't let me do that."

"Is it really that important?"

His hand around my waist tightened.

"No, but you can think about it rather than just outright saying you won't."

Think about it? I'd never even considered the possibility anyone would want that from me until today.

"I guess so."

"Now you've seen the truth, do you still want to stay with me? Do you want me like you say you do?"

I turned around, causing his hands to drop. I stared up into his grey eyes.

"Am I fucked up for wanting you? And don't list the things you did to me when we met because we're so far past that now."

"Yes, you are. You shouldn't want me. I'm not good for you. You're innocent and here all I want to do is corrupt you."

I came from a corrupt family. Corruption was in my blood at this stage. Aiden would set me free. He just couldn't see it.

"Fine. If I'm fucked up, then so be it. I'm tired of fighting. Aren't you?"

"Of course I'm fucking tired, Avery. Do you think I enjoy fighting with you?"

"Then stop pushing me away."

He sighed, running a hand through his hair.

"You don't know the whole truth."

It was one excuse after another with him. Excuses could go to hell.

"Then tell me."

"You can't handle it all in one go. Look at what happened today."

"Why does it matter so fucking much? Me knowing everything."

"It just does."

I wanted to tear my hair out. What was the point in him showing me his box of toys? What more did I have to do to prove to him how much I wanted this? Wanted him.

"I don't want to hear any more bullshit. I've laid my cards on the table. I am yours. All of me. What more do you want from me?"

Aiden opened his mouth and closed it again. The tension between us rippled and snapped. He felt so close but so far away. A deep fucking chasm lay between us and I couldn't cross it. He wouldn't let me.

"Fine. Not going to answer? Then I'm fucking done."

I stormed out of the room. Emotions warred inside me. I wanted to cry. Scream. Rage. I wanted to hit him. Show him how much he kept hurting me. Why the fuck did it even hurt? My heart wasn't built to withstand all these revelations. These feelings.

It cracked.

Fractured.

Disintegrated.

I slid down the wall outside his bedroom, trying to fight back the urge to cry. Had I not shed enough tears? Why was the world fucking doing this to me? Why did the one person who gave me the utmost joy and freedom also have the power to destroy me entirely?

The rumble of my stomach interrupted my thoughts. I'd barely eaten today. He'd promised me dinner, but after that shitshow, I doubted he remembered.

I hauled myself to my feet and shuffled into the kitchen. On automatic, I pulled things out of the fridge and cupboards. Stir fry would do. I wasn't in the mood to be creative.

I just finished cutting up the veg when two hands rested either side of me on the kitchen counter. His breath dusted across my ear as he leant down towards me. I expected him to say something, instead, he nibbled my earlobe. I stiffened and melted at the same time.

I put the knife down, fully prepared to turn around and ask him what the hell he was doing when his tongue trailed down my neck. My knees buckled. I gripped the counter to steady myself.

"Aiden…"

"Shh. Shh. I know you're angry with me. Let me make it up to you."

What? The world spun around me. *Aiden wanted to what?*

"I'm making dinner."

"It can wait."

He pulled me away from the counter and directed me toward the kitchen table. Spinning me around to face him, he sat me on the table. There he resumed kissing my neck and nibbling my ear. He trailed his fingers up my inner thighs. I could hardly breathe. Heat coiled in my stomach, flooding my veins with fire.

He pressed down on my shoulder, forcing me to lie back and moved me higher up the table. He crawled over me, his eyes molten silver as he stared down at me.

"You're so beautiful."

His fingertips trailed down my sternum, brushing across my stomach. My breath caught and my heart stuttered. I was his instrument and he knew exactly how to play me. Fuck. How could we go from fighting each other to this so quickly? Was fighting just a part of foreplay? I didn't have a clue. All I wanted was his hands on me.

"Give me time."

He pushed my t-shirt up slightly, exposing my midriff.

"That's all I'm asking. In return, I'll give you what you desire."

"What do you think I desire?"

He smirked as he traced circles along my stomach with his fingers.

"Me."

I raised my eyebrow.

"You want to be fucked. You want me to slide my cock inside you. Give it to you harder and deeper than you've ever had before. That's what you want. I know because I see it in your eyes."

I couldn't refute that statement even if I wanted to.

"Are you saying if I stop asking and give you time, then you'll do that?"

"Yes."

Oh. Oh shit. Oh fuck.

Was this actually happening? Had Aiden just agreed to fuck me sometime in the future?

"How exactly are you planning to make things up to me right now in that case?"

"Are you wet, Avery?"

I felt my face grow hot. I nodded, unable to say it aloud. He leant down and his teeth grazed along my ear.

"Wet at the thought of my cock, aren't you? Did you like it when it was in your mouth? When I fed you my cum?"

"Y…Yes."

His hand slipped below my jogging bottoms. I hadn't bothered to get dressed in jeans today since I wasn't exactly going anywhere. His fingers brushed over my clit, causing me to buck against him.

"Would you like me to fuck your mouth again?"

He moved my underwear aside and plunged a finger inside me. I moaned.

"Tell me."

"I want your cock in my mouth."

"Do you like it when I talk dirty to you?"

I nodded, moaning again when he inserted a second finger inside me. His tongue curled around the back of my ear and I squirmed beneath him.

"Mmm, you're so fucking tight. So hot. I bet you taste so fucking sweet. Shall I try you?"

I didn't have the wherewithal to answer him. Pent up and needy, I wanted Aiden like nothing else. Even though he told me to give him time, I wanted him to tear my clothes off and fuck me with abandon. This teasing had gone on long enough.

He pulled away and withdrew his hand from me. I felt bereft immediately. He stared down at me as he tasted me on his fingers. His eyes darkened. Desire, lust and need flickering in those silver depths.

"Fuck, you really are fucking perfect."

His hands went to his jeans, tugging open the fly and unzipping them. He took one of my hands, pressing it to his cock through his boxers.

"Do you feel that? Feel how fucking hard I am for you?"

"Yes."

He groaned as I brushed my fingers along his length. He shoved his hand back down my bottoms and plunged his fingers back inside my pussy. I bucked against the table, moaning as he thrust into me.

"Touch me, Avery, touch my cock."

I reached up with my other hand, freeing him from the confines of his boxers. I ran my hand along his cock, fisting it. I stroked him as he continued to fuck me with his fingers.

Both of us stared at each other, quite unable to look away. His thumb ran over my clit and I almost detonated on the spot. His words, his fingers and his cock in my hand set me alight.

"Aiden, I'm so close."

"Come for me. Come for me so I can fuck your mouth."

His thumb circled my clit harder. I exploded, crying out and bucking against him. The rush of sensations flowing through my body fizzled in my blood. I saw stars. And I saw Aiden. The most beautiful man I'd ever laid eyes on staring down at me with satisfaction on his face. He enjoyed this.

Sending me hurling over the edge. He left me a panting mess on the kitchen table.

He pulled away from me and stood up.

"Come here and open your mouth for me."

I somehow slid off the table and got on my knees for him. My whole body still felt like jelly.

He cupped the back of my head and fed me his cock. He wasn't gentle. He shoved his cock down my throat and I almost gagged. I didn't panic. I'd taken it before and I could do it again. He thrust into me over and over, grunting. I stared up at him. His eyes were glazed over, hazy with desire. I brought him pleasure and that's all I could ask for.

It didn't take long until he growled and came. I could feel his cock pulsating and hot sticky streams coated the back of my mouth. He pulled out when he was done, slamming his hand down on the kitchen table as he panted. I swallowed, but his cum still lingered in my mouth.

I dragged myself up off the floor, reached out and put him away, zipping up and re-buttoning his jeans. He pulled me to him and pressed his forehead against mine.

"For someone who claims to be so inexperienced, you have the most fucking amazing mouth."

"Aiden… you're the only one."

"What?"

"In the forest, that's the first time I sucked cock. That's why I was reluctant. I didn't want to be shit at it and disappoint you."

He ran a hand down my back.

"You didn't disappoint me. Fuck, so innocent. I'm going to take all that innocence away from you, piece by piece."

I shivered. I wanted him to. His desires were mine now.

"What were you making for dinner?"

I smiled at him.

"Just stir fry."

"Shall we resume then?"

I nodded.

As Aiden helped me finish up with the food, I couldn't help but wonder just how much time I needed to give him.

Would he really give into what was between the two of us finally?

Or was it just his way of trying to placate me after our argument?

I wasn't quite sure I wanted to know the answer because the latter would break me in half. Whilst the former would make it impossible for me to ever leave Aiden.

Because once we took that final step.

There really was no going back.

At least… for me, there wasn't.

But would there be for him?

Chapter Sixteen

Aiden

The burner phone buzzed on my desk. I checked it. Anthony texting to say it was done. A week had been and gone. Now it was time to check if he'd really followed through. Social media was the first place. There it was, plain as day. Avery. Her video trending on Twitter. Shared all over Facebook and Instagram. And there was nothing the police could do about it.

I'd made sure to tell Anthony to get it to his boyfriend in the first instance. Likely the police had sat on it this whole time. Idiots. Now Avery was viral.

I left the office, locking the door behind me. She was on the sofa, drawing with a film on the TV. Things between us weren't strained, but I knew she was waiting for me to give her what I told her I would.

I picked up the remote and switched it to the news channel. She looked up, then her eyes fell on the screen.

"The missing heiress resurfaces. A video of her was posted in the early hours of this morning and has since gone viral. Twenty-year-old Avery

Daniels, the heir to Daniels Holdings, has been missing since Mitchell and Kathleen Daniels were found murdered five weeks ago in their penthouse. Speculation as to what happened to Avery and her parents has been making headlines. This new development—"

"What did you do?" she asked.

"Just made sure they had proof of life and now the world is watching, waiting for the next move."

"Aiden, you said the video was for the police only."

I shrugged. It had been, but I needed to make sure everyone knew she was still alive and not doing anything under duress.

She shoved the drawing off her lap, stood and walked away to the window. The sound of the reporter in the background blared in my head, but all I could see was her. The way her dark hair lay across her back. Her curves. Everything about her enticed me.

"I don't even want to know how."

"It's not hard when you're already worldwide news."

"I didn't sign up for this. I hate being in the public eye and now I'm plastered everywhere all over again. Do you have any idea what it's like when you live under constant scrutiny? It fucking sucks."

"There's a lot of things you didn't sign up for."

"Yeah, well, I didn't sign up to be yours and look what happened," she muttered.

Avery wasn't in a rational mood to talk about this. I'd successfully managed to piss her off again. I had no desire to fight with her. Fighting always led to one thing and I wasn't going to fuck her yet. One more fight and I'd lose my control. One more battle between us and I'd be fucking lost.

Betrayal

After I'd shown her my true desires, I'd been sure she'd run away despite what she said. No. Avery surprised me. Instead of telling me to do one, she'd been accepting. What kind of girl with so little experience wanted a guy to tie her up, restrain her and fuck her?

I warned her I wasn't gentle. Warned her sex with me wouldn't be vanilla. She pushed anyway. She demanded. Insisted. I had little choice but to tell her I would give her what she wanted.

And when she fucking told me I'd been the only man to fuck her mouth, I just about fucking died on the spot. She let me have that piece of her and it made it so much fucking sweeter.

I wanted her every way I could have her. But she had to say yes. I wouldn't force her. No matter how much I wanted to take the last part of her virginity. No matter how much I wanted her to give me control, I'd never fucking force her. Not after what I'd been through. Not after what I'd seen. I vowed never to force a woman in my life. I wasn't a fucking rapist like those sick shits in Avery's family. That was my hard line. I might have twisted desires, but rape wasn't one of them. Neither was pain.

The sound of her sobbing broke my heart into a thousand tiny pieces. Every time she cried my soul howled.

"Let me help you, Miss Lockhart."

Tina was with her. I peered around the door. She lay on her bed. Bruises mottled her face and torso. One eye was swollen shut. Blood splattered the sheets from various cuts across her body.

"No, no, Tina, it's okay."

"It's not okay. You need help."

She allowed Tina to take the first aid kit and start cleaning up the worst of the cuts on her body.

"I want it to end, Tina. I need it to. I can't keep doing this. I thought if I just let them then they'd get bored and I could keep him safe, but it's worse now."

"You know you can't give up. He needs you. He needs his mother."

"What kind of mother am I? He sees too much. How can he grow up normal when I'm beaten, raped and abused weekly? He hears it. I cannot hide what happens from him."

"He's a strong boy, Miss Lockhart and you're still his mother. He loves you. You are his everything."

She dissolved into another fit of sobs.

"They'll destroy him. I can't let them turn him into one of them. I'm worried I won't survive long enough to keep him safe."

Tina stroked her hair, her eyes softening.

"They won't. You know they can't do anything to him because of his father. And I swear to you, Lizzie, I'll protect him. I'll make sure he knows what they've done. He'll never become like them. I'll raise him right, give him the life he deserves if anything happens to you."

"You'd do that even though they pay you?"

"The sick bastards need to be stopped. What they do to people is despicable. I stay because of you and Aiden, not because I want their money. The only way I can help you is from the inside."

She smiled for the first time.

"You really are a kind soul."

Betrayal

Tina finished up bandaging her cuts.

"There, now, you need to get some rest. We'll talk more when you're feeling better."

I backed away, knowing I couldn't be caught watching them. Whoever these people were, they would pay for hurting her. Pay for hurting my mother.

I got back in bed and lay there. Under the covers, I vowed I would avenge her. It didn't matter I was only seven years old nor that I had no idea how to achieve it. I would make sure they all paid the price for hurting my family.

And Tina would help me.

Pain. That's why I would never desire pain. Neither to inflict it on another or have it inflicted on me. Not after seeing someone go through the brutality she'd been through. Shaking off the sudden influx of emotions that memory caused, I focused on Avery again.

"I'm going to leave you to calm down."

She turned to me. Her eyes full of unshed tears. Fucking hell. Doe eyes. Never in my life had someone had such fucking power over me with one single look. Fuck. I wish I deserved her. I wish I fucking deserved to have her, but I didn't. And I was still the arsehole who'd take her anyway. I'd take what's mine.

My feet stuck to the floor. If she wanted me then she had to come to me. That's how this worked. The thread which bound us together rippled. She took one step in my direction before breaking into a run. Her arms wrapped around my back, her face pressed into my t-shirt.

Having her so reliant on me was a blessing and a curse. A blessing because I needed her to obey me when the time came to execute my plan. A curse because her submission was like a fucking drug to me. So fucking intoxicated on her need for my control.

"Don't go," she whispered. "I feel so alone when you're not with me."

"And here I thought I'd made you angry again."

"I know why you did it. Doesn't mean I have to like it."

She dropped her arms and stepped back. I hadn't returned her embrace. Fighting the urges coursing inside me to tear her clothes off. It kept getting harder to resist her. Now I knew how fucking sweet she tasted and how tight her pussy was. I wanted to be in her so much, my cock throbbed. I'd have her bound up with leather cuffs, open and exposed for my viewing. My fucking pleasure.

"If you keep looking at me like that, Aiden, I won't be able to keep my promise not to ask you again."

Her voice brought me crashing back to reality.

"Looking at you how?"

"Like I'm a meal and you want to devour me whole."

I grinned. Oh, I'd fucking devour her all right. That's what she didn't seem to understand. I wasn't Mr Nice Guy.

She reached out, taking my right arm.

"Will you tell me what these mean?"

She ran her fingers over the chain on my arm.

"I think you know now what that is to do with."

She flushed, the tips of her ears going red.

"Wearing your desires on your skin."

"The skulls and roses… even in death, there is beauty."

Her eyes met mine. I knew exactly what she was hoping I'd explain. The bird in the cage.

"Not that one, Avery. I don't talk about… her."

She frowned, releasing my arm.

"Who?"

"Avery…"

"Okay. I get it. I'm overstepping."

She put her hands up and backed away. I reached out, grabbing her arm and pulling her back towards me. How was she supposed to know who I wouldn't talk about if I didn't tell her?

"My mother. I won't talk about her, okay?"

She nodded, her gaze falling to the floor.

"I'm sorry."

I didn't talk about her because every memory haunted me. Every moment she'd been in my life. So fucking fleeting.

"You didn't know."

"I'm still sorry anyway. Is… No. I shouldn't ask you anything else. I'll just go."

"What?"

"Nothing."

I held her in place when she tried to move away.

"Does she have anything to do with why you hate my family? I know this is more than just what they've done to others. It's personal for you."

I froze. Fuck. She was far too perceptive for her own good.

"I've been trying to work out how you'd have known my family for so long and what they might have done to you. I'm not going to ask you what they did to her, but it is about her, isn't it?"

She finally met my eyes. There was immeasurable sorrow in those hazel depths.

"Just give me that, Aiden, please. I won't ask any more questions about it. Not ever."

"Why?"

"I want to understand you. I see you, but I still don't know what goes on inside your head. I still don't know who hurt you or what they did."

My heart cracked. Fucking useless organ. Bitterness encompassed me. I worked so hard to keep those emotions at bay, but she'd torn open the bindings.

"Yes. Yes, it's because of her."

A tear ran down her cheek. She pulled her arm away from me, hugging her own to her chest. The world fucking crashed and burnt around us. Her sorrow affected me. Reminding me of my own fucking pain. My own heartache. My mother. Fuck.

"They killed her, Avery. She's dead."

"When?"

"I was seven."

She choked on a sob and tears flooded her face. I felt helpless watching her come apart in front of me. This wasn't like when she'd discovered her family's secrets. She was crying for me. Hurting for me. Fucking sucker punching me to the gut.

"I'm sorry," she whispered. "I'm so sorry."

"It's not your fault."

Betrayal

She seemed to cave in on herself. Her entire body vibrated with sadness. I couldn't go to her even though my arms burnt to hold her. I needed to. She shook her head.

"I can't… I can't."

She ran past me out of the room. I turned on my heel, about to go after her when my fucking heart stopped. She opened the door of the cell, walked in and slammed it shut behind her.

What the actual fuck? Why the hell would she willingly go in there? Had she completely lost her mind? I couldn't let her stay in that room. Not when all it did was bring back all of her worst nightmares.

I strode into the hallway and wrenched open the door. She was sat right at the back, her head buried in her legs. I took a step in.

"Go away, Aiden."

"What the fuck are you doing in here?"

"Leave me alone."

"No. You're not fucking staying in here. You know what will happen."

"Please, please just leave."

I walked over and squatted beside her. I reached out, trying to touch her, but she flinched away.

"Don't. I don't want your comfort. I don't deserve it. I don't deserve anything. So just leave me alone."

"Avery…"

She raised her head. Her eyes were wet with tears and her face patchy and red.

"How can you even look at me? How can you want me after what they've done?"

How could I not want her? Didn't she see herself? How fucking beautiful and precious she was? Her fucking innocence called to me. And she wasn't her family. She'd proven that to me over and over again. Avery had compassion. Empathy. She saw right from wrong. She'd fucking drawn a picture of herself ripping her heart out for me. How could I not want her after all that?

"You're not them."

"But I am. I'm their blood. I was born into their corruption. I own the rights to their fucking company and all that money they've made off the backs of slavery, torture and pain. Dirty fucking money. I don't want it. They sicken me. They disgust me, but I'm still theirs. I'll always be a Daniels. Don't you see that?"

"No, Avery. Why the fuck do you think I stopped short at taking your life that night? You're not a part of that shit. Anyone who has an ounce of decency would be disgusted by their behaviour. Don't you fucking see? You're what's good in this world."

She shook her head.

"I don't deserve that. I don't deserve you."

My heart. My fucking heart constricted. It was me who didn't deserve her.

"You've got that the wrong way around."

"Do I? I can't believe that. I don't want to talk about this. Just leave me be, please. I can't right now. I just can't look at you. All I see is what they've done. How they've hurt you and it kills me so please, please just go."

She dropped her head back into her legs, clutching her arms around them. I couldn't see her like this. It fucking broke me. I didn't know how she could even lump herself in with those sick shits. And she hadn't even asked me who'd killed my mother or how. She hadn't asked any questions.

I didn't want to leave her. I knew deep down she needed me, but I also didn't want to upset her further. Cause her any more distress.

Fuck. Avery. Fucking hell.

Nothing could make this any better. Why did she have to push me into telling her? She always pushed me so fucking hard.

"Okay, I'll go, but I'm not shutting you in here. Do you understand?"

She nodded, hugging her legs tighter. I got up and walked out, not closing the door behind me. I only got two feet away before I slid down the wall and sat with my head in my hands.

I hadn't felt this kind of pain since her. Since I'd seen her hurt, abused, beaten, raped. And now, the girl who fucking turned my world inside out? She fucking hurt and I hurt for her. The pain might be emotional, but it was still real. All of it.

I couldn't leave her. I needed to know she wasn't going to have more nightmares. That she wouldn't hallucinate her parents again. Fuck. What had she done to me? Cleaved my fucking heart in two. Fuck. It shouldn't hurt this much. None of it should.

If telling her the truth about her family was this fucking awful, then how could I ask her to do what I needed? How could I fucking tell her what I had planned? She'd fucking hate me. Despise me. And I didn't want that. I wanted her to look at me like I was her everything because I was beginning to realise she was mine. The fucking balm to my bruised, battered and broken soul.

That fucking girl in there. She was mine. My responsibility. I didn't believe in fucking fantasies of love or soulmates. I didn't believe in stupid fucking fairy tales. What I believed in was the connection between two people so fucking real. So fucking raw and visceral that one couldn't be without the other.

And I had that with her.

With her.

Avery.

She was my woman.

Mine.

Chapter Seventeen

Avery

Pain. Every inch of me burnt with it. Indignation. Rage. Sorrow. Pain.

They'd stolen something from me. Something so deep. It ruptured the moment he told me. Fragments dug into my skin.

Pain.

No one told me when you had such an intense connection with another person, you'd take on their hurt. Their sorrow. Their pain. I felt it. I carried it. I burnt.

Aiden.

How could they do that? How could they have stolen a seven-year-old boy's mother? It didn't surprise me he wouldn't talk about it. Had she been one of their girls? If so, it was so much worse than I ever imagined. I could hardly blame him for wanting to end them.

My family were more than monsters. They were evil. Evil and corrupt. Was I the same? Did the same evil run in my veins? Aiden said I was different. I couldn't see it. How could I be anything else other than theirs?

Because you see how wrong it is. You want to end it. Destroy it all.

The words didn't soothe me. Didn't quiet my warring mind.

"You're what's good in the world."

Was I? Was I really? I inherited their legacy. And it was shameful. Disgusting. Inhuman.

Hadn't I been optimistic before? Determined to destroy it all?

Pain.

I sobbed.

I cried.

And then I wailed.

The injustice of it. The horrific injustice clawed at my soul. It didn't matter who'd done it or how. My family were responsible. Which meant I took on that responsibility too.

You weren't even alive. How are you to blame?

The rational side of me knew that, but I was too far gone to pay attention to it.

I knew he could hear me. He hadn't shut the door. He'd not gone very far. Did he care about me? Care I was hurting? Was that why he stayed close?

Pain.

I wept for the boy he'd been. The one who'd lost his mother so young. I wept for the man he was now. The one who'd suffered so much. And he had no one.

He has you now.

What good was I when I couldn't even deal with the truth of my family's actions? He was right. I couldn't handle it all at once. He knew me better than I knew myself. Knew what I needed. What I wanted. How to take care of me.

I was no fucking good for him. I'd interrupted his life. Completely inconvenient. A stupid girl. Too young. Too inexperienced. Too naïve. What good was I to a man like Aiden?

"I'm nothing. Nothing and no one," I whispered.

What would James say if he saw me now? He'd tell me to get off my arse and stop being a miserable bitch. I wasn't a defeatist. I had to be stronger than this. Fuck, I missed him. So terribly much. He always knew how to make me feel better. Blue eyes twinkled in my vision. Then they morphed into grey. Grey eyes which looked at me with such passion when he'd pressed me down on the kitchen table. Grey eyes I sought out every waking moment of my day and every night, they soothed me in my dreams.

I whimpered and lay on my side, curled up in a ball. I wanted Aiden but I couldn't have him. I wanted to talk to James. I needed to hear his voice. I just needed one normal thing in my life.

"Avery…"

Aiden's voice whispered across my skin. I cracked an eye open. He wasn't there.

"Please give me a sign you're still breathing."

My breath stuck in my throat. His voice washed over me. The deep, rich timbre of it settled into my bones.

"I'm alive."

I'm alive and I want to talk to James.

"Please tell me what you need. I know you don't want me, but what do you need?"

Was my pain hurting him too? Is that why he wanted to know what would help me? Would he let me have it if I asked? There was only one way of finding out.

"James... I need him."

A low rumble of frustration echoed through the cell.

"Avery, you know that's impossible."

"Is it? Is one phone call going to ruin everything?"

Silence. It echoed around my skull. I heard him move. Footsteps echoed, but they led away from the cell. Had he finally had enough of me?

Minutes later, his footsteps returned until I found his feet right next to my head. I peered up at him. In his hand, he held a phone.

"If I give this to you, you are only going to call him and you are to watch what you say. Understood?"

I nodded. He was going to let me. Let me speak to James. My heart tightened.

"I need to hear you say it."

"Yes, I understand."

"Do you know his number?"

I could never forget it. Branded in my memory because of all the times I'd lost my phone and needed to contact him. He called me a clumsy mare all the time because of it.

"Yes."

He leant down and placed the phone next to me. Before he could rise, I reached out and snatched his arm, keeping him there. His eyes met mine.

"Thank you."

"I don't enjoy seeing you like this. Whatever pain you feel, I feel too. Do you understand?"

I did. I hurt him just as he kept hurting me. Except I hadn't meant to. I just wanted to understand him and instead, I'd learnt something so terribly dark about my family. About myself.

"I'm sorry."

"Stop apologising to me."

He shifted until he sat next to me and took my hand.

"Avery, you did nothing. You weren't even born yet. I keep telling you this, but you are innocent. You are good. You are the only fucking light I have so don't you dare turn yourself off. You hear? You're mine and I won't let you."

My heart bled.

"Am I?"

"Yes. You're mine. Only mine. Now. Forever. Always."

I wanted so much for it to be true. So fucking much. I couldn't bear the thought of being anything but his. Completely and irrevocably his.

"Yours," I whispered.

The relief in his eyes fractured my heart all over again. He leant down and kissed my forehead.

"Good girl."

Then he got up and left. His footsteps echoed down the hallway. I reached out, picked up the phone and unlocked it. I knew it wasn't Aiden's actual phone because I'd held that before. Perhaps he had several.

Who cares.

There was only one reason I needed it. I dialled James' number. It rang once. Twice. Three times before he picked up.

"Hello?"

My throat felt tight.

"James."

"Avery? Is that you? Please tell me it's you?"

I cleared my throat.

"Yes, it's me."

"Thank fucking Christ. Do you know how fucking worried I've been about you? Fucking hell and when I saw the news today. Your face everywhere and that video. What the fuck happened to you?"

I tried to smile. Always asking too many questions at once and never letting me answer them.

"I've missed you too, dickhead."

"Fuck, it's so good to hear your voice."

"It's been too long."

"I'm serious, Avery, where the fuck have you been?"

I wanted to tell him everything but I wouldn't. Not when I had to keep Aiden's secrets.

"All you need to know is I'm safe and I'm okay."

"I call bullshit."

I sighed. I could've predicted this.

"James, you trust me, right? So trust that I'm okay. I just needed to hear your voice."

There was silence for a long minute.

"I don't believe you. This isn't like you. Christ, you would never disappear on me without a word. Tell me where you are. Tell me what the fuck happened."

The anger in his voice took me by surprise. I hadn't expected him to be angry. Worried, yes, but angry?

"I can't tell you that."

Betrayal

"I get your parents are dead and it's fucking tragic, but you don't just run away. How could you? Isn't our friendship worth more than that? Worth more than finding out you're fucking alive on a viral video?"

Tears welled in my eyes. I thought I had no more left to shed, but I was wrong. Even if I told him the truth, he wouldn't understand. Aiden left me no choice and I no longer wanted to go back to my life.

James wouldn't see it that way. He'd want to know why I hadn't fought harder. How could you fight against someone you wanted, needed so much it burnt? I wanted and needed Aiden despite what he'd done to me.

Yes, he'd ruined my life. Ruined it by showing me the truth and making it impossible for me to believe my family was anything but evil. He'd broken me over and over again. Made me reliant on him. None of it mattered. It was my soul that called to his. I needed and wanted him because he was Aiden, not because of any of the other bullshit surrounding our lives.

Deep down, he knew that.

Deep down, he felt it too.

"I'm sorry, James. I really am. It wasn't like that. I promise. Please, you have to believe me."

"Then what was it like? Because to me, it looks like you bailed."

Too much pain. My body overloaded with it. My mind so overwhelmed. I thought speaking to him would make me feel better, instead, I felt so much worse.

"I'd never bail on you. It's complicated."

Footsteps. Aiden stood in the doorway.

"Avery, I need to know where you are."

"I have to go."

"Avery—"

"James, please. I'm sorry. I love you, but don't try and call me back. You won't get through. I'll speak to you when I can, but I have to go."

I hung up. If I spoke to him further, I'd break completely and tell him everything. Aiden came into the room and took the phone off me. He fiddled with it for a moment before looking down at me.

"Are you okay?"

I shook my head, burying my face in my knees again. A moment later, I felt his hand on my shoulder.

"Avery, please don't shut me out."

"I…I…I can't. It hurts too much. All of it. He got angry with me. Said I bailed on him. I just can't."

I heard him shift. When I peeked out, he was lying on the floor next to me. He took one of my hands from off my knees and held it in his.

"I'm just going to stay here with you, okay?"

"But—"

"No, Avery. I'm not letting you be alone. If you won't come out then I'm staying here."

"You can't lie on the concrete floor with me."

"I can and I will continue to until you let me carry you out of here."

Arguing over it was futile. I saw the determination in his eyes. I shivered. The floor was cold. Just like I remembered from when I was last in here. My body felt freezing all of a sudden. How long had I even been here? Time seemed to have no meaning when I was so lost in my own misery.

"Why?"

He frowned.

"Why what?"

"Why are you insisting on being with me?"

"You're upset and hurting."

"Why did you say I was your light earlier? What does that mean?"

He stroked his thumb across my knuckles.

"My world is full of darkness. So much of it. All the things I've done and seen. Dark and twisted. You are full of compassion. You feel for those who've been wronged, who hurt. You take that pain and it becomes your own. You're so fucking innocent and pure. You talk about not deserving things, but you deserve everything. I can't give you that. I'm not a good person. I've hurt you and I'll keep hurting you. I don't want to dim your light, but I will because you're mine and I won't let you go."

He was so wrong about that. Aiden had goodness in him, he just couldn't see it. And pain from him? I'd take that any day over losing him. I'd let him hurt me if it meant I had him. I wanted him. And I wanted him mine too. Just like I was his. Whether that was selfish, stupid or naïve, I didn't care.

"I won't let you go either."

"You sounded like you were ready to earlier."

A fresh wave of tears hit me. If I said sorry again, he wouldn't be happy.

"I doubt you'd let me even if I wanted to."

That made him smile at me. And his smile made my heart flip-flop. How could I desire someone so much even after all the pain and sorrow I'd been through?

"I belong to you, leaving or saying goodbye, it'd be like tearing a piece of me out."

His eyes flashed with an emotion I didn't understand.

"Just like you drew yourself ripping out your heart and offering it to me?"

He'd seen it then. How could I explain it?

"I wasn't in a very good frame of mind when I drew those things."

"I noticed."

He squeezed my hand.

"I want to help you. Helping you means I have to turn my back on my family. It meant I have to tear out my feelings, my love for them so I can fight for you."

I still loved my family on some level, but every time I learnt something new about them, it eroded that love from my heart piece by piece.

"Avery… Will you let me take you to bed?"

How could I continue to make him lie next to me on the cold concrete floor when he looked at me as if I was breaking him inside too?

I nodded. Aiden shifted to his feet before he picked me up off the floor and held me to his chest.

"Fuck, you feel like ice."

Striding from the room, he kicked the door shut behind us and took me into the bedroom. He pulled back the covers and tucked me in. Then he went to the cupboard and tugged out my warmest set of pyjamas along with a jumper and socks. He tossed them at me.

"Put them on, please."

Betrayal

He kept his back to me. My body felt stiff, but I managed to peel off my clothes and dress in what he'd given me. I huddled in the covers, shivering.

When he got in bed with me, he wrapped his arms around me and held me against his chest. He'd changed, but I'd been too busy dealing with my own clothes to notice.

"How long was I in there for?"

"You cried for two hours. I didn't hear a peep out of you for another two. And I think we can add on a further hour just now."

"Five hours? Did you wait outside for me that whole time?"

"Yes."

"Aiden… why?"

"I had to. What if you saw them again? I can't listen to you screaming like that."

I hugged him tighter. He'd stayed to make sure I was okay. How did I remotely deserve that? And here he was trying to get me warm again.

"I didn't know you cared," I mumbled into his chest.

"You just haven't been paying attention."

He stroked my back, his fingers soothing.

"Are you hungry? You haven't eaten."

I was, but he'd done enough for me.

"Yes, but you've not eaten either. I don't want you to have to make me something though."

"I was thinking of ordering in."

I pulled away from his chest and looked up at him. Aiden never did takeaways, at least not since I'd been here.

"Really?"

"What do you want?"

I thought about it for a moment.

"Is it so terrible that I want to lie in bed with you and eat pizza?"

He laughed. The rumble of his chest against mine vibrating my insides.

"No, it's not."

Aiden ordered in from a local family run pizza place nearby and set up his laptop, putting a film on whilst we ate. It felt like we were doing something normal for once.

He held me whilst we sat up in bed and dotted my nose with tomato sauce at one point. And he licked it off. His face being so close to mine made my blood thunder in my ears. I'd never wanted to kiss someone so much in my life. I wanted his lips on mine, to taste him and have him take me under.

Those urges didn't go away, even after the film was done and I curled up by his side, my arm wrapped around his waist. I wasn't sure if I could fall asleep, but the exhaustion of the day caught up with me and I drifted off.

The very next thing I knew, I was screaming and Aiden was holding me so tightly I couldn't breathe.

Chapter Eighteen

Aiden

Bliss. I felt blissfully free from the nightmares and terror I usually felt when I fell asleep. Except my bliss was being disturbed. Something kept whacking against my chest. Was I still dreaming or was I awake?

The piercing sound of terror rang in my ears. My eyes flew open. It was still dark and it disorientated me. Something hit my chest again. Then it registered.

Avery.

The sound was coming from her. It was her hand flailing and hitting me in the chest. Was she awake? No. Her eyes were closed.

Fuck. She's having a nightmare.

I reached out, capturing her up and tugging her against my chest to stop her moving.

"Shh, shh, I've got you. I'm here."

She shifted in my grasp. I held her tighter. Her screaming was muffled by my chest, but it was still haunting.

"Avery, you need to wake up."

Nothing. Whatever she was dreaming about, she was stuck. Her t-shirt was drenched in sweat.

"Avery," I said louder. "Wake up. It's just a dream. I'm here. I've got you."

I shook her. Fuck. I needed her awake so she'd stop screaming. I wanted to help her. Make her feel better. Fuck. Knowing she was suffering tore at me.

"Please, fuck, please wake up."

The screaming abruptly stopped. She wriggled against me. I released my hold on her slightly. She took a few deep, gulping gasps. I looked down at her. Her eyes were open, terror evident in them.

"Avery….?"

She let out a rasping sob and buried her face in my chest.

"Shh, I've got you."

"Aiden," she whimpered. "There was so much blood."

I stroked her hair. It stuck to her neck. Fuck. Sweat everywhere, seeping into my clothes too. I needed to get her in the shower.

"It's okay. It wasn't real. Just a dream."

"It felt real."

"I'm here. We're real. It's okay."

I kicked the twisted up covers off us. I tried to shift away, but she held on tighter.

"I'm not going anywhere. You're covered in sweat. Let's get you cleaned up, okay?"

She nodded. I got off the bed and picked her up. Carrying her into the bathroom through the dark flat, I set her down. She clung to me. I reached into the shower and flipped it on.

Betrayal

"Avery, you need to let go."

She shook her head. Fuck it. She was clearly too affected by the dream. I guided her into the shower with me, not stopping to strip our clothes off.

The water cascaded down both of us. I held her for the longest time until her sobbing abated. Our clothes were drenched. Nothing mattered but her.

She pulled away and looked up at me. Doe eyes. Fuck. She looked so innocent. So lost. How could I ever look away from her? She was like the fucking sun to me. We'd been through so fucking much together in the space of a month.

I reached up, cupping her face with both my hands. I ran one thumb over her bottom lip, which trembled under my touch.

Fuck. I wanted her. I needed her. Why did I keep holding back? What was really stopping me? Avery wasn't like anyone else. She was unique and so fucking perfect. Her eyes set my fucking world on fire and her touch. Fuck, her touch. Skin so soft and delicate. I couldn't. I just couldn't stop all these feelings. All these emotions. My fucking heart bled. And nothing could save me but her.

I leant down towards her, mesmerised by her doe eyes and her slightly parted lips. Lips I wanted to taste. Water streamed down both our faces, but all I could see was her. Our breath mingled for a moment, so fucking close.

Then I kissed her.

Soft. Gentle. Tender.

Her lips made me drunk. She tasted so sweet. So fucking innocent. I couldn't tear myself away even if I wanted to. Her hand fisted in my t-shirt, tugging me closer.

Fuck. She felt so good. Fuck. This felt so right.

I pressed my mouth harder against hers, needing more. Her other hand snaked up around my neck, anchoring me to her. Her lips parted, allowing me deeper. Fuck. She was like fire. As soon as my tongue met hers, our kiss became ever more heated.

We ground into each other.

We drowned in each other.

Fuck.

I couldn't fucking hold back.

I needed more.

I needed everything.

My hands ran down her back, tugging her against me. I could feel her nipples pebbled on my chest through our clothes. I wanted to touch her. I needed to see her. Fuck. I needed her skin on mine. All these fucking barriers. I was done with them.

I couldn't stop kissing her. Her mouth was the sweetest damn thing I ever tasted. Her fingers dug into my neck. The need to be as close as possible overrode my senses. I had to have her. Now. Right fucking now.

My hands went to the bottom of her t-shirt. Releasing her mouth, I peeled it off her. Her eyes were wild with fucking desire. And her tits. Fuck. They were perfect. Her hard nipples were stark against her skin, just fucking begging me to taste them.

I leant down, capturing one in my mouth whilst I cupped her other breast, running my thumb over the nub. She moaned, arching into me. The sound of her only heightened my need. Fuck. My teeth grazed over her nipple before I bit down. She bucked, gripping my shoulders.

"Aiden," she gasped.

My name on her lips. Fuck. She vibrated with need. Fuck. She wanted me just as much as I did her. My hands found her shorts. I pulled at them, tugging them down with her underwear. When I straightened, she was naked before me. The sight of her made my cock pulsate and throb, already rock hard from just our shared kiss.

She was so fucking beautiful and perfect in every single way. Even though I hadn't turned the lights on, her skin glowed in the moonlight streaming in through the bathroom windows. This was it. There was no fucking going back now. I had to have her. Had to be inside her.

She reached for me, hands curling around the bottom of my t-shirt. Her eyes met mine, looking for confirmation it was okay. She'd never seen me without a shirt.

What the fuck would she think when she saw the rest of my tattoos?

Did it matter?

The way she'd looked at the ones on my arms told me she found them fascinating.

I put my hands over hers and encouraged her to help me take it off. It landed with a splat on the floor. Her eyes roamed down, falling on the two large depictions on my chest. Her fingers ran over the one on the right, her eyes wide with interest.

Now wasn't the time to explain them.

Now was the time for us to finally shed the last of our barriers.

To let go and have this moment we both wanted.

I tucked my fingers into my boxers, pulling them off.

For a long moment, we stood there staring at each other as the water cascaded over us. I reached for her first, tugging her to me as our lips crashed against each other again. Her body felt so fucking right next to mine. Her arms wrapped around my neck and mine curled around her back.

We were as close as two people could physically be but it wasn't enough. I fucking needed her. I needed to be in her. That way I'd feel her. Feel everything she felt. Every emotion. Every fucking thing.

I pressed her up against the shower wall, grinding into her stomach as she moaned in my mouth. Fuck. I didn't want to do this in the shower. Perhaps another time, but right now, I wanted her in my bed where I could lay her down and worship every inch of her. She deserved to be kissed everywhere. Her skin begged to be touched, stroked.

I pulled back from her and flipped off the shower. Taking her hand, I pulled her out with me. We were both dripping wet. I picked up a towel from the rack and wrapped it around her before taking another and drying her hair as best I could with it. She took the last towel and started drying me too. I grabbed it from her and tied it around my waist.

"Aiden—"

I put a finger to her lips, silencing her.

"Shh. No words."

She nodded. I took her hand and led her back to the bedroom. I ripped the covers off the bed, tossing them on the floor. They were drenched in her sweat, so I wanted to change the sheets, but I couldn't wait. Tearing off the bed sheet and leaving the mattress bare, I laid down our towels on it.

I pressed her down on the bed and knelt over her. I had no desire to restrain her. I wanted her to be able to touch me. To run her hands over my back.

"Aiden… I need to say something."

I cupped her face, wanting desperately to feel her lips against mine again.

"Tell me."

"I'm… I'm on birth control. I want to feel you. All of you."

The thought of taking her without barriers made my cock jerk. I always used condoms. Didn't want to catch anything and there was no fucking way I wanted to be a father.

"Are you sure?"

She nodded. Taking my hand, she brought it to her bicep, pressing my fingers down on it. I could feel a small rod under her skin. I didn't think she was lying about being on birth control, but proof made me feel a little more at ease about it.

Fuck. I couldn't deny her. If she wanted this, then so did I.

"Has anyone else had you without protection before?"

"No," she whispered.

I almost fucking lost it. The first. The first in her mouth and the first to feel her without barriers. Fuck. She was killing me. She really was mine, in every fucking way.

"Spread your legs for me."

She did so without hesitation. My eyes roamed down her body. Her skin glowed in the moonlight. I'd forgotten to shut the curtains and I was fucking happy I had. She was the most beautiful girl. Alluring. Stunning. Sexy yet still so fucking innocent. The way her nipples hardened under my gaze right down to the neatly trimmed thatch of dark hair between her legs. And she was mine.

Fuck. I had to swallow, my mouth watering at the sight of her. As much as I wanted to bury my face in her pussy and taste her until she came all over my tongue, my cock throbbed restlessly. It needed her and I was so fucking done denying it.

I leant over her and captured her lips again. Her tongue danced with mine. The taste of her so fucking intoxicating. My fingers ran down her sides before I cupped her breast. Her perfect fucking tits. Just the right size for my hand.

I settled down between her legs, my cock finding her pussy and sliding against it. Fuck. She was so wet. I fucking ached to fill her. To have her clenching around me.

Was she ready for me?

Her pussy was so tight, I wasn't sure she'd be able to accommodate me. But fuck, I couldn't wait any longer. I needed her.

I released her mouth, shifting back slightly. I gripped my cock and guided it to her opening. I watched her face for any sign of discomfort when I pressed myself inside. There was a little resistance.

When I sunk the head of my cock in her, she cried out, gripping my arm. Fuck. She was like a vice. Her pussy clenched around me, so tight.

"Am I hurting you? Shit, I should've known you weren't ready yet."

"No, no please, it doesn't hurt. Just give me a sec, okay?"

I brushed her hair from her face.

"Are you sure?"

"Yes… it's just… you're…"

"I'm what?"

"So big."

I bit my lip to keep from grinning.

"Oh, you've barely felt me yet, Avery. Did you forget what I told you?"

She shook her head.

"Mmm, say it."

"You said I want you to give it to me deeper and harder than I've ever had before."

Fuck. If I wasn't so concerned about hurting her, I'd have slammed into her up to the hilt.

"That's right… Now, we're not going to talk anymore. I want to fuck you and I'd much rather hear you moaning and crying out my name."

She squirmed beneath me. Fuck. She was so innocent. Her hands curled around my back. I took it as a sign she was ready. I thrust into her a little further before I pulled back. I fucked her with slow, shallow thrusts, only giving her as much as I thought she could take.

Her pussy was the tightest I'd ever felt. So fucking wet. She gripped me, pulsating with heat.

Her eyes were wild with desire, pleasure. Her lips parted as she breathed out small pants and moans. The sweetest fucking sounds I'd ever heard. And I fucking needed more. I thrust deeper, harder and her moans got louder.

"Aiden, fuck, please, I want all of you," she cried out.

Her wish was my command. I gripped one of her hips as an anchor. I pressed deeper. Her pussy. Fuck. She was so tight, it was almost fucking agony. I could feel her stretching, trying to accommodate the intrusion of my cock.

"Fucking hell, you're like a fucking vice."

"Aiden, please, I need it."

"I don't want to hurt you."

"Don't stop. You feel so good. I want this. I want you so much."

Her words spurred me on. I pressed harder, breaking through the last of her resistance and seated myself fully inside her. She felt like nothing else. Her moan, a mixture of pleasure and pain almost fucking broke me. How could she want this when it was clearly hurting her?

"Avery…"

"Fuck me, Aiden," she moaned, her eyes flying open. "Fuck me hard."

Well fuck.

I pulled back and thrust into her, setting a steady rhythm. She gripped my back, staring up at me with those fucking doe eyes. Only her doe eyes spoke of lust, need, desire and pleasure.

I captured her mouth again, kissing her without mercy. My fingers entwined with hers as I rode her harder.

No one fucking told me it would feel this fucking amazing. Fucking her was ecstasy. She moulded to me perfectly, her body so in sync with mine. With her, my need to restrain and control disappeared. She was so pliant, so fucking perfect, I didn't need any of it. I already had her submission and that was enough right then.

She moaned, panted and writhed beneath me. I didn't let up. I pounded into her harder until I set an almost punishing pace. The fingers of her free hand dug into my back, nails biting against my skin. And fuck, I really wanted her to come. Her pussy was so fucking tight, but I needed more.

"Avery, are you going to come for me? I want to hear you scream my name."

I shifted and gripped one of her legs, pressing it upwards so I could get a better angle on her. I pounded into her again, feeling her clenching around me. Fuck. She felt so good.

"Aiden, fuck, fuck me."

"Come for me. Fucking come all over my cock."

She cried out, her nails digging deeper. I could feel it. She was so close to the edge. I wanted to make her snap.

"That's it. Tell me how much you want it."

"Harder. Please, fuck me harder."

Harder. Faster. She was so fucking pent up. The tension inside her so close to snapping. And when she did, I wasn't quite sure if I could hold on either. I was too fucking close to blowing my load inside her.

"Fuck. Come on my cock. I want to feel you."

I shoved my hand in between us and strummed her clit. Once. Twice. Then she fucking detonated on me. Her scream of pleasure echoed around the room. And her pussy milked me for all it was worth.

I thrust once, twice, three more times and then I was fucking coming too. Coming inside her whilst she pulsated and trembled beneath me. I rode out both our orgasms, grinding into her. Making her take it all as my cock spurted again and again.

I almost fucking collapsed on top of her when both of us were spent. Shit. I'd never fucking come so hard in my life.

Nothing could prepare me for the sweet ecstasy she brought on.

Fuck. Avery was a fucking goddess. Just like the Aztec goddess of carnal pleasures and lust tattooed on the right side of my chest, Tlazolteotl. And on my left, Tezcatlipoca, the god of darkness and the lord of the night. They represented the darker sides of me. Partially why I kept them hidden so much. My desires weren't for public consumption. But Avery knew. I'd shown her. And I'd explain the meaning of the tattoos to her later.

Avery. Beautiful, strong and so fucking amazing.

I pulled out and lay beside her. She curled into my chest, her hand running down my back. Her touch so gentle. Her lips met my chest in a soft kiss, making me shiver.

"Am I allowed to tell you that was the best sex of my life?" she whispered.

I smiled.

"You're allowed to say what you want."

"Best. Ever."

I couldn't help laughing. Fuck. Too innocent, but really... she was right. It had been. No one gave me the same intense rush of feelings she did.

"Don't want to raise the bar too high, how do you expect me to top that?"

She shoved me, which only made me laugh harder.

"Aiden, it's not funny. Now I'm embarrassed."

I wrapped my arm around her and kissed the top of her head. I brushed her hair away from her ear and leant towards it.

"Don't be. Everything about it was fucking perfect."

She twisted in my hold, trying to shift away from me. I wouldn't let her.

"Be serious."

"I am. You've got the sweetest, tightest pussy. You're so sexy it hurts to look at you and the way you came apart on my cock was fucking amazing to watch. So yes, Avery, it was fucking perfect."

"So you don't regret it?"

I tucked my fingers under her chin and forced her to look at me. The hesitation in her doe eyes almost fucking fractured my heart in two.

"Never. Trust me, I won't be able to stop. Not now I've had you once. That's not fucking enough."

"You want to fuck me again?"

"I expect you to spread your legs for me daily."

She bit her lip.

"Will that include the use of your box of toys?"

I raised an eyebrow.

"Is that what you're calling it?"

"It felt apt."

"Yes, it will. I'll go easy on you though."

She trembled against me.

"Okay. Um… I need to go… Uh…"

I watched her squirm, knowing exactly what she wanted to say.

"Hmm?"

"Bathroom. I don't want to get it all over the bed."

"Mmm, did you like that? Knowing I came inside you without any protection?"

"Aiden…"

She tried to wriggle away from me again.

"Don't be shy."

"Yes, okay?"

I kissed her, trying to ease her embarrassment. Her fingers curled in my hair. Fuck. I wanted to kiss her all the time. I pulled away, cupping her face.

"You're so fucking beautiful, you know that?

"If you say so."

I grinned, releasing her. She shifted away and practically ran to the bathroom. I got up, pulling the towels off the bed. I snagged a clean set of sheets from one of my cupboards and remade the bed. I'd just finished putting the pillows back on when she stood in the doorway. Her body called to me. I put my hand out to her. She walked over.

I shoved back the covers, grabbed her and tossed her in the bed. I got in next to her and cradled her to my chest, kissing the top of her head.

"Go back to sleep. I'll protect you," I whispered.

Her palm flattened on my chest where my heart hammered.

I listened to her breathing turn steady before I let myself fall away into oblivion too.

Avery.

So fucking perfect.

And mine.

Chapter Nineteen

Avery

Waking up next to him felt like heaven. A dull ache settled between my thighs from the intense pounding he'd given me. I didn't care. It reminded me last night was real. It happened.

Aiden finally kissed me.

Finally fucked me.

And it was everything.

Neither of us had dressed before falling asleep. Aiden had thrown the covers off. His bare chest illuminated in the soft glow of the late morning winter sun streaming in through the windows. His tattoos were so beautiful. I traced my fingers over them. He shifted under my touch.

"Are you admiring them?" he grumbled.

"Yes."

"They're Aztec. Tlazolteotl in the right. Tezcatlipoca on the left."

He yawned, opening his eyes and blinking at me.

"And who are they?"

He smiled at me.

"Tezcatlipoca is the god of providence, the darkness and the invisible. Tlazolteotl is the goddess of lust, carnality and sexual misdeeds."

"Sexual mis… Oh. I get it."

My face burnt, but I did understand. She spoke to his desires. Ones I knew he thought were twisted, but they didn't freak me out. And the other, his darkness. It was Aiden all over. Complex. My avenging angel.

"There's one more you haven't seen."

My curiosity piqued. What had he hidden from me for all this time? He rolled over so his back was to me. I stared for the longest time. Then I ran my fingers over it. This huge, beautiful phoenix rising from a fire at the base of his spine. Holy hell. It was absolutely stunning. The artwork, divine. I had to meet the man who'd tattooed this on his flesh.

"It's you."

"Perceptive."

"Well, I do pay attention to what you tell me."

He rolled back over, grabbed me and held me close. His fingers danced across my skin. I arched against him, desire immediately flooding my veins. His cock nudged my stomach.

"Do you… want me?" I asked.

His grey eyes sparkled with amusement laced with the heady cocktail of lust.

"I always fucking want you. Especially now I've seen you naked."

My skin itched to feel his fingers. His mouth crashed down on mine, stealing away all my thoughts. His taste. Intoxicating.

Betrayal

I wanted more. I knew what Aiden brought out in me. I craved it.

"Fuck me," I whispered against his mouth.

Aiden shifted, pressing himself between my legs, pinning one to the bed. He rocked his cock against me. I grew wetter, hotter as it brushed against my clit relentlessly. I'd come quickly if he kept this up. My hand curled around his back, the other caught between us.

"I need to be in you," he growled.

I shifted, reaching down between us and gripping his cock. He groaned, thrusting against me. His lips sealed mine again. A kiss so deep, I felt as though I drowned in him. I pressed him to my entrance.

Just as Aiden thrust inside me, a loud sound rang through the flat. We both froze.

"For fuck's sake," he grunted. "Who the fuck is that?"

"Aiden…"

"I know. Fuck. All I want is to ignore it so I can fuck you senseless."

He thrust into me deeper, not making any attempt to dislodge himself. I moaned. His cock felt so good. Replacing the dull ache with pleasure.

"Fuck, you feel amazing."

I gripped his back, letting him fuck me how he wanted. I didn't want him to stop. Who knew if he'd withdraw from me again now he'd finally given into this thing between us.

The buzzer went again. He groaned.

"Seriously? They can fuck off."

I sighed. It seemed we were destined to be interrupted at that moment. He pulled away from me and got up. His cock slapped against his stomach, glistening and damp from my arousal. And I really wanted to stop him from walking away so I could take him in my mouth. Giving Aiden pleasure turned me on.

"Fuck, fuck, fuck," he muttered as he pulled on a pair of shorts.

He ran a hand through his hair as he stalked from the room. I never thought I'd see the day Aiden would get so worked up about not being able to fuck me when he'd spent so long denying me.

"Avery... Come here."

I frowned. Why did he want me? I hauled myself out of bed, not bothering with clothes and padded out into the hall. His eyes darkened when he saw me.

"You naked is not helping," he said as I approached him.

"Tell them to—"

I faltered when I saw who was on the monitor. Aiden wrapped an arm around me, tucking me into his side.

"Why the fuck is he here?"

My heart stopped. James.

"I... I don't know. I promise I said nothing about where I was to him. You know I was careful."

"Shh, I know."

He kissed the top of my head. I relaxed against him. Aiden pressed down on the intercom.

"Hello," he said.

"Oh, hi, um... look, I'm sorry to just turn up here, but Charlie said he'd tell you. I'm James—"

"I know who you are."

Betrayal

Aiden leant down and whispered in my ear, "Go get my phone for me."

He released me. I hurried into the bedroom, grabbing it off the bedside table and brought it back to him.

"I'm really worried about her. She didn't sound right on the phone yesterday and I was awful to her. Charlie said you could help me trace the call. I know the number was blocked, but he told me you were good at this stuff."

I handed Aiden the phone and he fiddled with it before cursing under his breath.

"I hadn't checked my phone, but I see Chuck text me. You've caught me at a bad time, late night."

"I'm sorry, I know I should've called first."

Aiden looked at me, his eyes wary. What the fuck were we going to do with James being here? He released the button on the intercom.

"How trustworthy is your friend?" he asked me.

"I trust him with my life."

"I really hope I don't fucking regret this."

I wanted to ask him what he meant, but he put his hand down on the intercom again.

"Hey, listen, can you give me like twenty minutes? You see, I just woke up. There's a coffee shop down the road if you want to wait somewhere warm."

James looked a little lost, but he nodded.

"Okay, sure thing."

Aiden released the intercom again and turned to me.

"What are you doing?" I asked.

He grabbed hold of me and pressed me up against the wall.

"First, I'm going to fuck you, then we're going to come up with a believable story as to why you're here."

I didn't get a chance to reply because his mouth crashed against mine. His fingers dug into my skin, holding me in place as he devoured me.

Wait, why did sex come first? And what did he mean a believable story? Was he going to let me see my best friend?

I pushed at his chest. I needed answers. He pulled away, staring down at me with hazy, lust filled eyes.

"Aiden, what do you mean?"

He grabbed both my legs and hauled me up onto his hips. I had no choice but to wrap my legs around him to keep steady. My hands rested on his shoulders.

"Shh, fucking first."

He reached between us, shoving his shorts down enough for his cock to spring free. He gripped my hip as he guided his cock inside me and thrust upwards. I yelped. He groaned and slapped a hand over my mouth.

"You're going to take it like a good girl," he growled.

Submission. Total submission. He commanded. I obeyed. My back rubbed against the wall with the force of his pounding. He let go of my mouth, gripped my other hip and thrust harder. He felt so good. My fingers thread in his hair. His mouth latched onto my neck, peppering it with hot kisses.

"Fuck, being in you is fucking ecstasy."

I moaned his name over and over as he took me on the ride of my life. Last night had been incredible, but this was hot, fast and furious.

"For fuck's sake, I'm so close."

He grabbed one of my hands and shoved it in between us.

Betrayal

"I need you to come for me," he grunted.

I touched myself for him as he continued to pound into me. The pressure built. Blood pounded in my ears. My body thrummed.

I felt him struggle to hold on. His growl in my ear spurred me on.

"Fuck, I can't."

His cock pulsed inside me as he came. It set me off. I cried out his name as the waves took me under and drowned me.

Coming up for air, my head lolled on his shoulder. He pulled me away from the wall and carried me to the bathroom, still connected to me.

When he set me down, I felt his cum dripping down my inner thigh. *Oh shit.* No one ever fucked me standing up before. This was all so new to me. I stumbled away, grabbing tissues to try catch it all. He was smirking at me when I turned to him again after cleaning myself up.

"Mmm, I could get used to seeing you like that."

"Like what?"

"Thoroughly fucked, but you know what I want to see more? My cum splattered all over your chest."

I felt my face burning. He really did have a dirty mind and most definitely was not afraid to share his dark thoughts with me. I hadn't let anyone do that to me either.

"Mind out of the gutter, Aiden."

His grin got wider.

"Go get dressed, we need to talk."

I nodded and slipped from the room. I just pulled a t-shirt on when he came into the bedroom. He went straight to the cupboard and pulled out his own clothes.

"Are you going to tell him the truth?" I asked.

"Not exactly, but I know I can't keep him from finding out you're here."

"Why not?"

"Are you telling me you'll stay hidden?"

I shook my head. I wanted to see James so badly, it burnt in my chest.

"Well then, I don't have a choice. If I send him away and it gets back to Chuck, he'll be suspicious."

Aiden had a point. And I felt responsible since I'd been the one who wanted to talk to James last night.

"I'm sorry, this is my fault."

He put a hand up.

"Don't. You didn't know he'd go to your uncle."

It didn't make me feel any better. If I had just handled his revelation about my family killing his mother better, none of this would've happened.

I froze. Would we have finally had sex though? Why the fuck was I even thinking about that? Since when I had I become so... sex crazed?

Since you met Aiden, my brain helpfully supplied.

I wanted to groan.

"What are you going to tell him?"

"Just play along. I have some ideas."

"Aiden, he's going to expect me to explain."

The buzzer sounded. He shook his head.

"We're out of time. Stay here until I say, okay?"

I wasn't sure how Aiden could be so calm about this, but I had to trust him. Trust he knew what to say. What to do. He slipped from the room and I walked over to the door, closing it over. I flattened myself against the wall next to it. I wanted to hear what they said.

Minutes ticked by until I heard him open the front door.

"Uh, it's nice to meet you, Mr Lo—"

"Just call me Aiden."

"Well, thank you for taking the time to see me, Aiden."

James was being his usual polite self to people he didn't know. Get him around his friends and he swore like a sailor.

"Just come through."

I heard the two of them walk down the hall, past the bedroom door. I barely dared to breathe.

"I'm not sure how this works, but I can give you my phone," James said.

"Okay, look before we get into that, there are some things you need to understand."

"Um, okay."

I wondered where Aiden was going with this too.

"Firstly, what I'm going tell you stays within these four walls. You don't tell Chuck and you most definitely do not tell the police."

"Whoa, what—"

"I know where she is."

There was a long moment of silence.

"What do you mean you know where she is?"

"Avery. I know where she is and where she's been this whole time."

"How? That makes no sense. Why wouldn't you tell the police or Charlie? You do work for him, right?"

I heard them shuffling around for a moment.

"I do. It's complicated. She asked me not to. Asked me to make she stayed out of the public eye until this blew over. Perhaps it would be better if she explained it to you herself."

That's what he was telling James? Fuck. How was I going to turn this into something believable? James would see right through me. He always knew when I lied. This was an idiotic idea.

I guessed it was time to reveal myself.

"What do you mean? Wait… you're not telling me she's here, are you?"

I pulled open the door and stepped out into the hall. Seeing him made me falter. James looked like he hadn't been sleeping well. His blue shirt rumpled, his hair sticking up in places. He hadn't noticed me yet, but Aiden had. He put a hand out to me. James looked at him funny before his eyes followed Aiden's hand. As I walked towards them, James spied me. The blood drained from his face.

"A… Avery?"

Ignoring Aiden's outstretched hand, I ran to James and barrelled into his chest, almost knocking him off his feet.

"I'm so sorry," I said, trying to fight back tears.

"No, I'm sorry. Shit, I missed you."

"Me too."

Despite being relieved James was here, I was still very much aware of the other man in my life and the tension radiating off him. It scorched into my skin. Shit. He really wasn't happy about me hugging James.

I pulled away, taking a few steps back until I managed to bump into Aiden. One of his hands curled around my waist.

"Careful," he said in my ear.

Betrayal

When he didn't let go, I stepped out of his grasp, not wanting James to suspect anything was between us. If we were going to convince James of our version of the truth, then he couldn't know about us sleeping together.

"Look, James, what Aiden said is true. I asked him to help me. When I found out about my parents, I just couldn't deal with it. I'm sorry. I knew of some people who worked outside of the company for my Uncle Charlie, so this was the first place I came. I begged Aiden to help me."

I hoped James bought this because we'd be fucked otherwise. I wasn't sure how he'd take finding out Aiden kidnapped me and my family's dark deeds. Not with the shit going on in his own family.

"And what, you helped her out of the kindness of your heart?" James asked, eying Aiden with suspicion.

"If you'd seen the mess she was in, then you might understand why I couldn't just leave her outside my building," Aiden replied, his eyes hardening to steel.

James ran a hand through his hair, confusion evident in his expression.

"Why hide yourself all this time? Why didn't you just tell me?"

"I was barely able to function for the first two weeks and then it just got harder to go back to reality," I said. "We staged the video so it would keep the police away. I know you don't understand, but I had to, James. I had to do this. For me."

The lies stuck in my throat. I hated it. Without thinking, I reached for Aiden's hand and tucked my fingers in his. Instantly, I felt calmer. My safe place was with him.

The gesture didn't go unnoticed. James' eyes went wide whilst Aiden's lip curled up at the side. He knew exactly what it meant. I was his. I hoped James wouldn't interpret it that way, but if I pulled away now, it would only make it worse.

"Can I speak to you alone, Avery?"

I eyed Aiden. He gave me a subtle nod. He knew I'd be careful of what I said. I'd proven I was trustworthy.

"Sure, why don't you come make tea with me?"

James nodded. I indicated with my head he should go first. When his back was to us, Aiden leant down and kissed the top of my head.

"Will you make me a shake?" he asked.

"Of course."

Neither of us had eaten this morning. He'd taught me a few days ago how he liked it done. He let me go and I went into the hall with James. He followed me into the kitchen, leaning against the counter as I flipped the kettle on.

"What the fuck is going on, Avery?"

I took a deep breath before I turned to him.

"What do you mean?"

"Between you and him."

I shrugged.

"He's been helping me deal with it, that's all."

"Helping you? Helping himself into your knickers more like."

"James!"

He shook his head, scrunching up his face.

"Christ, is that what you two were doing when I interrupted you? What about Peter?"

Betrayal

"What the hell? No. What do you take me for? You know me, is that something I'd do? Sleep with someone out of what? Gratitude for helping me? That's fucking sick. And things with Peter are over. You saw the video. How can I be with anyone after this? I'm so messed up. It wouldn't be fair."

I turned away from him, anger flooding my veins. I had to deny it. I had no other choice. Pulling out the bits I needed, I started on making Aiden's protein shake. I also dumped cereal into a bowl for myself.

"It's just hard not to jump to conclusions when you're fucking holding his hand."

"I'm allowed to hold hands with whoever I want. He's been there for me. It's complicated, James. There are things I can't tell you."

He put a hand on my shoulder, turning me to face him.

"What things?"

"Stuff about my family. Reasons why we think my parents were murdered. I don't want you getting involved with it. It's fucked up enough as it is."

His eyes betrayed the hurt he felt at me not confiding in him. How could I? He didn't need to be involved. Enough people were already. I didn't want James knowing how evil they were.

"You've never kept anything from me."

And now I was keeping everything from him. It killed me to do it.

"I'm sorry. Look, James, I hate to ask this of you, but you can't tell my uncle I'm here. You cannot tell anyone. We agreed to tell you because I told Aiden I could trust you."

He looked stricken for a moment as if conflicted on so many levels before he sighed.

"I won't tell anyone, but you have to promise you won't go off the grid with me again."

"I promise."

He tugged me into his arms, burying his face in my hair.

"Fuck, I missed you so much. So fucking much. I went crazy without you. Avery, Christ, don't fucking leave me again. It's been hell. My family have been hell. My dad is being a cunt again. I can't deal with it. Not without you."

Hearing that made me feel like the world's worst friend. I should've been there for him.

James nuzzled my neck. I froze. This wasn't just a friendly hug. I wrenched out of his grasp.

"James…"

"I'm sorry. Fuck. I just, seeing you, being close to you."

"Don't."

We might've had that shared connection once. A mutual need to escape, but everything changed for me. I wasn't the same girl I'd been before my parents had died.

He rubbed the back of his neck, looking away.

"Just help me make tea for both of us. I have to finish this for him."

I indicated the blender where I'd shoved the ingredients for Aiden's shake. James nodded and did the tea for me. I finished up and picked up my cereal and the glass for Aiden.

We went back through into the living room. Aiden sat on the sofa. His eyes narrowed when he saw us. He knew there was something wrong. I had to sort myself out. Aiden couldn't find out James and I used to sleep together.

Betrayal

He could never discover the truth.
He'd never let me see James again.
And I couldn't live without my best friend.

Chapter Twenty

Aiden

I had no idea what her and her friend had discussed in the kitchen, but Avery looked as though it hadn't gone well. She plastered on a fake smile. I knew for sure there was something wrong.

What the fuck had he said to her?

I hated seeing her with him. Honestly, I didn't think I'd ever like seeing her with another man even if they were just friends. The way she was acting had me wondering how close the two of them were.

She handed me a glass and sat next to me. James sat next to her, setting down two mugs on the coffee table. The tension between the three of us flared and permeated the air.

When he was gone, I would ask her what the fuck happened. He'd already interrupted my plans. I wanted to keep Avery in bed all day. Intended to make up for lost time. Fuck. I couldn't think about that now. I was already sporting a semi from her sitting next to me, her thigh pressed up against mine. It wasn't strictly necessary for her to sit so close, but I had a feeling she needed distance between her and her friend.

Fuck. What happened?

"Um, so… How's Gert?" Avery asked.

"She's not been dealing with you disappearing very well. Was convinced you were dead until yesterday," James replied.

Avery rubbed her forehead, eyes full of pain. The lying was getting to her. I could tell. And knowing she'd upset her friends hurt her. Fuck. This was really all my fault. I'd make her feel better later. Take care of her like I was supposed to.

"I didn't think… I'm so sorry. You can't tell her, you know she won't understand why."

"Hey, hey, it's okay."

He put a hand on her arm. She flinched. And when I tried to catch her eye, she refused to meet mine. Now I really was fucking concerned.

"Ave, it isn't like you, but your parents died, I don't blame you for needing space. I get it."

Ave?

Knowing he had a nickname for her made my blood boil. Fuck. What the hell was this? Jealousy? Shit. I needed to get a grip. I had her already. There was no need to get worked up over her best friend knowing her better than I did. They'd grown up together. I took a breath. She'd share those things with me in time.

"I still feel shit about it. Worrying you guys unnecessarily. The media attention would've sucked."

"Hounded day and night? Yeah, thanks for that."

She smiled at him. Fuck. I hated it. I fucking hated it. The need to stake ownership, my fucking claim on her grew. *Mine.*

Betrayal

Mine. Mine. My cock got harder thinking about how pliant she'd been last night. It also reminded me I hadn't asked her what her nightmare had been about. Fuck. I'd been so wrapped up in fucking her.

"You're used to it, twat."

She nudged him with her shoulder and he smiled back. Immediately, the tension between the two of them evaporated.

"Dozy mare."

I clamped my mouth shut on the instinct to tell him to take that back. Avery's grin got wider.

"Such an arse."

"Takes one to know one."

She put her cereal bowl down and launched herself at him. I almost fucking choked on my shake. She laughed, he grumbled and tried to get her off as she tickled him relentlessly.

"Fuck, Avery, get off. Point made."

She sat back, hands up, her smile radiant and her eyes glittering with amusement.

"Not sorry."

"You'll fucking get it next time."

Gone was the polite boy I'd met at the door. The love and friendship between the two of them was clear. And I fucking hated it. I wanted her to be that free with me. Instead, we fought each other more often than not. Freedom was had when we touched each other. I saw it in her expression. She craved the connection between us. Craved me. Craved my control.

Fuck. I needed to bury my dick in her. The quick fuck against the wall wasn't enough. No. I wanted to fuck her into next week. And I would as soon as he left.

Avery shifted closer to me, grabbing my arm off the back of the sofa and wrapping it around her.

"No, you won't. Unless you want to fight Aiden."

James blanched at the prospect.

"Hey, that is unfair."

"I don't play fair or did you forget the time Dante thought it was you who broke his Lego collection?"

"I still haven't forgiven you for that."

My hand curled around her stomach, holding her closer.

Dante? Why is that name familiar?

"Dante is James' older brother," Avery said, eying me with a smile.

Dante Benson. Eldest son of Zachary, the designer. Benson was a name you didn't mess with. Never met them, but Chuck always said they were a bunch of stuck up cunts. I guess it's why he tolerated James rather than sending him away.

"I remember," I said.

"Fucking Dante can go to hell," James mumbled.

"They don't get along," Avery said.

James stared at my arm around her. When Avery noticed, she sat up straighter and pushed me away.

What the fuck is she playing at?

She shot me an apologetic look before picking up her tea.

"So… It's okay for me and James to stay in touch, right? Now he knows."

"Yes."

Betrayal

I didn't see why not if he kept his mouth shut.

"Thank you."

She put a hand on my knee. My cock jerked. This touching had to stop. Did she have any clue how fucking much I wanted to bend her over the sofa? I wouldn't care if her friend saw.

"Um, Ave, where's the bathroom?" James asked.

"Oh, the door opposite the kitchen."

He got up and ambled off towards it. I took the mug out of Avery's hands, placed it on the coffee table and gripped her face. Her eyes went wide.

"Aiden…?"

"Shut up."

When I heard the bathroom door close, I kissed her. She mewed in protest, shoving against me, but I didn't let go. Shoving my tongue in her mouth, I tasted her sweetness. Fuck. I wanted her so much. My other hand ran up her inner thigh, brushing against her clit through her jeans. She jerked in my hold. Then she bit my tongue. I grunted, pulling away.

"What the fuck?"

"I should be asking you the same thing," she retorted, eyes wild. "What the hell is your problem? He doesn't know. Unless you want him finding out the whole truth, I suggest you cut it out and act like we're friends instead of trying to fuck me on the sofa whilst he's in the bathroom."

"You fucking say that again. I'm warning you. Do not test me."

She flinched.

"He already accused you of taking advantage of my fragile state, so don't start with me."

"He what?"

She pulled away from me entirely.

"Did you forget he thinks I've been under emotional distress and you've been helping me? What other conclusion would you like him to draw?"

I sat back. She had a point. I didn't like it. Fuck. Where the fuck was my control? Shot to pieces because of her. I had to reign it in. She was right. He couldn't find out about us. Not yet anyway. We needed him to stay quiet.

She cupped my face. Her entire expression softened. It fucking killed me.

"I'm sorry I bit you. Does it hurt?"

"No."

It stung a little, but she hadn't hurt me.

"Aiden, please, don't be angry with me."

"I'm not."

With her?

No.

With the whole situation?

Yes.

The bathroom door opened and she dropped her hand, looking away.

"Avery," I whispered. "I'm just frustrated."

She nodded.

James sat back down next to her, eying the two of us warily.

"Everything all right?" he asked.

"Yes," she said. "All good."

My phone started ringing in my pocket. I sighed, pulling it out and checking the caller ID.

Betrayal

"I have to take this and you two need to be quiet."

I got up and walked over to the window before answering.

"Hello Chuck, to what do I owe this pleasure?"

"Did you get my message?"

I ran a hand through my hair.

"Yes, just wished you'd called. I was half asleep when he turned up at my door."

"Yeah, sorry. Insistent little prick. Not as bad as the rest of his family though. Still, did you find out where she was yesterday?"

Time to weave some more lies.

"Not exactly. Couldn't pinpoint her location, the number was blocked and even if I did, she'd be long gone by now unless she was stupid enough to stay put."

Chuck sighed and I heard some banging in the background.

"Fuck. You're right. Little bitch is clever."

I almost fucking growled. He'd fucking pay for calling her that. No respect for his niece whatsoever.

"I wonder why she called him after all this time," Chuck continued. "That little stunt she's pulled with the media hasn't helped either. She had to have help. According to Ethan, they haven't been able to trace where the leak came from."

"So you didn't dispose of him?"

"No. He's useful. Besides, there would be too many questions if a pig disappeared. Don't need any more shit right now."

I turned back to James and Avery. The two of them were whispering to each other. I'd fucking pay to know what they were talking about, but I had to deal with Chuck.

"I'll keep working on it."

"Good man. I know I've not had much on for you recently, but when this blows over, I'm sure things will go back to normal."

I didn't much care about that. Gave me time to spend with Avery and work out my next move. I had enough to live on for life working for them so money wasn't an issue. I wasn't one to live in the lap of luxury.

"Don't worry about it. Got stuff to keep me busy."

"I'm sure. Right, better get back to the grind."

He hung up without saying goodbye.

Avery looked up when I approached the sofa.

"James has to go, but is it okay if he comes over again soon?"

I nodded. The sooner he left, the sooner I could get some answers. And fuck her. There would be no getting out of it.

"Well, it was nice to meet you," James said, standing up.

He didn't move to shake my hand again. Probably a good move on his part as my patience was wearing thin. She got up and saw him to the door. I sat back on the sofa and waited for her. She wasn't quick to come back to me, making a stop in the bathroom first.

When she finally walked in, her eyes were downcast and she looked tense.

"Aiden…"

"Come here. Now."

She didn't hesitate, walking over and standing before me. I grabbed her arm and tugged her down into my lap so she straddled me. I gripped her chin and forced her to look at me.

"What the fuck happened between the two of you in the kitchen? And do not lie to me, Avery. I'll fucking know."

"Aiden, please don't."

My grip got tighter. Her eyes flashed with pain.

"Tell. Me."

"I told you already. He accused us of sleeping together and I denied it."

"That is not all. I'm giving you one last chance to be honest with me."

Her eyes flashed again. This time with fear.

"I just feel shit. He's having a hard time with his dad again and I wasn't there. He's abusive, strict and a workaholic. I know my family's track record is sick, but what Zach has done to his kids is all kinds of fucked up. James hasn't told me everything, but I know enough."

I released my hold on her immediately. I knew Zachary Benson was a piece of work, but abusing his own kids? That's just fucked.

Tears welled in her eyes. Fuck. No wonder she'd been tense.

"It's my fault you weren't there."

"No. I'm not placing blame on anyone here. Please, can we just not talk about him? He won't tell anyone where I am. There's things I can't explain and I need you to trust me when I say it's better left in the past."

What the fuck would she have trouble explaining? A suspicion took hold and it wouldn't fucking leave.

"Avery, if this is what I think it is…"

Her face fell.

"Aiden, please, please don't." She took hold of my face with both hands. "I'm begging you. Don't. My life is an open book to you, but not my friendship with him. Okay? Please."

I didn't like it. Not at all. Her expression fucking killed me. Secrets only ended up hurting people. Was she doing this to protect me or him? Or was it both of us?

"Who are you protecting here?"

"It doesn't matter. I'm asking for one thing. Can't you do that for me? Please."

She kissed me. Her lips gentle. Fuck. How on earth could I deny her?

"Please," she whispered.

I cupped the back of her neck with one hand, deepening the kiss.

"Okay, I won't ask you about it, for now," I said as I pulled away.

"Thank you."

"However, you are going to tell me what the fuck you were dreaming about last night and I won't tolerate any excuses as to why not."

She sighed, her hands falling on my chest.

"I never told you what I saw that time you locked me in the cell again. My parents asked me to avenge them and take away your life."

"You saw both of them?"

They told her to kill me. What the actual fuck? All this shit had seriously fucked with her head. And who was responsible for that? Me.

"Yes. It was awful. I told them no. I wouldn't… You know I can't do that."

She looked away, her eyes full of pain.

"You should've told me."

"How could I? You forced me to watch those videos afterwards. You wouldn't let me talk."

Fuck. She was right. I'd been fucking terrible to her. Fuck. I was such a dick. This whole thing fucking broke me. Hurting her only made me feel worse. My fingers traced lines over the back of her neck.

"Would you believe me if I told you I'm sorry about those things?"

"Yes."

"Fuck. I really don't deserve you."

She kissed me again. I'd never fucking get over how amazing her mouth felt against mine. I rarely ever kissed women. Too intimate. Too easy to fall into fantasies of happiness and love. Things I didn't believe in. With her, it was fucking everything.

She leant her forehead against mine.

"It's not a question of who deserves who. I'm yours no matter what you do."

She really had no fucking clue what I planned. I wasn't sure if I could even go through with it at this point. The thought of it killed me.

We were getting off track here.

"Your dream, Avery."

"Nightmare more like. My whole family were there, taunting me. Telling me I'd betrayed them."

She pulled away from me, her hands falling to her sides. Her eyes filled with tears.

"And you… they had you. I couldn't fucking stand it. They put a knife in my hand and told me to end it. When I wouldn't, hands grabbed me and then they forced me. Over and over. So much blood. It went everywhere. I fought against them, but it was useless. When it was over, they let go of me. The knife dropped and I screamed when I saw what they'd made me do."

I tugged her against my chest, stroking her hair.

"I would never do that to you. Never. I can't. I care about you, Aiden, so much."

My heart. My fucking heart. That she even had to suffer through a dream like that made me feel sick. And I'd fucked her after that. How the hell could I do that to her when she'd just witnessed her family forcing her to kill me? Fuck. I should've fucking asked her first before I slept with her for the first time.

"You should've said something last night. You should've, Avery. I would've never—"

Her hand over my mouth silenced me.

"If you're going to say you wouldn't have had sex with me, then save it."

She raised her head from my chest. The look in her eye made my head spin.

"I waited. I tried to be patient. I gave you time to come to terms with our attraction to each other. So don't fucking take it back, Aiden. Don't you fucking dare. I wanted it. I needed it. After what I saw, it was the best fucking thing to happen. Do not tell me you would change it. Don't ruin it."

That told me. Hell. I'd never seen her look so determined. And it was fucking hot. My cock throbbed. If she wanted me that much, then I'd show her just what it meant to be mine. I would go easy on her, but it's time she learnt just how deep my need to make her obey ran.

I pointed at her hand over my mouth. She moved it away slowly. I reached up, running my thumb over her bottom lip.

"I want you to go into the bedroom, take your clothes off and lie on the bed for me."

"What?"

"You heard me."

Her eyes betrayed her confusion.

"I'm… not in trouble for what I said, am I?"

"No, but I suggest you do as I say if you want me to fuck you again."

Chapter Twenty One

Avery

Heat flooded my body from his words. What did he have planned? The way he was looking at me sent shivers down my spine.

"Go, Avery, before I get impatient."

I scrambled off him and made a beeline for the bedroom. I tore off my clothes in a hurry, making sure not to leave them lying all over the floor. I hopped on the bed and lay down to wait for him.

A minute later, he appeared in the doorway. His eyes roamed across me. He smiled, a wicked note to it. Goosebumps prickled all over my skin. He approached the bed.

"So compliant. Mmm, as long as you do as I say, I'll make you feel good."

"I will."

"Good girl."

He knelt down and pulled out the box under the bed. His box of toys. My breath caught in my throat. He'd promised to go easy on me last night, but I wondered if he meant it.

When he stood up, he had a few things in his hands. Two pairs of handcuffs, two lengths of silk and a blindfold. He kicked the box back under the bed.

"Now, you'll tell me if any of it is too tight. I don't want to hurt you."

I nodded. After placing the items on the bed, he hopped on and crawled over me. He leant down and kissed me. It was soft. I wanted more, but he released me after only a moment.

"You and I need a safe word, Avery. If ever it gets too much."

I didn't know very much about bondage. It made me nervous. Why would we need a safe word?

"You're not going to hurt me, are you?"

"No. Trust me, I have no desire to inflict physical pain. I want only to give you pleasure. Seeing you at my mercy and thinking about the ways I want to restrain you makes me so fucking hard. A safe word is necessary. It's about trust. I need you to trust me not to hurt you and I need to trust you to tell me when it's too much."

I nodded. I understood. It wasn't because he would do anything to harm me. I did trust him. I thought about it for a moment.

"Angel."

He raised an eyebrow at me.

"Is that not okay?"

He smiled at me again.

"I should've known you'd pick that."

"What? Why?"

He ran a finger down my arm.

"Because that's what I am to you."

I felt my face grow hot. I almost wished he'd never seen that picture I drew so he wouldn't know how I felt.

"It is just for this, right?"

"Yes."

He took my right wrist and placed it above my head before picking up the first set of handcuffs. He wrapped it around my wrist, securing me before he looped the other side around one of the metal poles on his headboard. He took my other wrist and did the same. He didn't make them too tight, but there was no way I could get out.

He moved lower and picked up a silk binding. He secured my ankle in a series of knots before he did the same to the other. He slipped off the bed and knelt by each end. I wasn't quite sure what he'd secured the bindings to, but when I tried to move my legs, I found very little leeway.

He looked down at me with desire evident in his expression.

"Fuck. You're so sexy. Is it okay? Not too tight?"

"It's fine."

Being unable to cover myself or move was disconcerting, but this was Aiden. I'd do anything for him. He said he wanted to give me pleasure. He nodded once before moving around and picking up the blindfold.

"Is that really necessary?" I asked.

"Yes. Being deprived of one of your senses heightens the rest."

I let him put it on. Everything went black instantly. I took several breaths, trying not to panic. This reminded me of the darkness in the cell. I couldn't let that rule me.

Today, Aiden would replace those memories.

"I'll be back," he said, his breath against my ear.

I lay there, the silence enveloping me. The only sound was the clock on the wall outside. Aiden could move silently when he wanted to. I strained to hear anything.

Shifting a little, I wondered just how long he'd be. My skin pebbled in anticipation. What did he have planned? He'd never explained exactly how this would work.

Why hadn't I asked more questions when he showed me the stuff in his box?

Because you were too busy trying to get him to fuck you, that's why.

Thanks, brain. Helpful. Not.

This waiting became torture. My body thrummed. The more I thought about what he was going to do, the wetter I became. Was he doing this on purpose? Making sure I was so worked up, I couldn't say no to what he wanted.

Then I heard it, something clinked in a bowl as it was set down on the bedside table. And his breath dusted across my ear the next moment.

"Are you ready for me?"

"Yes."

"Good girl."

He leant over and kissed me. He tasted so damn good. He was right. My senses were heightened. I could smell cedarwood and pine. Heaven. He fucking smelt like heaven.

All too quickly, he pulled away and I was bereft of his touch. I mewed, unable to keep the sound back.

Betrayal

"So needy already? Mmm, this is going to be sweet. Watching you unravel before my eyes."

I didn't respond. His fingertips ran down my arm, setting my skin alight. He replaced his fingers with his tongue. I bucked against the restraints. Again, he moved away too soon. It became very clear to me, he intended to tease me until I couldn't take it. Did he want me begging? Because I would. I'd beg him to fuck me.

I felt the bed dip and then he straddled my legs. He'd taken off his jeans, but his boxers remained. He leant over me and picked up whatever he'd brought off the bedside table. I heard the clinking again. I didn't have to ask what it was. I felt it the next moment. Fucking ice between my breasts. It sent jolts rippling down my stomach.

"Shit, Aiden, that's cold."

He chuckled. The sound rang in my ears. He dragged it across my skin. I arched up, unable to help myself. The ice left my skin. I tried to breathe, but oxygen wouldn't get in my lungs fast enough. Hell. This was not what I expected him to do.

When I felt the ice again, his breath accompanied it. Fuck, he'd put it between his teeth. This time he circled it around my breast before he sucked the ice into his mouth and latched onto my nipple. The sensation made my nerve endings go haywire. Hot and cold at the same time. I bucked against him. His hand went to my stomach, holding me to the bed.

"Aiden," I moaned. "Fuck."

His response was to switch breasts and it only made it worse. Everything tingled. I couldn't fucking breathe properly.

When he finally pulled away, I panted, my whole body flaming. He shifted lower. I should've known better than to expect him to let up. I didn't know where he'd settled until I felt the ice against my inner thigh, trailing upwards. Then I knew his intentions.

My heart thundered in my ears. All my focus was on what he was doing between my legs. His breath ran across where he'd trailed the ice. I could barely think straight. Cold followed by hot drove me nuts. I shifted, trying to get away from him, but he gripped my leg, holding me in place.

"Mmm, do you want to escape me? Doesn't it feel good?"

"Aiden, please."

"What do you want?"

"You."

He kissed my thigh, trailing upwards until I felt his breath hot against my clit.

"Do you want me here?"

"Yes, please."

I would literally do anything to have him touch my pussy. No one had ever gone down on me. Another first for me.

"Mmm, I don't have to touch you to know how wet you are. I can see. You're drenched and all of it is for me."

For once, I wasn't embarrassed. Aiden had stripped it away from me by depriving me of my sight. He ran a single finger down my clit and across my entrance. I almost cried.

"Do you know what I want to do, Avery?"

"No."

"Bury my tongue in your pussy. Fuck, you're going to taste so sweet. Do you want that? Want me to make you come?"

"Yes. I want you so much. Please, please."

He pressed his hands on my thighs, opening me up wider for him. The restraints pulled on my ankles until I couldn't move. And I didn't want to.

"I know you've never been tied up before, but tell me, has anyone tongue fucked you?"

I had a feeling he'd ask. It seemed to please him knowing he gave me a lot of firsts.

"No."

He growled.

"Fuck, you're killing me. Seriously, how do you expect me to think straight knowing I'm the first in this as well?"

"Did you want me to lie?"

"No, fuck, no. It does things to me. Fuck, I'm so hard, it fucking hurts. You have no idea how sexy you look right now."

My pussy throbbed. If he didn't touch me soon, I'd lose my mind.

"Please, I'm begging you. I'm so turned on, it hurts too."

He groaned, the sound vibrating across my clit. I took a gulping breath, trying to hold onto my sanity. Aiden had me so worked up, it really did fucking hurt, but I knew the sweet relief of him touching me would make it all worthwhile.

"Fuck."

His breath fanned across my clit, followed by his tongue lashing against it. I just about died. The sensation burnt through me, sending a shockwave up my back. I cried out, bucking into his face. His hand immediately pressed down on my stomach, securing me in place.

"Holy fuck, you taste so sweet."

I moaned his name as he continued to pleasure me with his tongue. He licked his way down, making sure he tasted every part of me. I didn't even care when his tongue went lower, meeting puckered skin. All I cared about was Aiden touching me, regardless of where it was.

The fact that it even felt good had me questioning what I was so scared of. Then I remembered how big his cock was. And it really wasn't the time to think about these things. Not when I was so fucking close to coming just from his teasing.

His tongue moved upwards again. He licked my pussy, then his tongue thrust inside, sending me spiralling upwards.

"Aiden, please. Fuck. Fuck."

His thumb brushed over my clit as he continued to fuck me. So close, but his pace was slow. No, he knew and didn't want me to explode just yet. Tease. Such a tease.

"Please, Aiden. I need to come."

I tugged on the handcuffs and felt the metal bite into my skin. I wanted to touch him so badly. My fingers itched to thread in his hair. Fucking hell. This was absolute torture but in the best possible way.

"Fuck, please. I can't take it. This isn't fair. I want you so much. Please."

He didn't respond, but his tongue found my clit again and lashed against it relentlessly, keeping me on the edge. His fingers brushed across my pussy. He slid a finger inside and began to fuck me with it. I wished it was his cock so fucking bad. I needed him inside me. No one felt like him. No one had been so deep and made me feel so full.

"Please fuck me or let me come. Please."

Betrayal

Still no response. He withdrew his finger, running it around my entrance and coating it with my arousal. I wished I knew what was up or down anymore because I would've realised why he was doing it sooner. Perhaps I would've stopped him, but nothing mattered except coming at that point.

He dragged his finger lower until it met my other entrance and he circled it. It registered then.

"Aiden... What... Wait..."

He pressed against me and I couldn't speak any longer. His tongue on my clit felt like fucking fire, but it was nothing compared to the sharp intrusion of his finger. He groaned when my resistance failed and the tip slid in. What the hell? He hadn't even asked me if this was okay. I sucked in a breath.

"What... what... what the... fuck?"

I bucked, trying to dislodge him, but his other hand was firm on my stomach. There was no let up from his tongue on my clit. Fuck. I was on the edge.

His finger thrust deeper inside me and I came. I screamed his name as the waves crashed over me. I barely registered what was happening to me any longer. There was nothing but the sensation of drowning in pleasure. My body shook and clenched around his finger.

Fucking hell. What did he just do to me?

I panted, unable to form words when I finally landed back on earth. Aiden moved back, his hands and tongue leaving me.

For a long moment, all I could hear was the sound of my heart in my ears and my laboured breath. The bed shifted. I heard the clink of a glass being put down on the bedside table and tissues being pulled out of the box.

"Are you pissed off at me for what I just did?" he asked.

I didn't know how to feel about it.

"Not exactly."

"What does that mean?"

"It means you should've asked me first, but I'm kind of glad you didn't because I've never orgasmed like that in my life."

The bed dipped again. Aiden crawled over me. I could feel the heat of him seeping into my skin.

"I'm sorry I didn't ask."

His finger traced my collarbone.

"If you kiss me, I'll forgive you."

I didn't know whether he smiled at that or not, but his lips met mine. It wasn't gentle. He took command of my mouth and I relented. His tongue swept over mine. I hated the fact I couldn't touch him more than this. I wanted to run my hands down his back. I desperately wanted to hold him.

His fingers went to my head, untying the blindfold. I blinked when he took it off me. He gave me a half smile. He was shirtless. Fuck. He was so ripped and his tattoos, so beautiful. I couldn't believe he was real half the time. And he wanted me.

"Do you want me to let you go?"

"Why? What did you have in mind otherwise?"

His grin turned wicked.

"Well, I want to fuck you and normally I would with you all tied up."

"But…?"

"Last night, I let you touch me and I enjoyed it. I don't want to restrain you now."

I raised an eyebrow.

"Are you telling me you don't let anyone touch you during sex?"

"Not very often, no."

What?

He never told me he had an aversion to being touched or was it something else?

"Why not?"

"Control, Avery. If you're tied up, I get to control what you do, but letting someone touch me during sex is unpredictable."

I really wanted to know why control was such a big deal to him, but pushing the subject was never a good idea. We always ended up in an argument when I pushed him.

"I like being able to touch you."

He reached up, unlocking my handcuffs one by one. My arms ached a little from being in that position for so long. He took my wrists and looked at them. There were red marks from where I'd tugged at them. He brought each one to his lips in turn and kissed the marks.

"Does it hurt?"

I shook my head. He moved away and untied my ankles. I sat up and stretched as much as I could. My legs felt a little stiff. How long had he had me tied up for?

He got back on the bed and crawled over me, forcing me on my back again.

"Touch me, Avery."

I reached for him, running my fingers down his chest. He groaned in response, shuddering.

"Fuck, don't stop."

I trailed my fingertips along his sides before curling my hands around his back and dragging my nails down his skin. He jerked, his eyes closing, the appreciation apparent on his face. I didn't stop there. I ran my nails down his arms, followed by his chest. He groaned again. Between us, I could see the tent in his boxers. He hadn't been lying about how hard he was.

Pulling him closer, I turned his head and nibbled on his ear.

"Fuck, Avery."

"Too much?"

"No, no, fucking hell, no. Fuck. I want to be inside you."

I bit down on his earlobe. He jerked again. I reached between us and tugged at his boxers. He helped me take them off. Settling between my legs, his cock jabbed at my entrance. I opened my legs wider. He slid inside me, grunting. I already felt full and he'd barely gotten halfway.

"Fuck me," I whispered.

He gripped my hip and slammed his cock right up to the hilt. I yelped. The pace he began to set was punishing. I held onto his back.

"That's it, take it. Fuck, take my cock."

His pounding almost rattled my teeth. His cock felt so good. Every part of him pressed against me was heavenly. I felt his need, his desire as he fucked without mercy.

He pulled away the next moment. Grabbing me by the waist, he flipped me over and dragged me up on my hands and knees. He slammed his cock back inside me, gripping my hips in an iron hold. Aiden held nothing back. Relentless.

My fingers curled into the covers, anchoring me to the bed. I cried out over and over, unable to keep my mouth shut. Fuck. His brutal pounding brought me almost to the point of pain. I couldn't breathe from the intensity.

"Aiden, I... please. Too much."

He froze. Letting go of one of my hips, he brushed my hair from my face and leant over me.

"Have I hurt you?"

"No, not really."

He kissed my cheek. Capturing my face, he turned it towards him and kissed my mouth.

"The last thing I want is to hurt you."

"I'm not used to sex being so intense. You teased me so much I thought I would lose my mind if you didn't touch me. I can only take so much in one go."

I had to be honest. This was about trust. And he'd stopped even though I hadn't used the safe word.

He kissed my cheek again, his lips trailing down my neck and my shoulder.

"Not so hard then?"

I shook my head. His fingers trailed down my spine. Gentle. Soft.

"Thank you for telling me your limit," he whispered, burying his face in my hair as he breathed me in.

"You can fuck me like that if you don't tease me first."

"Mmm, I'll keep that in mind."

He wrapped an arm around my waist and next thing I knew, we were lying down, his front to my back and his cock still buried inside me. He cupped my breast as he began to fuck me again, but now it was long, drawn out strokes. His face buried in my neck.

"Is this better?" he asked, pinching my nipple between his thumb and finger.

"Ah, yes, fuck."

"So innocent."

His movements increased in pace. My pussy throbbed and clenched around him. He'd have to let me take a break after this. Wasn't quite sure I could take any more sex.

"So tight, so fucking tight, fuck. Being inside you drives me fucking crazy."

Cocooned in Aiden's arms whilst he found his pleasure in me, I felt safe and free. He made me feel beautiful. Wanted. Needed. He moaned my name again and again as if he was lost in me. My heart slammed against my ribcage. *Holy hell.*

"So beautiful. So sweet. Tell me who's you are."

"Yours," I whispered. "All yours."

"Avery, I'm so fucking close."

I thrust back against him. I wanted him to lose it, come inside me.

"You're always telling me to come for you. I want you to come for me. I want to feel it, Aiden."

He grunted, fucking me harder.

"Fuck. Fuck. Avery. Fuck."

He lost it, shuddering against my back as his cock spurted and pulsed inside me. He pressed his forehead into my shoulder, panting.

"You really are like nothing else," he whispered.

I curled my fingers into his hand, resting on my stomach.

"I'm yours forever, Aiden. Don't forget that."

The truth of the matter… I was.

Of all the things which had happened between us, that day stood out the most. In those moments, lying in his arms after the most intense sex of my life, I realised something significant.

I would never leave Aiden no matter what he did. And that was just about the most fucked up I thought I could get.

But I was wrong.

So fucking wrong.

And I would pay dearly for thinking we could ever be normal or happy. Or that we were even in this together.

The truth hurt.

And the lies only killed us further.

Aiden broke us apart piece by piece until there was nothing left.

And I, the stupid girl I was, let him.

Chapter Twenty Two

Aiden

I never thought a single girl could make me lose all sense of rationality and control, but Avery did. Jealousy had taken up permanent residence inside me. And I fucking hated it.

Every fucking time she was on the phone to him, I wanted to punch something. Anything. I knew why. I hated she relied on someone else. Even though she belonged to me, she still had a life outside of us. One she outright refused to let me in on. Their friendship was out of fucking bounds. Fuck. I hated I couldn't say no when she asked for permission to phone him regularly. I hated it all.

When she smiled, laughed, called him a prick. Those things got to me. Avery might be in my bed every night. She might enjoy what I did to her, but she was withdrawing from me. I could fucking feel it. I had to do something about it.

"Why do you look so pissed off?" she asked, sitting next to me on the sofa when she finished her phone call.

"I'm not."

"Aiden…"

She ran a finger down my arm. I tried not to be affected by her touch. Tried and failed.

"It's him, isn't it? Because I refuse to talk about it."

"Just leave it alone."

She leant towards me and kissed my cheek.

"I'm sorry."

Fuck. She had nothing to apologise for really. I was being a dick.

"I said leave it."

She captured my face in her hand. Her lips trailed along my jaw. And I fucking lost it. She couldn't use sex to placate me.

"I'm not in the mood, Avery. Go and sit over there before I fucking make you."

She moved away from me immediately, her eyes flashing with hurt and confusion. It hit me. Avery wasn't withdrawing from me. I kept pushing her away. I ran a hand through my hair.

For fuck's sake, stop being a dick to her.

"Sometimes you make me feel like I'm completely alone."

She looked at her hands.

"Is it so wrong that I want to be close to you? That I want to know you? We sleep in the same bed every night. We have sex, but I'm not really a part of your life. I'm a toy you play with when you're bored or horny. I can't say no because I want you but I don't want to feel like this."

She thought I treated her like a toy. No fucking wonder she sought out her best friend. I was the fucking problem. Not her. I put my hand out to her.

Betrayal

"I want your help with something."

She eyed me with suspicion.

"Did you even hear what I said?"

I nodded. I wasn't about to respond to her outburst since I had no fucking clue what to say. All I knew was I had to fix it and stop making her feel like I only wanted her for sex. I wanted inside her head. I wanted to see her smile. And I fucking adored the way she always had a dimple in her cheek when she was concentrating too hard on her drawings.

"Why am I not surprised you won't say anything?"

"Avery…"

She shuffled over to me but didn't look happy about it. I didn't try to touch her, instead, I turned the laptop towards her. Her eyes fell on the screen. The moment it registered, she looked up at me.

"Why are you looking at artificial Christmas trees?"

"Because it's in three weeks."

"So?"

I rolled my eyes. Hadn't she gotten the hint yet? Perhaps I had to spell it out for her.

"So, I want you to have a proper Christmas since you can't go home."

Her eyebrows shot up.

"You do?"

"Yes."

"Is it just going to be the two of us?"

"Yes."

A smile played on her lips.

"Am I allowed to pick out the decorations?"

I nodded. She curled into my side, resting a hand on my chest.

"Aiden…"

"Hmm?"

I wrapped an arm around her, stroking my fingers down her arm.

"Can we have that one?"

She pointed at one which already had lights built into it.

"We can have whatever one you want."

Twenty minutes later, she'd picked out the tree and silver and blue decorations. None of it fancy or extravagant. She told me she preferred tasteful and understated. The light in her eyes when she'd chosen a silver star to go on top damn near fucking killed me.

"Do you even celebrate Christmas normally?" she asked me.

I shrugged.

"Not since I left the army."

She frowned, shifting ever closer to me as her fingers ran down my chest.

"Am I allowed to get you something?"

I turned to her. Why on earth would she want to do that? Gifts were traditional, but she didn't need to do anything for me. This was for her. Although, there was really no harm in her getting me something.

"If you want to."

She put her hand out. I raised an eyebrow.

"I can't exactly access my own accounts right now."

I rolled my eyes before handing her my credit card which we'd been using to purchase the other bits. She stole the laptop off my lap and sat away from me. I watched her fiddle with it and gave her the flat address when she asked for it.

"What are you planning?" I asked.

"You just have to wait."

"I don't like surprises."

She eyed me for a moment.

"Tough shit."

"Are you sure you want to play that game with me?"

She pouted.

"Don't be such a spoilsport. Why can't you just let me do this and not ask questions? I thought you wanted me to have a proper Christmas."

And that put the discussion to bed. If I pushed, she'd just get upset. The very last thing I wanted.

"Okay. You win. I won't pry."

It made her smile. So fucking radiant. When she was done, she handed the laptop and the card back to me. She'd closed down whatever she'd been doing. I wouldn't try check the internet browser history. I was going to be good for her sake.

I caught her face before she moved away from me and kissed her. She melted into me, her hands curling around my neck. When she pulled away, she rested her forehead against mine.

"Are we going to have a proper dinner and everything?"

"Yes. I'll get it all, don't worry."

"Okay, but I hate sprouts so don't bother with those."

I grinned.

"For the record, I hate them too."

"I knew there was a reason I liked you."

"Is that the only reason?"

"No…"

Her face flushed. I knew exactly what she was thinking. And she thought I had a dirty mind. She'd wound me up about it only last night in bed after I'd listed all the places I wanted to come on her. She hadn't said no.

Now I'd sorted out the bits for Christmas with her, there was something else we needed to get on with. I hoped this would show her I wanted her in my life.

"Do you want to go get dressed? We're going out."

"What?"

"You heard me."

"Why and where?"

"We're going to see someone."

"Who?"

I shook my head, pushing her back.

"No questions."

She frowned but got off the sofa and went into the bedroom. Ten minutes later, she was ready. She braided her dark hair down her back and wore a smattering of makeup. I made her put a hoodie on underneath her jacket.

The drive over was quiet. She stared at the streets passing us by. I should really take her out of the flat more often, but it was too dangerous. She could get recognised and then we'd be in the shit.

When I parked up, I made her flip up the hood. Her scarf covered half her face.

"Is this really necessary?" she mumbled.

"Yes, come on."

Betrayal

I took her hand when she got out the car after me. We walked up the street until we came to the right house. I pulled her up the steps and pressed on the doorbell.

A few minutes later, it opened revealing one of the only people in my life who knew everything there was to know about me.

"Well, I was wondering when you'd finally make an appearance," Tina said with a smile.

Her blonde hair was greying and her blue eyes shone with age, but she was still beautiful. She stepped back, allowing us both in. Avery's hand shook in mine.

Tina shut the door and I gave her a kiss on the cheek. Turning to Avery, I flipped down her hood and unwrapped her scarf for her. She looked nervous.

Tina's eyebrows were raised when I looked at her again.

"I'm sure you know who this is."

"Yes."

"Avery, this is Tina."

Avery looked between us, confusion evident in her expression. Tina smiled at her.

"Aiden, don't just leave the poor girl hanging. Honestly, I thought I taught you better." She turned to Avery. "I take it he hasn't told you anything about me."

Avery shook her head.

"I was Aiden's nanny and after what happened, I raised him. Although fat good that did. Grown up to be temperamental and sullen. Don't even get me started on all those tattoos."

Avery bit her lip. I knew she wanted to smile.

"He's not so bad," she said.

"No? Well, perhaps he's improved in the past couple of months. I hope you have a good excuse for not visiting sooner."

I shook my head, smiling at her.

"Come in then."

I helped Avery out of her jacket and took mine off, hanging them up on the hook by the door before taking her into Tina's living room. I got her settled on the sofa. She looked around. Her fingers fidgeted in her lap.

"Would you like a drink, Avery?" Tina asked.

"Um, tea please."

Tina eyed her for a moment before going over to the bookcase and picking up something I recognised. She placed it in Avery's lap. I was about to object when Tina gave me a sharp look.

"I'm going to have a word with Aiden. Why don't you flip through this?"

Avery fingered the photo album for a moment before opening it up. There were pictures of me from when I was a kid right up until recently. Tina was, for all intents and purposes, my parent. She was there when I'd gone through my exams and got my A-Level results. She'd come to my passing out parade when I'd joined the army. She meant the world to me and I to her. Tina would never replace my mother, but she'd been the only constant in my life since I was five years old.

"We'll be a few minutes," Tina said.

I followed her into the kitchen, knowing I wouldn't get out of this. I leant up against the counter whilst she filled the kettle.

"After the news broke, I knew you'd taken her. What were you thinking?"

Tina helped me devise the plan to take down Mitchell and Kathleen. She knew the hows and whys.

"I had no choice. She saw everything."

"Aiden, I told you to be careful."

I had been up until I reached their kitchen. Then I'd seen red and nothing else mattered but destroying them.

"Too late for that now."

I couldn't take back anything I'd done. Especially not to Avery.

"You care about her."

I crossed my arms over my chest. Fucking hated how well Tina read me.

"So what if I do?"

"You do remember what her family has done."

All too fucking well. Could never forget it. And neither would Tina.

"She's not a part of it."

She sighed, taking out three mugs from the cupboard.

"Except you've made her a part of it now, haven't you?"

"Are you going to tell me she doesn't deserve the truth?"

Even though it had fucked her up, I didn't regret telling her. What I still had left to tell her was another matter entirely. As difficult as the previous conversations had been. The ones to come were worse. So much fucking worse.

"Do you think this will end well, Aiden? I know you. Your plans have changed because of her."

My future plans, yes. Changed, adapted and expanded upon. And I wasn't going to involve Tina further. She deserved a quiet life without the Daniels on her case.

"Nothing ever ends well for me."

My life had been one shitshow after another.

She eyed me closely. Then she gave me a knowing smile.

"You're in love with her."

My heart fucking stopped. *What the fuck?* No, I wasn't. I felt things for her, but love didn't exist for me. Not romantic love. I loved Tina and Ben because they were my family. Otherwise, that fucking emotion could get fucked.

"Don't be ridiculous."

"I see you're in denial."

"I am not in love with her."

"But you are sleeping with her."

And now I just wanted to bash my head against the wall. As much as I cared for Tina, she was a certifiable busybody who'd only got worse with age.

"Are you done?"

"Not even close. Does she know what you intend to do?"

"No."

Her expression soured.

"I suggest you don't leave the poor girl in the dark much longer if you want to keep her by your side."

"You need to stay out of it."

She poured the water into the mugs. I didn't need Tina reminding me of a future I could never have. I didn't fucking deserve it. Avery was mine. Would always be mine. But eventually, I'd have to let her go. She needed more than me.

"Why did you bring her here then?"

Betrayal

"You're my family."

"And yet you won't admit you have feelings for her."

What did she want from me? Avery and I were complicated.

"I never said… Okay, fine, you win. I like her."

She smiled. I had to give her that.

"You've never brought a girl to see me."

None of them meant anything to me before. Not until her. I rubbed the back of my neck.

"She told me she feels like I don't let her in, that she's just a toy to me."

She raised an eyebrow, her expression amused.

"Do you treat her like she is one?"

"No. She's different. I'm trying but I keep upsetting her or hurting her or making her angry. I'm not good at this stuff. You know that."

She put a hand on my arm, giving it a squeeze.

"She's young, Aiden. Be gentle with her. Show her you care. You know how. Don't tell me you've forgotten everything I taught you."

"No."

"Then you know what to do. How to fix it."

She handed me two mugs and shooed me out of the kitchen.

Avery was running her fingers over a photo of me when I walked in the living room. I set the two mugs on the coffee table before sitting down next to her.

"Is that your tattoo artist?"

She pointed at a photo of me and Ben from our army days. His green eyes peered back at me. Reminding me it'd been too long.

"Yes, that's Ben."

I wrapped an arm around her and kissed the top of her head. She tried to pull away.

"Aiden, what if—?"

"She knows."

"Did you tell her?"

I laughed. I didn't have to. Tina knew me like the back of her hand. I was in no doubt the second she saw I had a girl with me, she knew that girl had to be important. Not wrong. Avery was the most important girl in my life.

I'd try to do what Tina told me to. Try to show Avery I cared, that she meant something to me.

"I've never brought anyone to meet her other than Ben and his wife. She guessed."

She turned to me, eyes wide.

"What, never?"

"No. Do you still think you're my toy now?"

She flushed, looking at her fingers.

"No," she mumbled.

I leant into her, nuzzling her neck and breathing her in.

"Good. You belong to me. I need you. I want you. I'm going to fuck you up against the wall in the shower later. I can't get the thought of it out my head."

She wriggled in my grasp.

"Aiden, that's not fair."

"Don't tell me you haven't been imagining it too?"

Betrayal

A cough interrupted both of us. I pulled away but kept my arm around her waist. Tina gave me a knowing smile before sitting down across from us. Avery pressed her hands to her burning cheeks. I picked up a mug and handed it to her.

"So, since Aiden is notoriously cagey about everything, why don't you tell me about yourself?" Tina said.

Avery took a gulp of tea.

"Um, well… I…"

"Why don't you tell her about your art?" I said.

"Oh. I like to draw. In my flat, I have a studio where I paint as well. I lived alone until well…"

"Until he took you," Tina finished for her. "Don't worry, I'm aware of your circumstances. Have you drawn Aiden?"

Avery eyed me for a moment.

"Um… yes. Although someone took my drawing and hasn't given it back yet."

"Now I'm intrigued."

My hand around Avery tightened. I still had it pinned up on the board in my office.

"She drew me with wings, Tina. Wings and a gun," I said.

And it still fucking killed me every time I looked at it. Avery had always seen me as something I wasn't. I wanted to be that person for her, but I was incapable of it.

"It was stupid. I told you that," Avery muttered.

"You're not some amateur, Avery. You've got skill."

"I'd love to see some of your drawings one day," Tina said.

"She can bring some next time."

Avery nodded, sipping her tea. She smiled at me. I wanted Tina to like her despite her family. Avery was the fucking brightest star in the sky. And if I could, I'd hold her close and never let go.

But that was never an option for the two of us. Not with my plans. Ones I was aware I'd have to tell her about sooner rather than later. I hated myself for it. Fucking hated every part of it.

Avery wouldn't forgive me. I wasn't even sure she'd agree at this point. She cared about me. Told me she'd fight for me. Help me destroy her family. What she didn't know is I wanted to take down more than just the Daniels. I was going to burn their empire to the ground and everyone involved. That meant going up against worse foes than just Chuck. So much fucking worse.

And I was about to throw Avery right in the middle of the lion's den.

Come the new year, everything would change.

And this thing between the two of us might just be lost forever.

The thing I refused to admit or acknowledge.

Avery Daniels had something of mine and I had something of hers.

If she left me when I told her the truth, I'd fucking break.

I let her have power over me.

And the day I realised that was the beginning of the end.

Chapter Twenty Three

Avery

Aiden taking me to meet someone he considered family was a big deal to me. It showed me I was someone to him. I hadn't really meant to tell him I felt like I was his toy. It just came out. My usual filter was wearing thin. My nerves fraying as I tried to work out what the hell he wanted me to do for him. He'd told me I'd hate him for it numerous times. There were things I hated about Aiden, but there were things I adored too. He was complicated. I didn't want to change him. I wanted to make him happy. The deep-seated unhappiness inside him killed me. My heart bled for his. My stupid heart.

I lay staring at the ceiling in the darkness. Aiden lay next to me, his arm draped across my stomach. When I brushed the hair from his face, he didn't stir.

It'd been a week since we'd gone to see Tina. All of the Christmas stuff arrived a few days ago. We'd spent a couple of hours decorating the living room together. I couldn't reach the top of the tree, so Aiden had helped me. I knew we weren't together, but it felt like we were a couple in those moments. I wasn't going to kid myself into thinking I'd ever be Aiden's girlfriend. A part of me craved it. The other part was realistic. I was just the girl he fucked because neither of us could stay away from each other.

There was no way I was getting to sleep with all this shit running through my head. I carefully moved Aiden's arm from my stomach, checking to make sure he hadn't woken up before I slipped out of bed and padded out into the living room. The Christmas tree lights twinkled. We'd set it up by the window.

I nabbed my hoodie off the sofa and shoved it on. It was a little chilly. In its pocket was the burner phone Aiden had given me so I could speak to James.

James.

I hated all the lies I'd fed him. It bothered me so much. I just wanted to strip them all away so we could go back to how we were before this happened. I checked the time. One in the morning. Would he still be awake?

I curled up in Aiden's old leather armchair by the window, tugging the blanket I'd left there over my legs. I dialled James' number.

"Hey Ave, bit late, isn't it?" James said after he answered on the first ring.

"You're still awake."

"What's up?"

I fiddled with the tassels on the end of the blanket.

"There's some things I haven't been honest with you about."

"I gathered, but I didn't want to push you with everything that's happened."

Not surprising. He always knew when I kept things from him. James and I knew just about everything there was to know about each other.

"It's about Aiden… and me."

"So there is something going on."

"It's not what you think. It's not like we're together or anything."

"No? So he's just fucking you? I fucking knew he'd taken advantage of you."

The frustration in his voice was evident. How the hell was I going to explain this without going into detail about how we actually met? And whilst Aiden had done some fucked up shit to me, I'd wanted him. I'd pushed so hard, he couldn't keep saying no.

"Don't put this on him. He said no to me for weeks."

"Wait a sec, are you telling me you went after him? Seriously? That's not like you."

"It's complicated, but sort of."

I shifted on the armchair. I'd known this would be a difficult conversation, but things needed to be said and I need my best friend to understand.

"Why are you being honest with me about this now?"

"Aiden can never know we've slept together."

"Well, I wasn't exactly going to going to come over with a banner saying 'I've had sex with Avery'."

"Ha-bloody-ha."

Trust him to make light of it.

"Can I ask why not?"

"I don't want him to hurt you."

"Why the fuck would he do that?"

"You must've noticed he's not exactly a sunshine and roses kind of guy."

He snorted. Aiden was dangerous and that danger excited me on some level. Not to mention he considered me his. Anyone else touching me would be a complete no-no. Aiden wouldn't hesitate to kill them. I'd seen the efficient way he'd killed my parents without remorse.

"Really? Can't think why… not like the whole boxing bag, seriously insane muscles and tattoos gave it away or anything."

I stifled a laugh.

"Were you checking him out?"

"What? No. Fuck off. I was trying to work out what you see in him. Not exactly your usual type."

He wasn't wrong. I couldn't explain it. Aiden's soul called to mine. The connection we shared made no sense. I shouldn't want a man so fucked up and broken and he shouldn't want the girl whose family killed his. And I was trying to ignore the glaringly obvious feelings we had for each other.

One day I'd stop lying to myself.

One day he'd admit to having them too.

"I have a type?"

"Yes, nerds."

"Are you calling yourself a nerd?"

"Again, fuck off."

I grinned.

"I just like Aiden, okay? I feel… free when I'm with him."

"If you like him so much, why are you keeping secrets from him?"

Betrayal

He kept more than enough from me.

"Some things should be left in the past, James. It's what we needed at the time and you've got other ways to cope now. We promised each other we'd never let it ruin our friendship."

"You're right. I'm sorry. I won't tell him. You can trust me. Anyway, as much as I love talking to you, I'm fucking tired."

"I'll let you go."

"Love you."

He hung up. I wasn't going to be able to sleep. Even though I'd sort of cleared the air with James, there were other things bothering me.

I got up from the armchair and walked over to where I'd covered the stuff I'd got for Aiden. I pulled away the sheet and there lay a canvas along with paints. He might not like surprises, but it wouldn't be Christmas if I didn't do something for him. He liked my art. It was the first thing which came to mind when I thought about what to get for him.

I set the canvas against the window. I didn't have my easel, but this would do. I picked up a pencil and began sketching out the initial design. By the time I was done, my hand ached a little, but I was happy with my progress. I could start painting next.

I checked the phone. It was three in the morning. I tucked the canvas back where it'd been with the sheet over it.

When I turned around, Aiden was standing in the doorway in just his boxers watching me. I'd never get over how beautiful he was. His tattoos, everything about him.

"How long have you been there?" I asked.

"Don't worry, I didn't see it."

I walked over to him, wrapping my arms around his back and pressing my face to his chest. He stroked my hair.

"I couldn't sleep."

"You should've woken me up."

"You looked peaceful. Didn't want to disturb you. Besides, I know what your idea of helping me sleep would've been."

"Are you saying you wouldn't have liked it?"

I shook my head. He knew I wouldn't say no to a workout session with him even though he'd more than satisfied me earlier in the day.

"No. This just gave me a chance to work on something without you peering over my shoulder."

"Is that something for me?"

"Maybe."

He leant down and nibbled my ear.

"I still don't like surprises."

"You'll like this one."

He spun us around and pressed me up against the wall. His mouth found my ear again.

"What I'd like right now is my cock in your tight pussy."

And just like that, Aiden made me ache and grow wet with one sentence. I clenched my thighs together, heat pooling in my core. His fingers went to my shorts, tugging them down along with my underwear. He bit down on my earlobe when he pressed a hand between my legs.

"Always ready for me. You make me fucking crazy. All I can think about is you. How much I want you. Need you. Fuck."

"Need me?"

"Yes, I fucking need you. You're mine."

He plunged two fingers inside me without warning. I cried out, hands clutching at his waist.

"Don't you get it by now, Avery? Don't you know how I feel?"

How he felt? He'd barely told me anything about his feelings other than his innate desire to stick his cock in me. Aiden was very vocal about that part. About all the ways he wanted to fuck me. But his real feelings? He was silent on those.

"No, I don't."

He pulled me away from the wall and walked backwards towards the sofa, tugging off his boxers in the process. He sat down and stared up at me.

"Sit on my cock."

I straddled him and sunk down on his length, inch by inch. He grunted, tugging off my hoodie and t-shirt and running his fingers over my breasts. He leant down and sucked a nipple into his mouth. I gripped his shoulders, stifling a moan. He held my hips, encouraging me to ride him.

"So fucking beautiful. So fucking tight. So fucking perfect."

I stared down at him. His eyes were full of heat.

"Tell me how you feel," I whispered.

I was desperate to know now. Desperate to have confirmation it wasn't just me. He reached up, holding my face in his hand as he ran his thumb across my lips.

"You're my sun. You fucking glow like a beacon. Whenever you're not with me, I'm fucking lost. I hate fighting with you, upsetting you. When I hurt you, it hurts me too. None of this makes any fucking sense, but I don't care. I need you. Promise me you won't leave. Promise me you'll stay right here where you belong."

My heart threatened to burst out of my chest. My nails dug into his shoulders. I read between the lines. I knew what he was trying to tell me but couldn't. I knew because I damn well felt the same thing.

"I promise I won't leave you."

How could I leave when he had all of me? He held my entire life in the palm of his hands. He owned me.

I rode him harder, needing fall deeper into this fucked up pit of insanity I was in with him. He grunted, his fingers digging into my hips.

"Fuck, that's it. Fuck me, Avery."

I groaned, throwing my head back as one of his hands snaked between my legs and his fingers brushed over my clit. This was the part I couldn't explain to James. The insane chemistry and connection between Aiden and me. We burnt for each other. Craved each other. I was about ready to throw away my entire life just so I could be by his side. Be what he needed me to be. His.

How the fuck did I end up feeling this way about the man who'd murdered my parents in cold blood?

The honest truth.

I'd already forgiven Aiden for doing it. I understood. My dad wasn't a good person. I had no clue why he'd taken away my mother too, but some part of me knew there was a good reason. No matter how much it hurt, Aiden soothed away the pain. Every time he was inside me, I forgot about the shit in my life. I forgot my family were evil and corrupt.

Betrayal

I leant down, pressing my face into his neck. He thrust back, matching my movements.

"I'd do anything for you," I whispered. "Not just because I'm yours. I want to."

My fingers threaded into his hair.

"And I forgive you for what happened that night. It doesn't matter why you did it any more. All I care about is you and me. Promise you won't leave me either."

His fingers brushed over my clit faster. I cried out into his neck as shockwaves radiated from my core. I came apart in his arms, just as I always did when he was inside me.

When my trembling subsided, he picked me up and carried me into the bedroom. He got on the bed and lay me down, whilst still remaining inside me. He gripped my hip and thrust into me, over and over.

"I promise," he whispered against my neck. "I fucking promise."

Aiden came and came fucking hard. He moaned my name, pressing his cock so deep, it almost hurt. I could feel each pulse and spasm radiate through me.

And then he collapsed on top of me, pinning me down on the bed with his weight. I lay there for several moments until it became harder to breathe. I pushed at his shoulder.

"You're squishing me," I squeaked.

He grunted before rolling off me, throwing his arm across his face. I slipped from the bed and went into the bathroom. I didn't linger when I was done, hurrying back to the bedroom. Aiden hadn't moved. I curled up against his side, running my fingers across his chest.

"Did I wear you out?" I whispered.

I looked over at the clock blinking on the bedside table. An hour had passed. It wasn't the first time we'd had sex in the middle of the night.

"What happened between you and Chuck?"

I froze. Where the hell had that question come from?

"Um, what? Is that really what you're going to ask me right after we've just fucked?"

He lowered his arm from his face. His grey eyes glinted, his expression serious.

"Yes and if you don't answer me, I'm going to fuck you again until you do."

"What kind of threat is that?"

"Just tell me, Avery."

His fingers threaded in my hair, massaging my scalp. I looked down at his chest. I didn't want to talk about my uncle. Especially not that incident. The one that made me hate him for life.

"Why? What difference does it make?"

"It makes a fucking difference to me."

I guessed my time avoiding this conversation was up. The only person who knew this story was James other than the people who'd been there.

I traced the lines of one his tattoos.

"When I was twelve, he came into my room one day. I think he might have been drinking. Started asking me all sorts of weird questions. Like had I ever kissed a boy and what I knew about things adults got up to. For the record, my first kiss didn't happen until I was sixteen."

Aiden's fingers tightened in my hair.

Betrayal

"He told me I was very pretty and that one day I'd grow up to be just like my mum. Which was stupid because I don't really look like her."

I felt funny telling Aiden this story. I knew he didn't like my uncle even though he worked for him. This was only going to make it worse. Charlie had done the one thing I never expected him to and I would never forget it.

"He sat next to me on my bed, wrapped one arm around me and put his hand on my thigh. I didn't think anything of it until he nuzzled my neck. He told me I was old enough to understand now. It's not like I didn't know what went on between adults, it's just I never thought my uncle wanted that from me. When he tried to touch me between my legs, I shoved him away from me."

I'd known then what my uncle was trying to do. And it sickened me.

"Except he was a lot stronger than me. He pushed me down on the bed and pinned me there. Before he could push my dress up, I did the only thing I could. I kicked him in the balls. He got off me pretty quickly. I ran straight to my dad. From that day on, he was never allowed to be alone with me. I don't know what my dad did or said. It never got spoken about again. All I know is my uncle likes little girls because he stopped looking at me that way after I went through puberty."

Aiden didn't say anything at all for several long moments. When I looked at his free hand, his fist was clenched. Tension and anger radiated off him, seeping into me.

"I'm going to kill that sick motherfucker. I'm going to do it slow so he's in agony the entire time."

I'd never heard Aiden speak with such venom, hatred and conviction. And the weird part? I wasn't even upset about him wanting to kill my uncle. A part of me was glad he was going to take away Charlie's life. The fact is, he'd tried to act out his sick obsession with kids with me and that was unforgivable.

Aiden sat up abruptly. My hand fell into his lap.

"You were just a fucking kid. Sick motherfucking cunt. I knew he had issues, but you're his niece. Fuck. How could he fucking try that shit with you? He is a fucking dead man."

I retracted my hand from his lap and placed it on his arm. It wasn't so much I was surprised by his reaction. Aiden was a little overprotective when it came to me. It was the way his expression darkened and his eyes hardened to steel when he said he was going to kill Charlie. I knew that expression. It was the same one he'd worn when he'd killed my parents. Cold, calculating Aiden terrified me to my very core. I wanted the Aiden who looked at me like he was drowning in me when we fucked back.

"Hey, Aiden, I know you're mad, but you're scaring me."

He looked down at me, his eyes softening immediately. He lay back down and pulled me into his arms.

"I'm never going to let anyone touch you or hurt you again. You understand? No matter what I ask you to do, I won't let them hurt you. I'll keep you safe. You'll only be safe with me."

"I know."

I just wished Aiden had kept me safe from himself.

Chapter Twenty Four

Aiden

The buzzer for the door went. I picked myself up off my office chair and stalked out, locking the door behind me. Avery told me to stay out the living room as she was painting. It was only a few days till Christmas now. I'd been good and not looked at what she was doing for me. I wanted to know, but in order to make her happy, I kept away.

Fuck knew who was at the door. I walked over to the intercom camera and froze. What the actual fuck? This could not be fucking happening. Standing there was a police officer and a woman in plain clothes. A detective. Fuck. Why the hell were the police at my door? This didn't fucking bode well. I had to act now. No fucking doubt they'd want to come up to speak to me.

"Avery, I'm going to need you to put all your shit in the cell, right fucking now," I called.

"Why?" she called back.

"Because the police are here."

The buzzer went again.

"What? Why?"

"I'm going to find out. Just do as I said."

She appeared in the doorway of the living room, eyes wide. I pointed at the cell door. She nodded and disappeared. Putting her back in there killed me, but it was the only place she'd be safe from them. The only way I could hide her.

I pressed down on the buzzer.

"Hello."

"Mr Lockhart? My name is Detective Reynolds and this is PC Yeoman. Might we have a few moments of your time?"

"What is this about?"

"It would be better if we came inside, Mr Lockhart."

"And I would rather you tell me what you want with me. Isn't that within my rights?"

The detective frowned.

"We have some questions regarding the disappearance of Avery Daniels."

I fucking wanted to punch the wall. Fuck.

"What would I know about her?"

"You work for the Daniels, do you not? We simply want to ask you some questions, but if you would rather we conduct this down the station, then you're welcome to come with us."

I had no choice. No fucking way I was going with them. I couldn't keep her safe then.

"I'll buzz you in."

I pressed down on the button for a moment before turning away from the camera and intercom. Avery had the cell door open and a bundle of stuff in her arms.

"You got everything?" I asked.

Betrayal

"All my art stuff, toiletries from the bathroom and any clothes I left in the living room. I don't think there's anything else other than my stuff in the bedroom."

I wanted to kiss her. She hadn't questioned any of it. She knew.

"Just leave it. I'm not fucking letting them search the place. They need a warrant."

She put the stuff down in the cell and turned to me.

"You want me to stay in here, don't you?"

I approached her, curling my hands around her waist.

"I'm sorry to ask it of you."

"I'll be okay, Aiden. I promise. You fixed it when you blindfolded me. I'm not scared of the dark anymore."

I leant down and kissed her. Tasting her lips made my cock twitch. Fuck. No. Really didn't need a reminder of how much I needed to be inside her. How much I worshipped her body. How fucking perfect she was.

"They want to ask me about you. I don't fucking know why, but whatever it is, I'll deal with it."

She ran a hand over my cheek and smiled. The last week had been too fucking perfect between us. This shit wouldn't change that. I had to give her a perfect Christmas before I told her what I planned to do.

"I know you will."

She walked into the cell. The light was on and I'd leave it that way for her. I shut the door but didn't lock it. Next, I pulled out the hidden panel and secured it in front of the door. Unless you looked closely, you wouldn't be able to tell there was something behind the wall.

The bell for the door rang. I walked over and opened it.

"Please come in," I said, stepping back.

The detective and the officer walked in. I pointed down the hall towards the living room. I shut the door and followed them. I indicated they could sit down. Reynolds took a seat but the officer remained standing. I sat on the sofa and turned to the detective.

"So, you want to ask me about the missing Daniels girl?"

"Yes," she replied. "Have you met Miss Daniels?"

"No."

That was easy enough. It wouldn't be the end of it. Something in her eyes told me she was suspicious of me. I didn't have my tattoos on show so who knew why she'd already made up her mind about me.

"How long have you worked for the Daniels?"

"About four years."

Reynolds cocked her head to the side.

"Is it not the case that you've known them for most of your life? I am aware your mother's missing persons case was never solved."

She's dead. It'll never be solved.

I tried not to clench my fists. Fucking police bringing that shit up. I bet she thought I was directly involved in all the shit going on.

"Looked me up, did you?"

She didn't flinch. Where the fuck was this line of questioning going?

"You've known the family for your whole life, worked for them for four years and you've never met Miss Daniels."

I shrugged.

Betrayal

"I'm not a family friend if that's what you're getting at. I do their security. That's it."

She leant back in her seat.

"Care to explain why we had an anonymous tip placing you with a woman matching Miss Daniels' description on the 4th December?"

That's when we'd gone to see Tina. Fuck.

"I was out with a friend."

"She was seen getting into your car. Care to tell me who it was if not Miss Daniels?"

I'd need to pull in a favour to deal with this shit.

"Skye Andrews. Married to my best friend, Ben. You're welcome to ask her. I'm sure she'll clear up this little misunderstanding."

Fucking lucky Skye looked a little like Avery with dark hair. Or I'd be absolutely fucked.

Reynolds looked put out for a moment. I'm sure she hadn't been expecting me to have an immediate answer. I smiled at her.

"I see. Well, I'm sure you understand why we are required to follow up on matters such as these."

"Yes."

Reynolds stood up.

"If you'd be happy to provide me with Mrs Andrews details, I would like to verify this information before I put this to bed."

Happy to? No. I would just to get them off my case. I needed to get in touch with Ben and Tina, but not by normal means. Didn't need them tracing that crap.

I pulled out my phone, picked up some paper and pen from the coffee table and wrote down Skye's details for them.

"Well, thank you for your time, Mr Lockhart. We can see ourselves out."

I got up.

"No need. I'll show you out."

No fucking way I was letting them do any snooping. The sooner they left, the fucking better. I led them to the front door and nodded when they left. Slamming it shut, I strode to my office, unlocked it and rummaged through my drawer. I sent a message to Ben and one to Tina via another burner phone.

It rang two minutes later.

"Mate, how you been?" Ben said.

"Good. How are you, Skye and the bump?"

"All good here. Baby is due in a few months. You should come see us. I still need to touch up that fucking girly phrase on your arm."

The tattoo Avery had first asked about. My latest. I'd see him to deal with it soon.

"Listen, I need a favour. If the cops ring Skye, I need her to say she was with me when I went to see Tina on the 4th of December."

"What shit have you got yourself into this time?"

"They think I have something to do with that missing girl."

"Your employer's daughter? I saw that shit on the news. Why the fuck would you know about it?"

I wanted Ben to meet Avery. He wouldn't fucking say anything to the cops. Ben and I trusted each other with our lives. Brothers in fucking arms.

Betrayal

"Because it was her with me when I went to see Tina, but they don't need to know that. Some prick tipped them off."

"Aiden, what the fuck?"

"I know, but she needed help. The chick was messed up as fuck after the shit with her parents."

"Why the fuck would she have gone to you? Not exactly gentlemen or therapist of the year."

Ben knew me all too well. Except I'd sort of fucked away her pain with my cock. Least she kept telling me whenever we had sex, she felt free. Free from the burden of her family.

Shit, I'd left her in the cell. I walked out of the office, shutting the door and locking it behind me.

"She didn't. I found her. It's a fucking long story."

"Always getting yourself into shit. And for a girl? Don't tell me you've gone fucking soft."

"Says the shithead who got married and has a baby on the way."

"Prick."

I pulled back the panel.

"Listen, I'm sorry I haven't been in touch."

"Yeah, yeah. Just text me the regular way when you're free. I'll make sure Skye covers for you."

"Thanks."

"Anytime dickhead."

He hung up. There was a missed call from Tina. I texted her again to let her know I was done with Ben. I opened the door of the cell just as the phone rang.

"What's wrong?" Tina said.

"Some prick tipped off the cops that Avery was with me when I saw you. If they talk to you at all, tell them it was Skye. I have to go."

"I will. And Aiden, stay safe, okay?"

"Sure."

I hung up. Avery turned and smiled at me.

"I finished it."

"Finished what?"

"Your gift."

She walked out and wrapped her arms around my back. I didn't look in the cell. I buried my face in her hair. Fuck. I was so relieved she was okay.

"What did the police want?"

"Had a tip-off you were with me at Tina's, but I sorted it. Don't worry."

"Saving me from the big bad police officers hunting me down?"

I chuckled.

"Something like that."

"Do you have a story ready for them when I do finally make it back into the real world?"

Not quite yet. I'd work it out soon.

"I will when it's time."

She stepped back from me.

"I'm going to ring James. I'll clean up afterwards, just don't go snooping."

She went up on her tiptoes and kissed my cheek.

"Snooping? Me?"

"Yes, you. You said you'd let me do this. It's only a few more days."

Betrayal

I smiled and tucked a stray hair behind her ear.

"Okay, but later, you're going to make up for it for all this waiting."

"How exactly?"

"By letting me cuff you to the bed."

She bit her lip before running her fingers across my chest.

"I'll make sure to wear something nice for you then."

My cock twitched. I'd bought her all sorts of underwear, but I not asked her to wear any of the more revealing sets. I leant down and brushed my lips over her ear.

"Now you're just teasing me."

She ducked away and hurried down the hall.

"Patience, Aiden."

Fuck patience. I stalked after her. I caught her hand before she could escape into the living room. I tugged her back and pressed her into the wall. She stared up at me with a raised eyebrow.

"Don't you know anticipation only makes it sweeter?" she asked.

"You know what is driving me fucking crazy?"

"No, what?"

"Every time you walk away from me, I can't take my eyes off you."

Her brow furrowed in the cutest fucking way.

"Why?"

I brushed my hands down her sides and curled my hands around her behind.

"Because I want this. I want to touch you here."

"Aiden…"

"Did I say fuck? No. I won't unless you agree to it, but I want you to let me touch you here. I know you liked it when I did last time."

A flush crept up her neck.

"I… I want to let you fuck me there, but I'm scared."

She looked down at our feet.

"The thought of you taking the last bit of my virginity. It… feels sort of right. I want to, Aiden."

I couldn't speak for a long moment. I hadn't meant to pressure her. I'd tried not to bring it up, but I wanted her there, so fucking much.

"Are you sure?"

"How can I be sure of something I have no experience in?"

I took her hand, pulling her into the bedroom. She shifted nervously on her feet as I left her by the bed. I knelt down and pulled out the box, selecting what I wanted to show her. I set it out on the bed. She stared at the items with curiosity.

"Sit."

She hopped up on the bed. I shifted so I was kneeling before her. I picked up the bottle of lubricant, putting it in her hands.

"You know what this is for, right?"

She turned it over.

"Yes."

I picked up a small plug and handed it to her.

"And this?"

"Yes."

She didn't look nervous. Putting down the bottle of lube, she ran her fingers over the plug.

"And what do you think to using these next time we have sex?"

"You mean you want to put this in me?"

I smiled.

"That's the point of it."

"And do you want to fuck me at the same time?"

My cock couldn't take it. The thought of her having that in her arse whilst I fucked her pussy made it stand to attention.

"Yes. Fuck. Yes, so fucking much."

"This is new, right? Not one you've used with anyone else."

I nodded. I wouldn't do that to her. I always replaced those types of things. It didn't feel right otherwise. She placed it on the bed.

"Then yes, we can use this later. I want to know what it feels like."

Later? I wanted her right fucking now. She'd just agreed to let me play with her arse. Something I'd been so fucking hesitant to wish for. If she liked this, then maybe she'd let me stick my dick up there. I wanted her so fucking much. Her pussy was so tight, but fuck, being in her virgin arse would be like heaven.

"Later?"

"Yes, later. I need to call James and I doubt you want me leaving a mess in the cell even if you never go in there."

All of that shit could wait. All of it. My fingers went to her jeans, unbuttoning them.

"Aiden!"

"No. I want you now. Right fucking now. I want to stick my tongue in your pussy. Don't fucking deny me."

Her eyes were wide, but she didn't stop me when I tugged off her jeans and her knickers. I tugged her hips to the end of the bed, draped her legs over my shoulders and buried my tongue in her pussy. Fuck. She tasted sweet.

"Fuck, Aiden. Oh, oh, fuck."

Her fingers threaded in my hair. I'd make her come now and later, I'd fuck her. After I called Chuck and sorted out the rest of the shit with the police.

I promised myself I'd keep Avery happy until after Christmas. That meant making this shit go away. We'd have a few more days of bliss. A few more days of her being my solace.

A few more days before everything went to hell.

Chapter Twenty Five

Avery

Christmas. The day I'd always spent with my parents. I'd never wake up to the smell of pastries for breakfast again. Never wear ridiculous matching Christmas pyjamas. Never watch my parents smile and cook dinner together.

I shook myself. They were gone. It still hurt. Worse now I had all those perfect memories tarnished by the knowledge of who they'd really been. I had to lock that pain away. That part of my life needed to be let go. I'd always love them, but it wouldn't be the same.

A hand curled around my waist and lips pressed to my shoulder.

"Happy Christmas," a deep voice whispered in my ear.

His voice always had me melting on the spot. Deep, rich and sexy. That was Aiden all over.

"Happy Christmas."

"Shall I give you a gift now or would you like breakfast in bed?"

"Gift?"

His hand slipped below my underwear, brushing over my curls. I whimpered when his fingers met my clit.

"Mmm, my fingers are your gift."

I arched against him as he strummed me. This was one way to wake up on Christmas morning. Aiden was the first man I'd share this day with. And he was already making me forget all about not spending it with my family.

"Today is all about you," he told me. "Feeding you. Making you smile. Making you come over and over again."

"You promised we could watch Christmas films."

He growled in my ear.

"Talk of that isn't permitted when my fingers are on your clit, Avery."

I wanted to laugh but he circled my clit harder. *Shit*. I cried out. His cock dug into my back as he ground against me.

"Aren't you going to fuck me?"

"Don't tempt me."

"Even if I want you to fill me with your cock?"

"For fuck's sake."

He tore my underwear down, pulled his cock out and pressed it inside me.

"I wanted to wait until later and take my time with you, but no, you just have to say such provoking things."

He thrust into me, still circling my clit with his fingers. It didn't take long until we both shuddered in a mutual conclusion.

"I'm going to make you breakfast and start on dinner," he said, kissing my neck.

"Mmm."

Betrayal

He slipped from the bed. I watched him stretch, taking in all his tattooed glory. Definitely the sexiest man I'd ever seen.

"You're so beautiful," I mumbled.

He turned his head.

"I'm what?"

I buried my head under the covers.

"Beautiful."

"You think?"

"I thought you'd tell me off for using a girl term."

He laughed. His deep voice vibrating through me. I peered out at him.

"From you, it's okay. Just don't tell anyone and ruin my image."

"Yeah, okay. Off you go tattooed bad boy, make your lady friend breakfast."

He cocked an eyebrow.

"Bad boy?"

"Yes. You've got that air about you. Making all the ladies want to drop their panties for you."

He shook his head.

"I only want yours dropping for me."

I threw a pillow at him, which he ducked away from and strolled out of the room without putting a shirt on. I hopped out of bed and had a shower.

When I dressed in a plain t-shirt and jeans, I found him in the kitchen, still very much shirtless. I needed to stop looking at him or I'd quite possibly drool all over the kitchen table.

I sat down and he deposited pancakes in front of me. He hadn't made me these since the first day he'd taken me. It seemed like a lifetime ago.

He sat next to me, giving my thigh a squeeze.

"Eat up, princess."

"Is that a new nickname for me?"

"Maybe."

His grey eyes glittered with amusement.

"I like it."

I stuffed my face with as many pancakes as I could. Then I helped him prep the rest of the vegetables for Christmas dinner. It was just the two of us so we didn't need much. Aiden still insisted on having all the trimmings minus the sprouts.

"Tina is coming over tomorrow. We usually spend Boxing Day together," he said. "Leftovers are a must."

I grinned. The turkey was in the oven, the veg ready to go. Now, I could get him to sit down with me and watch a film. I took his hand, dragging him away from the kitchen.

"Are you going to put clothes on today?" I asked.

"Do you want me to?"

I pointed at his chest.

"As much as I like all this, you are rather distracting."

He nudged me with his shoulder.

"Go put on what you want."

He slipped away from me into the bedroom. I went into the living room and stopped dead.

What the...

Aiden had seriously gone all out. Those presents had not been there yesterday when I went to bed. When did he have time to do all this and why?

I walked over to the tree and knelt down, checking one of the labels.

For the light in my darkness. Aiden.

His handwriting was a little messy, but it made me smile.

"I thought we agreed to do those after dinner."

I glanced up at him.

"That was before you decided to go all Christmas crazy on me."

"I told you, I wanted it to be as normal as possible. Besides, some of those are from James, not me."

I stood up before throwing myself into the sofa and grabbing the remote. Aiden sat next to me.

"Are you mad?" he asked.

"No. When did he drop those off?"

"You were asleep very early last night, remember? I wore you out."

I felt my face burning. He really had. We barely left the bedroom yesterday.

"Shh you."

I picked a film and we settled in to watch. He groaned most of the way at how ridiculously over the top cheesy it was and kept leaving to check on dinner. It was almost ready by the time we were done.

We ate so much, both of us could barely move from the kitchen to the living room. I lay on the sofa grumbling with my head in his lap.

"Presents?" he asked.

"Too much effort."

"I'm not a patient man."

And didn't I know it. I dragged myself up and we sat next to each other by the tree. He made me open mine first.

Various art supplies, new trainers and several sets of barely-there underwear which I raised an eyebrow at.

"Is this even considered clothing?" I asked, holding up a very low cut, lacy see-through bra.

"You're going to look sexy in it regardless."

"I see. These are really for your benefit, aren't they?"

He kissed the top of my head.

"Caught red-handed."

James gave me some clothes from his father's new collection, which admittedly I'd been eying up before the shit with my parents had happened. I fired him off a quick text to say thank you.

"Okay, so this is your proper present," Aiden said.

He handed me the present I'd read the label off before. The light in his darkness. I opened it carefully. Inside was a box and in that box lay a silver necklace. Hanging off the chain was the letter A. I put a hand to my mouth. Holy shit. So simple yet it meant the fucking world to me.

Underneath the necklace was a business card. I looked it over. It had an intricate rose design on it which reminded me of Aiden's tattoos.

Ben Andrews. Tattoo artist.

Aiden had written something on the back.

I want you to meet my best friend. And perhaps you'll let him ink you too.

"Do you like it?" he asked.

I nodded, unable to speak. He was letting me in. That was what this meant. He took the necklace from my hand and secured it around my neck. He fingered the A.

"A reminder that you're mine. Now and always."

Betrayal

"Thank you," I whispered.

I put down the box, curled my hand around his neck and kissed him. He'd really made my Christmas perfect. My heart threatened to burst from my chest. Shit. I totally adored this man. Broken parts and all. All of him was perfect to me.

He cupped my face when I pulled away, staring at me intently.

"Can I open mine now?"

I nodded. I'd spent a lot of time perfecting it. I desperately wanted him to like it. I twisted my hands in my lap as he got up and went over to where it was leaning against the window. He turned it over and carefully undid the wrapping paper. I tried not to flinch when he pulled it off and flipped it back around. He set the canvas down on the floor and took a step back.

He said nothing. I couldn't see his expression from where I was sitting.

I'd painted us as angels. Aiden had black wings. He stood before me, cupping my cheek with one hand. I knelt on the floor, my white wings flared out behind me. One of my hands rested on his. It was simple, yet I'd spent forever painting the feathers on our wings. Making sure to get the details just right. I'd even taken the time to try my best to replicate his tattoos as I'd depicted him shirtless.

"Aiden…?"

He knelt down on the floor and reached out, touching my wings. He ran his fingers over them before he traced the outline of his own wings.

"It's…"

I didn't prompt him to continue. My hands shook.

Does he like it?

I couldn't tell. I wished he'd look at me.

"Avery... I don't have any words." His voice was quiet.

I crawled over to him. He wrapped his arm around my shoulder when I drew level with him.

"Do you like it?"

"I love it."

I looked up at him. His eyes shone with admiration.

"You do?"

"I'm going to hang it above the bed."

When he'd told me I was the light in his darkness, I'd known I wanted to paint us this way. I wanted so much for him to understand the depth of my affections. Explaining it in words was impossible.

"You are?"

He turned to me, cupping my face.

"I'm glad you made me promise not to look until it was done. I can't begin to tell you how fucking incredible you are. Shit. Avery... I really don't fucking deserve you at all."

I didn't get a chance to respond. He kissed me. A kiss so deep and heartfelt I could barely breathe. He pressed me down on the floor, covering my body with his own. His fingers curled into my hair, holding me still. My heart thudded in my chest. The relief I felt at him loving my gift overwhelmed me. I needed Aiden. I needed him like air. I couldn't live without him.

"I don't want to hurt you, but I will," he said to me between kisses. "I've never been good at this. Fuck. I wish we could stay like this forever. Just you and me."

He kept telling me he was going to hurt me.

Betrayal

"We can."

"No, we can't."

His words tore at my soul. What the hell was he going to ask me to do? The need to know threatened to consume me. Why couldn't he just let go of all of this shit and be in this with me?

"Why not? I'm yours."

He pressed kisses to my cheeks, my jaw and down my neck.

"I've lied to you. I said I'd protect you. Keep you safe. I can't do any of those things if you do what I'm going to ask of you."

I froze. The room suddenly felt very cold. I couldn't catch my breath. Having him on me was suffocating.

He's admitted he's lied to me. How the fuck can I be okay with that?

"Aiden…"

"Shh, let me have this last moment with you before it all goes to shit."

"No."

He stilled. His lips left my neck.

"No?"

"No. You can't just tell me you've lied to me and then expect me to sleep with you. I'm not letting you kiss or fuck it away, Aiden."

He raised his head from my neck. His eyes were dark.

"Yes, you are."

He took my hands and pinned them to the floor. I struggled in his grip. What the hell was he doing?

"You're going to let me fuck you because you're mine and you will obey me."

There was no way we were having sex now. Not after what he'd just said. I couldn't.

"Get off me. I thought we were supposed to have a nice day without any bullshit. Why did you have to ruin it?"

Tears pricked at my eyes. I wanted so much for him to take those words back. To tell me it was okay. After everything, our promises to each other, this felt like a slap in the face.

"Is everything you've told me a lie? Do you even care, Aiden? Or is this just some kind of game to you? Because I care about you. So tell me if I've been stupid to believe you could ever feel anything for me."

My heart shattered. Aiden's eyes flashed with pain. He let go of my wrists, sitting up on top of my legs.

"You think I don't care?"

His expression told me he did, but I was so confused. I couldn't think straight. I wanted to believe him. So much.

"How the hell am I supposed to know when you just told me you've lied to me?"

"I've never lied about how I feel. Not once."

"Then tell me, do you care?"

His grey eyes flashed with anguish as if my questioning him was physically painful.

"Of course I fucking care. What more do you want from me, Avery? You've taken every fucking ounce of my self-control. I never wanted to feel anything for you, but I do. I feel so fucking much for you. Fuck. You drive me fucking insane. I don't know how to do this. Everything I say and do hurts you further. What more do I have to do? Tell me because I can't keep doing this. I can't. It's fucking hurting me. Every time you cry. Every fucking time I have to watch you break apart. All I want is to make you fucking happy. What do you want from me? Just fucking tell me already."

I want you to love me because I love you.

Chapter Twenty Six

Aiden

Avery stared up at me. Her doe eyes full of tears. Pain. So much fucking pain and heartbreak in her expression. Shit. I hadn't meant to say any of those things. I hadn't meant to do anything to hurt her. Not today of all days. This wasn't a conversation for now. It was a conversation for later, but I'd fucked it up. Just like I fucked up everything else between us.

That fucking painting killed me. It was everything. Every fucking thing. She laid bare our relationship. She was the light. I was the darkness. And she'd submitted to me. Her light was fucking dimming because of me. Fuck. I hated myself. And I hated what I was doing to her.

I'm fucked up. So fucked up.

"I want you to tell me the truth," she said finally.

"The truth?"

"The truth about what the hell it is you want me to do."

My heart stopped. Not today. This wasn't meant to happen today.

"Now? You want to do this now?"

She looked away from me. Her small hands fell on my legs, wrapping around my thighs. She'd never looked so tiny. I didn't fucking deserve this girl. Not at all.

"No, I don't want to, but we have to."

I wasn't ready. I couldn't. I reached down, running my fingers through her hair.

"Why do you have to push me?"

"I don't mean to."

Her fingers dug into my thighs. She turned her head back to me. A tear slipped down her cheek. I brushed it away.

"Please don't cry."

"I don't want to fight you. I hate it. I hate it so much. Please just tell me. Please, can we get this over with? I'm tired of these secrets."

I knew as soon as I uttered those words, she'd either tell me to go fuck myself or worse, actually agree to it. Fuck. She wouldn't let it rest. I knew her well enough now. She'd push me until I gave in. I didn't want this escalating further. It needed to end. I only had one course of action left and no matter how much it killed me, I had to do it.

I leant down, brushing her hair and tucking it behind her ear. Then I whispered in her ear. The more I spoke, the tighter she held me and I felt her break further. I cupped her face, feeling wetness underneath my fingers. She quietly sobbed as I told her exactly what it was I had planned. Every fucking word tore at my soul. I never wanted to ask this of her. I never wanted her to be this involved. And nothing between us would ever be the same again.

Betrayal

When I was done, I pulled back and rested my forehead against hers.

"No," she whispered. "No, no, no, no."

"I'm sorry."

"How can you ask me to do that? How?"

I shook my head. That wasn't something I could answer. Too many fucking reasons. Too much she didn't know or understand.

"Please, please take it back."

"I can't," I whispered, stroking her face.

"Please, Aiden, please. Do you have any idea how that makes me feel? Do I really mean so little to you?"

She meant the fucking world to me. That was the problem. When I'd decided on this plan of action, I didn't know the girl below me at all. She was supposed to be someone I could manipulate and use. Instead, she'd become the girl I couldn't fucking live without. The girl I needed. She'd fix me if I let her. She'd soothe me if I allowed her in. And the fucking worst part was I had. She'd began to heal my fucking broken soul. Just by being her.

"I'm sorry."

"Sorry? I don't want you to be sorry. I want you to take that back and find another way. Don't do this to me, Aiden. Just don't."

If I had another solution, I'd have gone out of my way to work it out. This plan was better than my last one. It meant the end of all the sickening, disgusting things her family had done. And it meant the end of the man who covered it all up. That was why it was so important. That was why I needed her.

"Do you think I want to ask you to do this for me?"

"I don't know. I don't know if I even know who you are any more. I thought I meant something to you, but if I did, then you'd never ask this of me."

Fuck. She was destroying me with every fucking word she said. I could see myself reflected in her eyes. See how sick and twisted I was. See the fucked up man I'd become. The one who couldn't do anything right by this girl. And fuck, if it didn't cleave me in two.

"How can you think you mean nothing? You are the world. My world."

"Am I? Am I really? What happened to you telling me you'd kill anyone who tried anything with me? Huh? Does that still stand now?"

I would fucking destroy them if they tried. They weren't allowed her. No one was. No one except me.

"Yes."

Her doe eyes filled with tears again.

"And yet you still expect me to… No. I won't do it. You don't understand. I already told my father I wouldn't. It was my only stipulation regarding the company. I wanted to be free to make a choice and he fucking agreed. You can't make me do this. I won't."

"Avery…"

She shoved at my chest, but it was a weak, half-hearted attempt.

"Stop. Just stop. I can't. I won't. You know I'd do anything for you. Anything but this. So don't fucking ask me to do it."

I cupped her cheek, running my thumb along her lips. I'd known she'd say no. A part of me always knew. Even if we hadn't ended up like this, she'd never have agreed to it.

Betrayal

"I have to."

"No, you don't."

"I really do."

Tears slipped out over her cheeks again. Fuck. I kissed her. She pushed at my chest again, refusing to respond to me. I didn't care. I needed her. I wanted her to know how much I needed her. Her submission. Even though I'd done the fucking worst thing possible to her, I had a sick need to prove she was still mine. To show her she wouldn't be free of me because I could never be free of her.

"Kiss me, Avery," I whispered before I pressed my lips to hers again.

I held her face in place when she tried to turn away.

"Kiss me."

"No, stop it. I don't want this."

"You do. You want me even though I've hurt you. Let me take away the pain."

She shook her head, more tears spilling from her doe eyes.

"Stop it, Aiden."

"Kiss me."

I pressed my mouth to hers and she did. She kissed me like she was drowning. Her hands threaded in my hair. Her tongue curled around mine, fighting against me for dominance. I wouldn't fucking let her take control. She was mine. I owned her.

I pressed her legs open, settling between them. She ground against me, causing lust to flood my veins. Fuck. I needed to have her. She moaned against my mouth when I cupped her breast, my thumb running over her nipple. I tugged up her t-shirt, needing her skin on mine. I released her mouth so I could pull it over her head. Her hazel brown doe eyes stared back at me with desire and pain.

I unhooked her bra and threw it halfway across the room before I bit down on her nipple. She arched up against me, crying out. Fuck. Such fucking perfect tits. Her fingers went to my t-shirt and I let her take it off me. She dug her nails into my chest, scraping them down my skin. Fuck. She knew that made me crazy.

"I hate you," she whispered.

"I know you do."

I claimed her mouth again and she dug her nails in my back, holding me closer. I tugged at her jeans, unbuttoning them before I tore them off her legs. I didn't even bother taking her underwear off. I ripped it in half, desperate to see her naked beneath me. Fuck. She was so beautiful. So stunning. And I needed in her.

I unbuttoned my own jeans and struggled out of them, freeing my cock from my boxers the next moment. I pressed her legs open and lined myself up against her opening.

"Do you want this, Avery? Do you want my cock?"

"Yes. I want you even though I hate the sight of you right now."

That was enough for me. I pressed inside, feeling her heat encase me inch by inch. Our mouths crashed together again. I pinned her to the floor, thrusting into her without any sort of gentleness or mercy. I made her take all of my cock and she whimpered in my mouth. Fuck. She was so wet. Even when she was angry and hurt, her body responded to mine. Something she could never hide and neither could I. Couldn't hide my need for her. The need to own her. Possess her. To make her understand she'd be mine forever.

"Are you still mine?"

"Yes, I'm still yours. I'll always be yours," she whispered. "Please, fuck me. I need you so much."

I thrust harder. She cried out. Her nails dug into my back. Fuck. She felt so fucking sweet. So fucking tight. I could feel the anger and desire radiating off her. The hurt. The pain. So I fucked her because it's what we both needed. Two lost souls drowning in each other. That's exactly what Avery and I were.

And I'd just fucked everything up between us.

"Aiden, fuck, please. More, give me more."

I gripped her hips, grinding into her harder, faster. Fuck. Too perfect. She was much too perfect for me. Her body fit mine like it was made for me.

"Only me, Avery. You'll only ever want me for the rest of your life. My cock in you. My mouth on you. Me. The only fucking one who gives you what you need."

"I'm yours. Aiden… My heart is yours."

I almost fucking stopped in my tracks, but I was so hellbent on driving us to an explosive climax. Had I fucking heard her right? Who fucking knew because the next moment, she screamed. Her pussy fucking clenched around my cock so hard, it almost hurt. I couldn't hold back. Grunting in her ear, I came too, my cock pulsating and spurting wildly inside her.

We lay there in a sweaty mess together. I couldn't get up. I knew as soon as I did, she'd bolt. She'd run from me. So I kept her there instead. I kissed her and she cried.

"Please don't do what I know you're going to," I whispered.

"I have to. You've hurt me too much."

I knew I had. She could only stand so much pain. I'd already given her too much. By telling her the truth about her family. By wanting her. Needing her. Caring for her. All I'd done was cause her pain even though I'd brought her so much fucking pleasure too.

"Don't break your promise."

She let out a rasping sob. Her hands met my chest and she pushed me.

"Let me go, Aiden. Please."

"No."

"Please."

How the fuck could I keep saying no when she begged me like that? I felt like I was fucking dying inside. This type of pain was unwelcome.

"I don't want you to leave me."

"You don't have a choice."

She was right. I moved, letting her get out from underneath me. She left the room, her chest heaving with every step. And mine fucking burnt. I pulled my boxers and jeans back up, not bothering with my t-shirt. I sat against the wall, running my hands through my hair. Fuck. Everything was utterly fucked.

I had no idea how long it was before she came back. She was dressed. Her shoes were on and a coat and scarf.

"I don't want to do this, but I have to, Aiden. I can't do what you want me to. It's better this way."

I stared at her. Her eyes were bloodshot and her face still wet with tears.

"How is it better, Avery? How is us being apart better?"

"It's better for me because you can't hurt me if I'm not with you."

As if her words couldn't fucking kill me any further, those just about tore my fucking heart to pieces. The stupid fucking useless piece of shit organ I wanted to forget. But she'd made me remember. She'd made me feel and now those feelings threatened to destroy me entirely.

I got up off the floor and strode over to her, taking her face in my hands.

"Don't leave me. You promised."

"You've made me break it, Aiden. This isn't my fault. It's yours. You broke us."

"Let me fix it."

"You can't. You can't just kiss me and fuck me and expect it go away. It doesn't work like that. You've never let me in. That's the problem. You expect me to just obey you and do everything you want. I can't do what you're asking. You have to find another way. But I know you won't. You're leaving me with no choice. I have to go because if I don't, then you'll destroy this entirely. You'll ruin me."

She took my hands from her face and placed them by my sides. Rising up on her tiptoes, she kissed me. She was fucking leaving me on Christmas Day. The one fucking day I promised myself I'd give her without there being any shit between us.

I'd broken everything.

She was right.

I broke us.

And I really fucking died inside.

She wrapped her arms around my neck and brought her lips to my ear.

"I'm sorry. Please believe me when I tell you I don't want to do this. I don't want to leave you. The stupid fucked up part about all of this is I thought I'd found the one person in this world who made me feel complete. I thought we'd get through everything. I believed in you. I trusted you. And the stupid girl I am fell in love with you. I love you. I love you so much it hurts."

She let go, not meeting my eyes.

"Goodbye, Aiden."

And then she fucking walked away. My heart fractured entirely. She loved me. Avery loved me. I couldn't comprehend it. Why the hell would a girl like her fall in love with a man like me?

I wanted to chase after her, but my feet stayed stuck to the floor.

She opened the front door of my flat and walked out, not looking back at me.

And I fucking let her go.

This hurt worse than anything I'd ever experienced before. Not even that fateful day my whole world fell apart compared. I thought it was my worst fucking memory. I was wrong. So fucking wrong.

"Mummy? Wake up, Mummy."

I shook her. Her eyes were glazed over. Blood poured out of her neck sluggishly.

"Please, please wake up."

Betrayal

Blood everywhere. Covering her clothes and seeping into the rug. Blood that now coated my hands. I lay my head on her chest, holding her in my small arms.

"I love you. I love you. Please don't leave me, Mummy, please."

In the back of my mind, I knew she was dead, but I didn't want to believe it. I couldn't cope. How could my mother be gone? I cradled her to me for the longest time, humming the lullaby she always used to sing to me. Rock-a-bye baby. Stupid really. I wasn't a baby any longer. But I wasn't a man either. I was just a kid. A kid who'd lost his mother.

"Aiden? Lizzie?" I heard Tina's voice.

I couldn't move. All I wanted was my mother back. I heard the gasp as her footsteps stopped next to me.

"Oh my god, Aiden? Are you...?"

"Hello, Tina. Mummy has gone to heaven. I tried to wake her up, but she won't. She's gone."

She gently pulled me away from my mother. She looked down at the body between us. Another gasp caught in her throat.

"Oh god. Oh god."

"She's dead, isn't she?"

Tina looked at me.

"I'm sorry, Aiden. I'm so sorry I wasn't here."

Her eyes reflected my own pain. Shaking herself, she put a hand out to me.

"You're covered in blood, Aiden. I think we should get you cleaned up, okay?"

I nodded, placing my hand in hers. She led me into the bathroom and ordered me to strip. Turning on the shower, she pointed at it.

"Make sure to wash thoroughly, okay? I will deal with this. I'm sorry, Aiden. I'm so sorry you had to see her like that."

I didn't respond. I got in the shower and did what she asked of me. I made sure to wash away all the blood coating my skin. When I got out, the bloody clothes were missing. I went into my bedroom and put some clean ones on.

Tina was in the kitchen on the phone when I walked in.

"Look, you get over here and deal with it… I don't care… Yes. I've kept him away. He hasn't seen her… I really don't care how it happened or why he did it. Unless you want me to phone the police and report her murder, then I suggest you clean up his mess… Of course, I know it was him. Who else would it have been?"

Tina looked up at me, her expression grave.

"Good. I'm taking him and you aren't going to stop me. Understood?"

She hung up a moment later, giving me a tight smile.

"Aiden, honey, go put your coat and shoes on."

I nodded.

It was just me and Tina now.

My mother was dead.

And whoever killed her was going to meet the same fate one day.

I dropped to my knees and did something I hadn't done in a very long time. I cried. Tears ran down my face. Fuck. My heart hurt. It physically hurt.

Avery.

What the fuck did I do to you?
What the fuck did I do to us?

I could hardly breathe.

Betrayal

Pain.

So much fucking pain.

I hated how she made me feel.

I hated myself.

I hated everything.

Avery… I'm in love with you too.

To be continued in Sacrifice…

I sincerely hope you enjoyed reading this book as much as I enjoyed writing it. If you did, I would greatly appreciate a short review on Amazon or your favourite book website. Reviews are crucial for any author, and even just a line or two can make a huge difference.

Acknowledgements

Thank you so much for taking the time to read this book. This has been quite the journey. Writing in a completely different genre has been a challenge for me as my previous published works have been paranormal romance. This book came about after reading a lot of dark romance books and deciding I really wanted to follow in some of those author's footsteps. I didn't have any intention of writing a new series whilst still in the midst of writing my After Dark series, but Avery and Aiden came along and demanded I write them.

It all started with a single question – what would happen if you fell in love with the man who murdered your parents? I didn't really know going in how their story would end up as I'm not the type of writer who plans anything. I just started writing and the words flowed and flowed until I ended up with Betrayal. I knew at this point their story wasn't finished, which is why they have two further books on the way. Writing these two has been an absolute joy. I really hope you all love these characters as much as I do.

Sarah Bailey

Thank you to Sabrina for being my sounding board and encouraging me to write this story. You're my best friend and number one fan. I couldn't ask for anything more. I very much doubt this book would even be in existence without you since you're the one who recommended I start reading dark romances. And yes, I fully respect your claim on Aiden as your book boyfriend for life.

Huge thank you to Thunder Team Alpha Force - Sean, Katie, Gil, Corry, Kenny, Jordan and Paul. Your support is invaluable. You all make me laugh every single day. Having you in my life is an absolute blessing.

Thank you to everyone who supports and follows me on Twitter. You guys are the best. The writing community has changed my life. I had no idea there was such a huge support network out there until I joined up. And I can never forget you gave me #TTAF!

Thank you to my family, friends and everyone who supports me in my writing endeavours. I value each and every one of you. Especially my mum who proofreads all my books for me. I've long since got over the embarrassment of having her read the steamy bits.

And last, but not least, I have to thank my husband. He's made it possible for me to pursue my dreams to be a writer. I love you to the moon and back!

About The Author

Born and raised in Sussex, UK near the Ashdown Forest where she grew up climbing trees and building Lego towns with her younger brother. Sarah fell in love with novels when she was a teenager reading her aunt's historical regency romances. She has always loved the supernatural and exploring the darker side of romance and fantasy novels.

Sarah currently resides in the Scottish Highlands with her husband. Music is one of her biggest inspirations and she always has something on in the background whilst writing. She is an avid gamer and is often found hogging her husband's Xbox.

Corrupt Empire

Avery & Aiden's Trilogy
Betrayal
Sacrifice
Revenge

Dante & Liora's Standalone
Provoked